# The MEDICI CURSE

Matt Chamings lives in Devon with his wife and four noisy children. He studied archaeology at university and now works a bit in a library. The rest of the week he divides between writing, doing the housework and telling his kids to be quiet. He likes being an author because he can spend hours looking at eBay while his wife thinks he is writing. His other interests include reading, watching films, going to church and supporting Leeds United.

# MATT CHAMINGS

*faber and faber*

First published in 2007
by Faber and Faber Limited
3 Queen Square London WC1N 3AU

Typeset by Faber and Faber
Printed in England by Mackays of Chatham plc,
Chatham, Kent

The right of Matt Chamings to be
identified as author of this work has been asserted
in accordance with Section 77 of the Copyright, Designs
and Patents Act 1988

A CIP record for this book
is available from the British Library

ISBN 978-0-571-23177-5

2 4 6 8 10 9 7 5 3 1

*For Eleanor, Jack, Tim and Alice*
*You're all my favourites*

# One

TERRIFIED, the boy peered out between his fingers. Always it was the same. He opened his mouth to scream but no sound came. He tried to move but found himself rigid with fear. He watched the scene again. The wounded man lay on the bed, blood seeping through the rag on his thigh. The dark figure entered the room. Then it all became a rush of tumbling images. The shouts, the threats, the cries for help. The swish of metal as the sword was drawn. The look on the man's face as his head was pulled back by the hair to expose his neck. The raised sword . . .

Arnaldo woke with a jolt and lay there, breathing hard. His body was bathed in sweat and the sheet was a tight ball, screwed up in his hands. That dream again. He sat up and ran his hand across his eyes, trying to rub the scene from his mind. But it wouldn't go. It never did. It was getting light outside so he might as well get up. Quietly. No need to disturb the others still sleeping. Today was the day.

He was silent at breakfast, chewing on his bread slowly, forcing himself to swallow though he wasn't hungry. The other artists had to speak two or three times to get his attention. Soon they stopped trying and began to joke instead. 'I heard him talking in his sleep last night.' 'Which girl's name was it this time?' They all laughed but Arnaldo didn't even notice. He sat there long after they had finished. Then he collected his things and stepped outside.

He waited for a moment in the street, his back to the cold stone wall. Alone apart from a stray dog that sniffed around his feet. He kicked at it irritably and it backed off, growling, the hair on its neck standing up. Then he began to walk, slipping among the crowd that made its way past the old market towards the great dome of the cathedral. Under his right arm he clutched his box of brushes and paints but his left hand wandered to the hilt of the dagger that hung at his waist. It was short and plain and he had spent an hour the previous evening working on the blade until it was razor sharp.

Beneath the great church the narrow street opened out into the Piazza del Duomo – a wide square, teeming with life. Arnaldo instinctively kept to the shadows, working his way along the marble wall. He stepped over a crippled beggar sitting behind his bowl, ignoring the hands held out. He kept his head down as he brushed past a group of noblemen – their voices loud and confident, their hands resting lightly on their swords. Then he stopped suddenly, his heart thumping. A pair of bright, terrifying eyes were glaring at him and a pointing finger seemed to fix him where he stood. It was a monk preaching on the steps of the church. He held Arnaldo in his gaze – looking right into his heart. What did he see there? Revenge? Hate? Murder? The boy shook his head and tore himself away, trembling. This would not do. Today he had to be strong.

He hurried on, the voice of the monk following him, unsettling his resolve. Soon he was at the Palazzo Medici and stopped in front of the big double doors. He straightened his tunic and steeled himself before knocking. He would do what he had come to do. Then let God decide his fate. One of the doors swung open and a servant appeared. She was middle-aged and very round.

'Yes?'

'I . . . I've come from Signor Verrocchio,' he stammered. She did not seem to understand but stood there, her hands resting on her enormous hips. 'The portrait,' he added. Slowly the woman nodded and stood aside.

He passed first through an unlit corridor and his eyes could make out no detail as they adjusted from the strong sunshine outside. In a moment they had entered a shady courtyard flanked by pillars and statues. Later the place would be busy with clients of the bank but for now it was deserted. That was good. He glanced around, wanting to be sure of his escape route. Coats of arms were carved on the roundels above the archways. The three feathers entwined in ribbon, the symbol of the house of Medici. A face looked at them from an upstairs window but whoever it was stepped back quickly as his eyes settled there for a moment.

'This way, signor, please.' The servant spoke impatiently and her footsteps echoed as they clattered on the flagstones. He hurried after her and soon she had left him, standing in a pleasantly furnished room with brightly coloured frescoes on the wall. He saw they were the work of his master, Andrea del Verrocchio. On any other day he would have looked closer and marvelled at their beauty. But they reminded him of home so he turned away quickly.

A figure was sat at a table in the centre of the room. Arnaldo's heart beat faster. At last he faced his enemy. How long had he waited for this? He had a sudden vision of himself drawing his dagger and plunging it into the chest of the man who was even now rising to greet him. He saw the look of surprised horror, the spurt of blood from the wound, the hands clutching at the desk as he staggered to support himself.

Arnaldo's hand tightened on the dagger's hilt.

'Good day, Signor . . . ?'

Lorenzo de Medici stood in front of him looking suspicious. He was holding out his hand. Slowly Arnaldo released the dagger and cursed himself for his cowardice. His chance had come and his nerve had failed him. What would he do now? He had made no plans for not stabbing Medici. He trembled as he transferred his paintbox to his other arm and noticed that his palms were sweating.

'Rossi.' He gave his false name quickly. He fumbled and tried to wipe his damp hand on his breeches before taking Lorenzo's, cringing at the man's touch.

'Arnaldo de . . . de Rossi.' The master of the house eyed him sharply as if he could tell it was a lie. He was not a handsome man. His black hair was lank, his nose was long and his lower jaw jutted out beyond his upper lip. But his eyes were bright and his movements quick and animated.

'My master has sent me to work on the portrait of your daughter, signor.'

'Has he?' Lorenzo seemed surprised and not too pleased. 'Verrocchio cannot come and so he sends this boy to me instead.'

Arnaldo flushed. 'My master gives his apologies, signor. He has not been well of late. I may be young but Verrocchio would not send me unless he knew my work was good.' He gazed steadily at Lorenzo.

'Very well,' Medici said at last. 'You have earned Verrocchio's confidence. Now you must earn mine.' He turned away and opened a door to call up a flight of stairs. 'Alessandra, come quickly.' Then he faced Arnaldo again. 'You can work in the room above. The easel is already there. The light is good. Ah! Alessandra, you are here. Good. Meet Signor Rossi who will be painting your likeness.' The girl in the doorway bowed her head to greet him. She was the most beautiful girl Arnaldo had ever seen.

∞

He made his way up the stairs, his mind racing, glad of the chance to be alone. At first he thought the door was locked but then he realised it was only stiff.

Pushing harder, it gave way grudgingly and creaked open. Inside he found a room more softly furnished than Lorenzo's study. This was a private chamber where the women of the household spent their days. There was a woven rug on the floor and tapestries on the walls. Bundles of dried flowers and herbs sweetened the air and there were countless other touches that made the room warm and welcoming. Unlike Alessandra. She had not spoken at all. Was it modesty or just contempt he wondered as he waited for her to change.

When she entered the room ten minutes later she was in a dress of pure white with silver embroidery threaded across the front and around the neck and cuffs. Her auburn hair was braided and a single band of gold encircled her head. She had removed a purple ribbon from around her neck which she now clutched tightly in her hand as if she didn't want to lose it. Without a word she took her seat on a wooden stool by the window. Her hands lay in her lap, her back was straight and she stared into the distance, as cold as the white of her dress. Equally quiet was the servant who had answered the door earlier. She entered after Alessandra, having helped her into the dress. She untied her apron and heaved her great body into a chair in the corner. Then she took up some sewing but her real purpose was to guard her young mistress's honour. She had been Alessandra's nurse.

Still bewildered by the unexpected turn of events, Arnaldo began to make his preparations. The board and easel stood in the centre and he laid his box on a low table next to them. He had not been boasting to Medici when he had claimed to be a good painter. He was one of the best. One by one he selected his paints and mixed them to a paste with a little oil. Vermillion, ultramarine, orpiment – the names were as alluring as their colours. Most workshops were still using tempera paints mixed from egg yolks of course. But not in the House of Verrocchio. Oils were easier to work with and gave richer colours. This was Leonardo's discovery.

He worked automatically, acutely aware of the girl by the window. He dared not look at her in his confusion. Everything about her was faultless. Her slender neck, her creamy white skin, her deep-brown eyes. He guessed she got her looks from her mother. How could he despise such beauty? But he must not think kindly of her. He must remember who her father was.

He worked in silence. The smell of the oils was soothing and the colours were enticing. Together they blended into a rich buttery paste. Little children who saw the paints couldn't resist taking a fingerful and licking them. They did not taste as good as they looked. Slowly his troubled mind became quiet. The wood panel already had the figure marked out by his master Verrocchio. The design had been done on paper and then transferred on to the board by pin-pricks through the lines of the drawing. The back-ground was not to be this room but an open landscape in the new natural style. Even with rough charcoal marks the old painter had captured the girl's likeness well. The tilt of her head, the elegance of the upheld hand that would hold the flower garland – it was perfect. Arnaldo was eager now to bring the picture to life.

'I must ask you, *signorina*, to assume the pose that Signor Verrocchio showed you last time.' His eyes were bright and feverish. Alessandra stiffened as if offended by his enthusiasm. Without speaking, she turned her head to her left and raised her arm with her palm turned upwards. Arnaldo looked at her and then at the sketch. 'You need not bother with the arm, signorina. You will tire if you try to hold it there.' She dropped her arm with a flash of irritation. '*Grazie*. And your face just a little more to the left.' She clenched her jaw and her eyes were cold with fury as she moved her head a fraction. If Arnaldo noticed any of this he did not show it. 'Perfect,' he said. He picked up a brush, dipped it and began to paint.

The servant continued to sew but shot shrewd glances at Arnaldo as he worked. There was much in her mind that was not betrayed by her face. 'Soon you will know,' she said at length as if continuing a conversation that had begun before Arnaldo arrived. Her needle darted in and out of the dress she was mending. Arnaldo was startled by the sound of her voice and lowered his brush. Alessandra flushed angrily and turned to face her.

'Hush, Marietta! You speak too much.' It was the first time he had heard her voice and although her tone was severe he felt an unwelcome thrill at the sound.

Marietta shrugged. 'Yes, Marietta talks too much. Stupid Marietta. Who wants to listen to Marietta? I remember a little girl who used to beg me to tell her stories. She didn't say hush then. Tell me another one –'

'I said be quiet!'

An uneasy silence returned but Arnaldo found he could not regain his concentration. He was clearly not the only one with something on his mind.

The servant was not to be quieted for long in any case. 'Soon you will know the responsibilities of being a woman,' she said sulkily.

Alessandra stiffened and clenched her fist. Arnaldo looked at her warily, not knowing what she would do. Slowly she stood up and faced her old nurse. She opened her mouth to speak but then shut it abruptly and turned and ran from the room. Marietta put in a last stitch and then snapped the thread between her teeth.

'Silly girl,' she said. 'She does not listen to Marietta but Marietta is not as stupid as she thinks.' She appeared to be talking to herself.

Arnaldo looked regretfully at the painting which was hardly begun. 'I will return tomorrow,' he sighed.

# Two

THERE was a moment of hush in the busy piazza as the sound of breaking china made people turn and stare. Tommy gazed sadly down at the pieces of broken vase that lay at his feet, while his sister, Maria, looked at him in exasperation. 'Oh, Tommy, how many times do I have to tell you not to touch things?' Then she groaned as she realised what she had just said. She sounded just like her dad. Bit by bit the crowd returned to their shopping leaving the pretty thirteen-year-old to sort things out. She wasn't really angry with her brother. He couldn't help it. When he lifted his eyes again they were big and blue and brimming with tears.

I didn't want to hurt it,' he said. 'I only wanted to touch it. It's pretty.' Maria shook her head in resignation and turned to the lady behind the market stall who was watching them closely.

'How much?' She switched to Italian to ask how much the break was going to cost.

'Twenty,' said the stallholder without hesitation. Twenty euros! That was more than she had in her purse. There was no way she was paying that much for a pile of broken pot.

'Five,' she said firmly. The woman threw up her hands as if she had been insulted and launched into a rapid stream of protest. Five euros for the beautiful vase! Not nearly enough. Wasn't it a magnificent vase? Never had she heard such a ridiculous offer. She might take eighteen but she was robbing herself. Maria waited calmly until the outburst was over and offered her eight. Eight! What did she take her for? The bargaining went on until they eventually agreed on twelve euros. Maria handed over the money and the lady smiled broadly as she thrust them deep into her apron. Perhaps the little girl would also like a plate to go with her beautiful vase which so sadly had got broken? Or maybe another vase seeing how the sweet little boy liked it so much? It was true. Tommy had picked up a piece of the broken pot and was running his finger fondly along the shiny coloured glaze. 'Put it down,' said Maria irritably. 'You'll cut yourself.' Tommy didn't put it down. He slipped it into his pocket and stared at her stubbornly. 'Oh well,' she shrugged. 'You may as well keep it. I've paid for it. Come on. Let's go and find Dad.' She took her brother by the hand and led him across the piazza, picking their way through the crowd of milling tourists.

'How about this lovely dish?' the woman called after them.

∞

Not far away, John Clayton led a group students along the top storey of the Uffizi building. Big, square windows – with ancient rippled glass – allowed the sun to pour in, making the rooms perfect for the display of fine art. The Medici family had discovered this in the sixteenth century and now some of the greatest treasures of the Renaissance were housed here. The teenage students were chatting and laughing but fell quiet when John stopped in room fifteen and turned to address them. He was in his forties but looked younger with dark hair and a pleasant smile. He had been a student here at Florence University and now, twenty years later, he had jumped at the chance to become a visiting professor.

'Staying with the School of Verrocchio,' he said, 'we can now see examples of the earliest work of his most famous student.' His Italian was good with just a trace of an English accent. 'Some of the paintings in this room are attributed to Leonardo da Vinci and although still heavily influenced by his master the signs of his later style can be clearly –' He broke off with a look of alarm as a crash came from the corridor. All the students turned to look in the direction of the noise. A moment later Maria and Tommy appeared in the doorway with the girl pulling her brother firmly by the elbow. 'Tell me that wasn't a priceless Renaissance sculpture,' John said weakly.

'No, just a wooden sign.' The children's father relaxed. 'He did break a vase in the market though.'

John nodded and pulled his wallet out. 'How much?'

'Twelve euros.'

He took out a ten and a five and handed them over. 'Here, keep the rest. Cheaper than a Michelangelo.'

The art students watched this exchange with amusement. 'Sweet little boy,' one of the girls said and stroked Tommy's fluffy, blond hair. He was ten years old but girls always treated him like a baby. He stared at her impassively and then walked away to look at one of the paintings. Maria looked shyly at the group of young Italians who were now all smiling at her. With her dark hair and complexion she could have been one of them. But that wasn't surprising – her mother was Italian.

'OK. If we can turn our attention to Leonardo again, my son – don't touch it, Tommy – is looking at an interesting example. This is a portrait of Paolo Orsini of Rome, cousin of Clarice Orsini who married Lorenzo Medici, the Magnificent in 1468. The first thing you'll notice is –'

'He is ugly.'

The students giggled. 'Thank you, Tommy. He is quite ugly. Stand back a bit please. What I *was* going to say is that the painting is done by at least two different artists. This happened a lot, of course. It allowed the master craftsmen to paint the main subject while the assistants filled in the background. What's strange about this portrait is that Leonardo appears to have collaborated with Verrocchio on it some time in the 1480s, long after he had finished his apprenticeship and moved on to Milan. No one has ever been able to explain why. Unfortunately parts of the work haven't aged well.' The students leaned closer and saw that the face was cracked and discoloured whereas the verdant green of the landscape and the deep red of Orsini's tunic were still rich and fresh.

'The painting is due for cleaning soon, so maybe something can be done to restore it. There is something else unusual about Orsini here. Anybody notice what it is?'

The students all stared intently at the painting. 'He has a big nose and his eyebrows join up in the middle?' More laughter.

'True, Andrea. Anything else?'

Orsini was not looking directly forwards; he had been painted three-quarters on, facing to the left. His right hand was raised and in it he held a garland of flowers which draped to the left and disappeared off the edge of the painting. Finally, a short girl with black ringlets had a suggestion. 'I think there must have been another painting to go with this one.'

'Very good, Marta! Yes, as it stands the picture is quite unbalanced. Orsini is clearly focused on something to his right but there is nothing there. Try and imagine another portrait to the left of this one. What would it look like? Fabio?' A tall boy who had been whispering to the girl next to him suddenly assumed a look of concentration.

'Er . . . perhaps it would be a woman facing in towards the man?'

'Yes?'

'And the woman, she would be holding the other end of the flowers.'

'Excellent! And that's the mystery. The history of this portrait is well documented but there is no record of there ever having been a companion to it.'

'The picture would be of his wife?' Marta suggested.

'Yes. It's the sort of thing that would be commissioned to celebrate a marriage but here Orsini is an old man and we know he married when he was twenty-eight.' The students were intrigued and gazed at the scowling old man in the painting with his heavy brow and prominent nose. 'There is one possible clue to the puzzle but in a way it only deepens the mystery. Does anybody have a copy of *Italian Renaissance Art* with them?' Marta nodded and rummaged around in her bag for her textbook. 'Thank you, Marta. Turn to page 274 and read from the second paragraph please. Tommy, stay away from that.' John caught his son's wrist just in time to prevent him from setting off the fire alarm.

Marta began to read.

*Another example of a lost Renaissance treasure is the* White Lady of San Arnaldo. *Now known only from an early photograph of a nineteenth-century copy, this portrait is believed to have perished in the fire that destroyed the Giannotti family home in 1873. Little is known of its history before this, but it is probably the same portrait listed in the inventory of Elisabetta della Porta when her estate was sold after her suicide in 1811. Here it was attributed to the School of Verrocchio. Similarly a* Young Lady with Flower Garland *is*

*described by the English traveller John Taverner during
his tour of Tuscany in 1786. He is said to have sketched
the portrait but the copy has not survived. Possibly it
was lost when the ship went down on his return journey.
The painting itself —*

'*Santa Maria!*' One of the students crossed herself and
another closed his fist with the forefinger and little
finger extended. The sign of the horns, believed to
ward off bad luck.

'What?' John was taken aback by the reaction.

'Fire! Suicide! Shipwreck! This girl is bad luck.'
Some of the other students nodded in agreement.

John laughed and then stopped himself when he
saw that they were not joking. 'She may have been a bit
unlucky,' he admitted. 'But if you look at the reproduction of the painting you'll see what I mean about the
possible partner to Orsini's portrait.'

The students clustered around the open textbook,
and Maria joined them. She had become strangely
absorbed by the story. At first glance, the picture was
disappointing – a grainy black and white photograph
and very dark. It was a girl, probably in her teens. What
was most striking was the pose she was in. It was the
mirror image of Paolo Orsini in his painting. She was
facing to the right, her left hand was raised and holding a garland of flowers. They looked up at the picture
on the wall and then back to the book. Side by side the
two would make a perfect pair.

'It's not right,' said Fabio at last.

'You don't think they match?' asked John.

'Oh yes, certainly they go together but they shouldn't. This man is an ugly old dog, but this girl is young and very beautiful. I can't believe she would bring bad luck. *Bella Bambina!*' he added appreciatively, which got him a frown from his girlfriend.

'Thank you, Fabio. Ignoring your somewhat romantic sentiments, you've made a very good point. That's why I said this picture only deepens the mystery. This girl, the White Lady, can't be Orsini's wife. So who was she?'

They all gazed at the mysterious painting until a loud thud behind them broke the spell.

'Tommy! That is over five hundred years old. Will you please stop fiddling with things!'

# Three

$\mathcal{A}$ VERY different Arnaldo left the Palazzo Medici to the one that had arrived less than an hour before. The knife still hung at his belt and his paints were under his arm, but the thought of killing Lorenzo de Medici was no longer driving him. He was in a thoughtful mood as he walked under the shadow of the Cathedral of Santa Maria del Fiore. Its giant dome dominated the city skyline of red-tiled roofs and occasional church towers with the green slopes of the Arno valley beyond. Slowly he made his way through the crowded marketplace. Carts were piled high around him with bread and fish and fruit and vegetables. Women with baskets, servants mostly from the great households, gathered around them bargaining. It seemed like a different world to Arnaldo and twice he unwittingly stumbled into people who turned on him angrily. Each time he mumbled an apology and walked on until he was able to leave the crowd and head south towards the Ponte Vecchio. Here he would have lingered and watched the Arno flowing lazily by, but the stench from the butchers' and tanners' workshops was particularly foul today. Sometimes the noble river ran red from the blood and offal that they tipped into it. The smell brought him back to his senses and, covering his nose, he hurried away.

The studio of Andrea del Verrocchio was as busy as ever when Arnaldo returned. It was a big, airy room with large windows. A few men were painting or sketching while models posed for them. Outside in the courtyard others were carving in stone where the dust and chippings could not affect the artists' paint.

'Back so soon?' Verrocchio glanced up from his work as Arnaldo entered and placed his paintbox on a bench.

'Yes,' he replied. 'The girl, she . . . I don't know. She didn't want to sit. I came away.'

'Did you offend the fair Alessandra?'

'I . . . I don't think so.'

Verrocchio lowered his brush. He had shoulder-length grey hair and although his movements were slower now, his hand was still steady and sure. He smiled mysteriously as he turned to his young assistant. 'She is very beautiful, no?'

'She is just a girl.' Arnaldo tried to sound indifferent but his old master did not miss the sudden blush that coloured his cheeks. He returned to his painting.

'No, she is not *just* a girl.' He filled his brush and made a smooth even stroke of brilliant red on the panel in front of him. It glistened wet like blood. 'She is a rose that is in bud,' he said. 'She is as fresh as the dew in the morning.' Arnaldo found himself becoming hot and bothered. 'Her young body quivers like –'

'Enough!' Arnaldo snapped. The old man looked at him in surprise and some of the other painters watched in amusement.

'What is wrong, Arnaldo? You seem warm. Perhaps you should take a dip in the Arno.'

'I'm all right.'

'I'm not so sure. Maybe I cannot trust a hot-blooded young man like you to paint the lovely Alessandra. Perhaps you should paint the old dog Orsini whom she is to marry.' Arnaldo fell quiet. He did not want the Medici job taken away from him. He came and stood quietly behind Verrocchio who was working on the other portrait. It was the mirror image of Alessandra's with the figure of Paolo Orsini facing to the left, his right arm raised. Orsini was still in Rome so one of Verrocchio's assistants was modelling for him. When the man himself arrived, his face could be added to complete the portrait.

'But no,' Verrocchio said at length. 'I am too old to take the walk to the Palazzo Medici each day. I feel the cold so.' Arnaldo felt himself relax. He was troubled by the strength of his desire to return to the Medici household and persuaded himself it was because he wanted another chance to steel himself for the kill. He half succeeded. 'Why are you wearing that dagger?' asked the old artist.

'I wanted to kill Medici and carry off his beautiful daughter,' Arnaldo said moodily. Verrocchio and the other painters laughed.

'Very funny, Arnaldo. Good. Keep your spirits up.

Laughter is a great healer of troubled minds. Since you are here, why don't you relieve Leonardo? He has been in that pose for over an hour.'

Leonardo da Vinci sat motionless with his curly hair and beard flowing down over a bright red tunic. He had been Verrocchio's finest student twenty years before and even now retained close links with his old master. He had been in Milan for the last three years but had returned to his old rooms in Florence while plague swept through Milan making it dangerous to stay there. Arnaldo nodded and waited for Leonardo to vacate the chair so he could take over. He didn't move. Perhaps he hadn't heard Verrocchio.

'Hey! Leonardo.' No response. Arnaldo noticed he was staring glassily so he waved his hand in front of his face and snapped his fingers. 'Leonardo. You can stop now.' Still no reaction. He turned back to Verrocchio. 'Can he sleep in that position?'

The old man shrugged. 'It wouldn't surprise me. He can do many things.' Arnaldo laid a hand on Leonardo's shoulder who immediately came to life as if newly animated by the divine spirit. Arnaldo jumped and snatched his hand away.

'I have observed . . .' Leonardo said in his high-pitched, excitable voice, '. . . that every man at three years old is exactly half his full-grown height. Most curious don't you think?' With that, he stood up abruptly, pulled the red tunic over his head and handed it to Arnaldo. Then he walked over to a bench and began to make rapid left-handed jottings in his notebook.

He didn't appear to notice that he was stark naked. Arnaldo looked back to Verrocchio who shook his head, baffled.

'I sometimes think that Leonardo moves in a different sphere from the rest of us.'

∞

When Arnaldo arrived at the Palazzo Medici the following day, the servant Marietta admitted him as before and accompanied him to where the portrait was waiting. The master of the house did not come to greet him on arrival. He was deep in discussion with his steward in the office, poring over the household accounts. Even from the courtyard Arnaldo could hear Medici's voice raised in anger. He managed to glance through the open door as they passed and saw Lorenzo impatiently grab at a roll of parchment, and stab a forefinger at it while the servant remained unruffled, answering all his questions calmly.

Alessandra was not in the upstairs room but joined them a few minutes later and although she was courteous, she had no more warmth than yesterday. She was not in the white but wearing a simple blue dress. Her hair was tied in a braid as before.

'Do you require that I wear the white dress, signor?'

'N . . . no, signorina. There is no need. Today I will work on your face.' She inclined her head briefly and took her seat. 'The blue becomes you well, signorina.' Her eyes hardened and she ignored the compliment. Arnaldo blushed and looked down feeling foolish. He would know not to try that again. She said nothing to Marietta who again took up her post in the corner. Arnaldo sensed they had reached an uneasy truce on whatever had been between them. He began mixing his paint and soon the sweet smell of walnut oil permeated the room. A restful peace descended as he began to work. A fly buzzed about the window, the old nurse occasionally shifted in her chair but otherwise there was silence – a silence where each person was lost in their own thoughts.

For Arnaldo the chance to look undisturbed at Alessandra was welcome. She, with her head turned slightly away, could not return his gaze so he could linger over the shape of her nose, the tilt of her chin, the dark curve of her eyelashes. Marietta, as she glanced up shrewdly from her sewing, did not miss his attentions. For nearly three-quarters of an hour he was able to work and bit by bit the picture took shape under his skilful hand. He applied the base coat of flesh tones to which he would later add more layers, building up the skin texture until the picture looked so real it might be alive. Inspired, his heart raced with pleasure.

Then, just as he stood back to observe his progress, there was a noise at the door. Medici cursed quietly as he struggled with the difficult door and finally it swung open to admit him. He appeared to be in a foul mood and Arnaldo felt a sudden knot tighten in his stomach as he looked again on the face of his enemy.

'I see you have deigned to show your face,' he began irritably. 'I suppose I am to be grateful.'

Arnaldo was taken aback. 'I am sorry, signor. Is there some problem that I am not aware of?'

Medici's eyes darkened. 'Indeed there is, *signor.*' He spat the word as if it were an insult. 'Yesterday, after a bare twenty minutes work you decide you have had enough and leave. This is intolerable. First Verrocchio cannot be bothered to come and then he sends an idle boy who only works when he feels like it. I have always favoured Verrocchio but there are others who would welcome the patronage of the Medici.' This was harsh but he had not had a good morning. Trying to understand the household accounts always exasperated him. He had a suspicion that his steward was cheating him but lacked the diligence that was necessary to catch him out. He turned his sense of frustration against the first available target, which today was Arnaldo.

The young painter flushed angrily. 'I am sorry if I have offended, but –' A sudden movement from Alessandra's direction made him pause. She had turned her head and Arnaldo noticed that her face had paled. There was a brief flash of fear in her eyes but then she looked away – too proud to plead. Marietta kept her head down as she sewed. These two were very hard to fathom. He chewed his lower lip as he deliberated. Why should he apologise to Medici of all people? Then he thought of Alessandra's frightened eyes. 'I am sorry,' he repeated as he hurriedly concocted a story. 'I . . . I found I did not have enough pigments with me. I assumed I would be working on the sketch not knowing that my master had already completed it.'

Medici grunted dismissively. 'So you replace the sin of laziness with that of incompetence.' Arnaldo had to bite his lip to hold back his anger.

'The portrait will be finished on time, I assure you.'

'We shall see.' Medici walked around to stand behind the easel. He stopped and surveyed the work, then bent closer to look. Finally he straightened up. 'We shall see,' he said again, more thoughtfully. 'Carry on.' He left the room and Arnaldo smiled to himself. Medici had been impressed.

Neither Alessandra nor Marietta spoke as Arnaldo returned to work but he sensed a subtle shift in the atmosphere – a slight thaw in the frostiness. After another hour he decided that he had done enough and lowered his brush. The paint would need to dry before he could do more. 'Thank you, signorina, that will be all for today.' He began to pack away his paints and clean his brush on an oily rag. Alessandra stood but did not leave the room. Arnaldo sensed she was watching him and began to feel uncomfortable. He looked up. 'Did you require something, signorina?' He tried to sound at ease, and failed.

The girl opened her mouth to speak but no word came out. 'You protected me from the anger of my father earlier,' she managed at last. She sounded agitated and her next words tumbled out in a hurry. 'It was nobly done and I thank you.' Then she stiffened as if she regretted her lack of composure. She turned and left the room without another word leaving a bemused Arnaldo to stare after her.

'You are welcome,' he said to the empty chair.

# Four

MARIA rested her chin on her hand and gazed out of the window at the changing countryside. They had left Florence behind nearly an hour ago and now they were on the winding roads heading west. They would struggle up one hill in their old Fiat, then descend into a valley populated with scattered villages, only to climb a higher slope on the other side. Olive trees and vines grew on the terraces around the villages, giving way to yellow grass and dark green, flame-shaped cypress trees further up. Her mother in the front seat leant forward, hungrily absorbing all the sights. In the fifteen years they had been married, Elisabetta had not been home more than a few times. Now a chance to stay for the whole summer. The car laboured slowly. John changed down a gear and looked at the dashboard anxiously.

'We ought to stop.'

'Why?'

'The car's overheating.'

Elisabetta glanced at the warning light on the dashboard as it winked on and off. 'It's nothing. Giorgio will look at it.' John smiled at his wife and took her hand. 'Nearly there now,' she said as they struggled over the brow of the final ridge. Then she fell silent as San Arnaldo came into view.

Maria sat up and peered across the valley at the small town perched halfway up the opposite slope. It was still early morning and hazy. The trees were draped in mist and the walls of the town seemed to rise out of the cloud like a castle in the air. She had visited once before, when she was six. She dimly remembered the town – the bright sunlight shining on the pale stone and red-tiled buildings of the town square, the piazza. Better she remembered her grandmother. They called her Nonna. And Uncle Giorgio. Hugs, kisses, noise, food, sweets pressed into her hands, seemingly endless faces crowded around the table. All these visions flitted through her mind and she felt a thrill of excitement swell inside her. She nudged Tommy who was sleeping on the seat next to her. He woke and looked at her blearily. 'Look. We're nearly there.' He gazed sleepily at his mother's home. He had only been three on their previous visit and could remember nothing of it.

John's eyes strayed to look at the town and then as a corner approached he let go of his wife's hand to take the wheel again. It was a good thing he did. Around the bend, a figure dressed in black stood in the centre of the road. Elisabetta's eyes widened. She screamed and instinctively threw up her hands in front of her face. John spun the wheel wildly to avoid a collision and the children clung on to each other in the back seat. Their father slammed on the brakes as he fought to bring the car back under control. All the while the figure stood stock still, staring straight at them. John just had time to see that it was a tiny old lady in widow's blacks. Then they passed her. The car skidded to a halt sideways across both lanes of the road. John breathed hard and it was a while before he could bring himself to unclench his fingers from around the steering wheel. 'I said we should stop,' he said finally.

He restarted the engine, moved the car into a safer position and then got out to check on the old lady. 'That was a close thing,' he said as he approached her. 'Are you all right?' The woman stared blankly and didn't answer. Perhaps she was still shocked from the near miss. He gently touched her arm and slowly her eyes focused. She mumbled something that was meaningless to him. He turned to Elisabetta who had followed with Maria. 'I can't understand her.' Elisabetta tried. First she spoke in pure Italian and then switched to the local dialect which she knew from her childhood. The woman nodded in recognition and answered her. Maria stared at the woman fascinated. Her face was so old and wrinkled it looked like leather, but her eyes were bright and wide. Her wispy hair was snowy white and when she spoke it was in a singsong rhythm and the words were strange. She recognised the name *San Arnaldo* though, and the shakes of the head were obvious enough.

'She's not hurt. She's going to the festival at San Arnaldo.'

'Let's give her a lift,' said John. 'It's another ten kilometres at least.'

'I already offered. She won't accept.'

They didn't want to leave her alone, but nothing would persuade her. In the end she set off walking and the Claytons had no choice but to return to their car and drive past her as she hobbled down the hill.

∽

When they arrived at San Arnaldo the festival was already well under way. The town itself always looked medieval with its crumbling walls and narrow twisting streets. Now the costumed procession seemed to transport them back to the time of Arnaldo himself. Knights in mail armour, ladies in colourful silk dresses, heralds with huge banners fluttering behind them. Today was the feast day of their favourite saint and everybody had turned out to celebrate.

Tommy's eyes were filled with delight as he hung out the window. John inched the car through the crush of people, anxiously watching as the engine overheated again. Elisabetta waved to old friends eagerly as they passed them and it was another twenty minutes before they managed to pull up outside the family home on the far side of town. Steps led up to the bright yellow door and there were low windows covered by metal grilles at street level. It was a narrow building but Maria remembered it went back a long way and there was a basement as well.

'They're here! Giorgio, come quickly!' The door was thrown open and Nonna was at the top of the steps, her arms held wide. Then there were hugs and kisses and cries of delight. Maria and Tommy were pressed to their grandma's aproned bosom and given bone-crunching handshakes by Uncle Giorgio. The children were informed that they had grown, and Elisabetta was chastised for being too thin. It was clear that English food didn't suit her. And so pale. Did the sun never shine in England? Giorgio's wife, Adriana, smiled shyly at them all . . .

' . . . but where is Beppe?' Elisabetta looked around for her nephew. At this Nonna clutched her head theatrically and uttered a stream of anguished dialect which the children couldn't follow. Uncle Giorgio smiled indulgently. 'He isn't here. He is going to be in the Palio.'

'The what?'

'It's a donkey race,' said Elisabetta.

Maria looked confused. That didn't sound so terrible. 'Why is Nonna so upset then?' She noticed the sound of shouts and pounding drums had started in the background.

'Wait till you see *this* donkey race,' said Giorgio mysteriously.

The noise in the piazza was deafening and Maria had to shout to make herself heard. 'Where are the donkeys?' There were plenty of spectators – the inhabitants of San Arnaldo mingling equally with knights and damsels, and modern tourists with camcorders. But there was no sign of any competitors.

'In the church!' Uncle Giorgio bellowed and pointed to the ancient stone building with its red-tile roof and square bell tower. Even as he spoke the wooden doors were flung open and a herd of donkeys poured out wildly, tumbling down the steps, braying and tossing their heads. Each was mounted by a rider in bright colours — reds, yellows, blues, greens — in checks and stripes. The crowd erupted into another massive roar as Maria's mouth fell open in disbelief.

'In the church? What for?'

'For the blessing of course.' The last donkey left the building, ushered out by Father Romano who emerged smiling in his long black robes.

'But don't they . . . poop?'

Her uncle laughed and nodded enthusiastically. 'Oh yes. If they are lucky. But look, there is Beppe.' Uncle Giorgio shouted to his son and the boy waved back. He was small for his ten years with dark curly hair.

The race clearly stirred strong feelings in the supporters. Giorgio explained that each rider represented a region of the town and that local rivalry was fierce. Their section had not won it for twenty-three years. 'Not since I last rode,' he added with pride. The beasts were brought under control and Father Romano prepared to start the race. He was a short man with a smiling red face. He had a large white handkerchief and the crowd hushed in expectation as he held it over his head. The donkeys jostled with each other, struggling for the best position and the old priest waited until they were still. Then, with every eye trained on him, he let go of the handkerchief which quietly drifted to the floor.

The moment it hit the ground they were off. All except the three that absolutely refused to move. The crowd let out another shout and surged forward to follow the donkeys' progress as they raced away along the edge of the square. Beppe was somewhere in the middle of the pack wearing a blue and yellow shirt, urging his animal on as they began to spread out. The race was only once around the square and usually lasted less than a minute. There was no time to make up lost ground if a rider fell behind. Past the church they raced, past a row of shops selling pictures and antiques, to the first corner. Here the leader's look of triumph turned to horror as his donkey stopped dead at the bend. He flew over the animal's head and landed hard on the stone floor, skidding into the wall. A moan of sympathy rose from the crowd and Nonna clutched her head in anguish as she let out a wail. All the other donkeys raced on around the bend and disappeared from sight momentarily as they went under a low canopy hung over the entrance to a restaurant. Only the sound of crashing tables and chairs revealed their progress.

On they went down the second straight. This was an important stretch because when they reached the next corner they would be at the town hall where the mayor and council met. Along the front of the hall was a covered colonnade of stone arches, very cool and pleasant to sit under on a hot afternoon, but not that good for racing donkeys through. To enter the walk-way the riders would have to negotiate a very narrow arch almost in single file. Whichever contestant got there first would have a real advantage over the others and it wasn't going to be Beppe. He was fifth or sixth. Uncle Giorgio roared a mixture of encouragement and threats which were lost in the general racket.

Then disaster struck. Just as the leaders reached the archway, one of the donkeys panicked. It stopped short, hooves skidding to a halt. It turned braying madly, eyes wide with terror. The other donkeys piled into it and began to rear up twisting and throwing their riders. Everything became a jumbled mass of grey fur and coloured shirts, mad shouts and frightened braying. No one seemed able to clear the confusion and make it though the archway.

'Beppe! Oh! Where is Beppe?' His grandma made the sign of the cross and prayed fervently to Mary and the Blessed Anthony, patron saint of donkeys. '*Santa Patata!* Where is he?'

'I don't know,' Giorgio said and searched vainly for his son but there was no sign of the blue and yellow shirt anywhere. Maria could understand now why her grandma was so anxious. She strained to look as well but then she saw something that made her forget the race completely.

In front of the donkeys the swarm of spectators was pressing against the barriers, waving and shout-ing. All she could see was the backs of people's heads as they struggled to make out what was going on.

Then the crowd parted and she gasped with surprise. There was a girl staring back at her. The noise around her seemed suddenly muted. The girl was a little older than her, standing deathly still and quiet. She caught Maria's eye, seemed to stare right into her, but her face didn't show a flicker of greeting. Nor did she look away. She had long auburn hair and was wearing a simple white dress with long sleeves and a bodice that hugged her figure closely. This wasn't unusual in itself – half the people seemed to be in some sort of medieval costume. For a moment Maria wondered why she was so struck by the girl's appearance. Then with a jolt of fear she realised. She was exactly like the girl in the lost painting.

Maria grabbed her uncle's arm but her voice wouldn't work properly. 'Uncle Giorgio!' she managed to croak. 'Who is that girl?' Giorgio wasn't listening. Something had happened among the donkeys that was causing a ripple of excitement to spread across the crowd. 'Uncle Giorgio!' She turned and pulled his arm more urgently.

'What?'

'Who is that girl?'

'What girl?'

'The one in the –' It was too late. She was gone. In the moment that Maria turned her head she seemed to have disappeared. The crowd must have closed around her again. 'She's gone!' But Uncle Giorgio was no longer listening. He let out an ear-splitting roar of delight. Somehow, Beppe had won the race.

Leaving Nonna on her knees in grateful prayer, Giorgio pushed his way through the crush of people to where Beppe waited triumphantly at the finishing point. 'Bravo! Beppe. Bravo!' The boy stood up in his stirrups to greet the crowd and his father lifted him off and on to his shoulder. They both raised a fist to the people who cheered again. Then the brightly coloured banner of red and yellow checks was thrust into Beppe's hands and he waved it with delight, nearly poking his dad in the eye. This was the trophy that they would hold for the whole year.

Not everybody was happy though. Some of the riders were arguing and a fat man in a black suit was mopping his face with a handkerchief and looking indignant. Father Romano nodded gently, ignoring them all. Giorgio frowned. The disturbance was spoiling his moment.

'What's the problem, eh?' The grumblers fell quiet as Giorgio turned to face them. He was six feet three inches tall and had the build of a man who spent his days working heavy machinery. No one wanted to be the first to suggest his son had cheated. 'I said what's up?' The fat man finally found the courage. As mayor he didn't mind who won the race, but he did object to animals running through his office. The church might find donkey poo on the floor acceptable but he did not. He had carpet. The riders agreed. Beppe, they alleged, had avoided the confusion in the archway by riding down an alley, into the town hall by a side door, right through the offices and out at the other end of the building. This was not the official route so he should be disqualified. Giorgio listened, with Beppe slightly anxious on his shoulder. Then he looked at his son with raised eyebrows. Beppe gulped nervously only to hear his dad let out an enormous laugh. Father Romano gave a knowing smile.

'But there is a precedent, no?' said Giorgio happily.

The old priest nodded. 'Yes. It happened once before. Twenty-three years ago, a young Giorgio Rossini won by doing exactly the same thing. Beppe is the winner.'

Father and son turned back to face the crowd in triumph.

# Five

ARNALDO took the lid off his jar of white lead to find just a few loose grains rolling around at the bottom. That wouldn't be enough. He quickly went to the large tub on the workbench but found that was also empty. He cursed quietly. Why did the person who used up the last not make sure it was refilled? Guiltily he realised he might be the culprit. He pushed this thought away. He had made good progress yesterday and didn't want to spoil it by being late today.

'Master Verrocchio?'

The old man looked up from where he sat at a table, leafing through some papers. 'What is it?'

'We have no white lead.'

'Then go and fetch some.' He sounded irritable at being disturbed over a problem that had so obvious a solution.

'I have no time. I will be late and Medici is already angry with me.' He could not hide the anxiety in his voice and Verrocchio raised an inquisitive eyebrow.

'You are keen to impress the girl's father?'

Arnaldo scowled. 'With respect, Master Verrocchio, I have had enough of your jesting.'

'Yes, yes,' Verrocchio said wearily. 'I'm only an old fool.' He returned to his papers and Arnaldo began to think he had forgotten the question in hand. 'Leonardo might have some,' he said eventually.

Arnaldo knew where Leonardo would be and reluctantly made his way upstairs. Late the day before they had managed to acquire the body of a man hanged for stealing. It had been hauled in unceremoniously on a cart after dark by the hangman's assistants – foul old men hardened by the nature of their work. Insensible from the pint of liquor they always drank whether it was a hanging day or not. The dissection of corpses was not illegal any more, but still frowned upon. Particularly by the church. Just the day before Arnaldo had heard that monk again, standing in the piazza outside the cathedral and preaching against unnatural practices. His name was Girolamo Savonarola and, daily, more people were listening to him.

Arnaldo had seen enough of Leonardo's dissections. They were useful in a way but he was glad of the excuse not to attend this one. The smell was strong and he recoiled as he opened the door. He put a hand to his mouth as he entered. The body of the unfortunate man lay on a table of rough boards while Leonardo da Vinci stood over it brandishing a fine, sharp knife. A group of five young apprentices stood around, watching nervously.

'Observe!' cried the excited Leonardo. He pulled back his sleeve and raised the knife high above his head as if he were about to plunge it into the chest of the man before him. It was a dramatic pose – like a pagan priest about to make a sacrifice. Everybody shrunk back in anticipation of the blow. Some turned away, others screwed up their eyes determined to watch. Leonardo continued to stand there flexing and unflexing the fingers around the knife handle. 'There, what do you see?' Slowly they unscrewed their eyes and faced the front, looking puzzled. As far as they could tell nothing had happened yet. 'My arm, you fools. What do you observe happening in my forearm?' His skinny arm was tensed and the tendons stood out clearly under the skin, shifting and sliding as he tightened and loosened his grip. 'The tendons. Don't you see?' He tutted in exasperation at their blank looks. 'If you are to be artists you must first gain a knowledge of anatomy. How else will you be able to paint the body if you don't understand how it works? The muscles and tendons in my arm control my hand. Here I'll show you.'

Arnaldo realised Leonardo was about to start the dissection and hurried to make his request first. 'Signor, have you any white lead? The tub is empty.'

Leonardo noticed Arnaldo for the first time. 'I have a little. Who would like to run and fetch it for Signor Rossi.' Five hands shot up. For some reason they all seemed keen to leave the dissecting table. 'Antonio, you may go. You others pay attention.' Arnaldo groaned inwardly as he realised he was going to have to watch the dissection after all.

With rapid but delicate movements Leonardo made an incision down the forearm from the elbow joint to the wrist. 'In the barbaric lands of the Mohammedans,' he said enthusiastically, 'they cut off the hand of a thief.' He pulled back the skin to reveal whitish tissue which in turn he deftly slit and pulled away. 'It prevents the thief from stealing again.' A few more incisions and the muscles and tendons of the forearm were laid bare over the white of the bone. 'This hand will never steal again, but behold . . .' Very carefully Leonardo gathered the tendons under his fingers and lifted them as if he were a harpist plucking at strings. There was a low moan of horror. As Leonardo pulled on the tendons, the hand of the dead man closed slowly, grasping like a claw.

'Catch him!' cried Leonardo as one boy gently keeled over, unconscious.

Arnaldo was more than relieved when Antonio returned with the paint. It was getting a little hot in the dissecting room. He quickly made his thanks and set off for the Medici household.

'Anybody else want a go?' Leonardo asked brightly.

∞

Arnaldo need not have worried about being late. Medici himself was in the courtyard when he arrived and greeted him warmly. He seemed in excellent spirits.

'Good day, Signor Rossi. The painting progresses well, yes?'

'Greetings, signor. I hope so.'

'You will have to wait now I am afraid. Alessandra is . . . indisposed. Stay a while here with me. Do you like to fight?'

Arnaldo was taken aback. 'Fight, signor?'

'Yes. We might fence a little while you wait.' Arnaldo noticed Medici was wearing a sword and felt suddenly strange. He still wore the dagger, concealed beneath his tunic today, but that was no match for the longer weapon.

'I . . . I have a little knowledge. My father taught me . . . when I was a boy.' His heart beat faster.

'As every father should.' Medici threw his head back and gave a rich laugh. Arnaldo noticed a scar on his neck and the sight of it filled him with anger. He knew where that scar came from. 'You must send my regards to your father,' said Medici.

'He is dead, signor.'

A frown passed over Medici's face. 'I am sorry to hear it. Forgive me.' Arnaldo said nothing and the man seemed momentarily at a loss. 'So, shall we fight?' he asked.

'It would be a pleasure,' Arnaldo said coldly.

Lorenzo called for another sword and while they waited he drew his own and gave a few practice swings. When the weapon arrived Arnaldo took it, felt its weight and tested the edge with his thumb. It was long and tapered, good for thrusting and cutting. Not razor sharp, but it would do. He turned and faced Lorenzo de Medici. He was now standing in front of the man he hated most in the world holding a sword. He couldn't ask for more. This time his courage would not fail him.

'Ready when you are, signor.'

Medici bowed, always keeping his eyes fixed on his opponent. Then he straightened up and held out his weapon in readiness. Arnaldo also held out his sword and together they circled, neither taking their eyes off the other for a moment. Arnaldo made a lunge which Medici parried easily. The first clash of metal seemed to invigorate them and things began to speed up. Arnaldo made a second thrust and another. Medici defended easily and then followed up with an attack of his own but Arnaldo stepped aside to allow the blade to pass safely by.

'Bravo, signor!' Medici seemed delighted at the move. 'That was good, yes?' He broke into a little song as he resumed his fighting stance. Arnaldo did not reply. He was struggling to keep a cool head and the song infuriated him. He attacked again. This time more forcefully. He made a sweep to Medici's left shoulder which was deflected. He feinted low and then lunged again but the man was not fooled. With a clash of weapons the sword thrust was brushed aside. 'Yes! That is more like it. But be quick, signor . . .'

Without waiting for Arnaldo to recover Lorenzo lunged and Arnaldo had to recoil, struggling to bring his sword up into a defensive position. 'I have you now.' Medici pushed forward relentlessly, Arnaldo fighting desperately to deflect his blows. All across the courtyard their weapons clanged until Arnaldo found himself by a pillar which he quickly ducked behind. Emerging the other side he lashed at Medici who now had to defend. 'Excellent! Yes! That's right, signor.' The harder they fought the more happy Medici seemed to become. The happier Medici became, the more enraged Arnaldo grew. His swordplay became more frenzied and erratic until he lunged hard at Medici who stepped lightly out of the way. Arnaldo fell head-long on the flagstones, his sword clattering away out of reach.

He stayed there on his hands and knees, breathing hard while Medici stood over him, sword still in hand. What would the man do now, wondered Arnaldo, if he knew his name was not really Rossi, but Pazzi. Thankfully he didn't know. He was laughing heartily and quite unguarded. Arnaldo's sword lay just out of reach but he still had the dagger. He put his hand to his chest as if to quiet his racing heart. There it was inside his tunic. He could feel the smooth bone handle nestling in his palm. It would only take a quick thrust up between the ribs. Leonardo's anatomy lessons would prove useful for something at last. Then he could be gone in moments.

'Ah! The eagerness of youth,' Lorenzo went on, unaware of the danger he was in. 'I believe you became quite angry then. That was your undoing. Here.' He held out a hand and Arnaldo looked at it with loathing. 'What? Not still angry? Come, take a glass of wine with me to restore your spirits. My daughter will be ready soon.' Arnaldo froze. His fingers had already tightened around the weapon. But if he used it, then there would be no more Alessandra. He would never even see her again. He tried to tell himself that that

~ 44 ~

didn't matter. But it did. Medici's hand was still there, open. Hating himself as a traitor, he accepted it grimly and was helped to his feet. Together they entered the house.

## Six

MARIA did not see the girl again. The crowd thinned out after the race and she thought she saw a glimpse of white dress but whoever was wearing it slipped away and was gone before she could get near. She told herself it was nothing, just a girl in costume. But the doubts in her mind lingered. She hadn't liked the way she stared with that unchanging expression.

Beppe eventually managed to wriggle out of the mob of delighted neighbours who all wanted to slap him on the back or ruffle his hair or push sweets into his hand. He emerged still in his blue and yellow shirt to find his cousins watching some jugglers in harlequin outfits tossing fire sticks into the air.

'Want some?' he asked, his mouth full of chocolate. The crowd gasped as one of the jugglers spat a jet of flame from his mouth.

'Thanks.' Maria looked at her cousin. He was the same age as Tommy but smaller. His eyes were bright and restless and he looked a bit wild. She took two chocolate bars from him and unwrapped one for Tommy who didn't take his eyes off the performance. He held the chocolate untasted in his hand. The fire arced from one juggler to the other, faster and faster, while Tommy stared, mouth open. Beppe looked at him curiously.

'Is he all right?'

Maria frowned. 'Of course he is,' she said. Her brother might be a pain but that didn't mean anyone could laugh at him.

'He doesn't say much.' Beppe's expression was interested but there was no cruelty there. Maria softened a little.

'No, he doesn't. He's a bit clumsy as well. He's always been like that. Mum says he was too long being born and he didn't get enough oxygen.'

'Oh,' said Beppe simply. He finished his chocolate while the three of them watched together but he was already growing impatient. The jugglers made one last throw high into the air. Then they caught their sticks, extinguished the flames and bowed low to the applause of the audience. 'Come on. Let's go up there?' he said while they were still clapping. He pointed to the bell tower of the church.

The inside of the church was cool and quiet after the heat and bustle of the piazza. The floor was tiled a dusty white and pillared archways supported the vaulted roof, dividing the interior into three aisles. 'This way,' said Beppe. His footsteps sounded loud as he raced across to a wooden door in the corner but Maria was in no hurry to follow him.

'What are these?' She passed through an archway and stood in front of a series of frescoes painted on the wall.

'They're just old pictures. C'mon. If we hurry we'll have time to ring the bell before Father Romano finds us.'

'Ring the bell? You never said that.'

'So I'm saying it now. Are you coming?'

Her gaze returned to the wall paintings. They were faded and cracked and obviously very old but something about them intrigued her. 'No. I want to stay here. You can go with Tommy if you like.' She looked around for her brother but he was already occupied at the altar, entranced by the bright cloth and shiny candlesticks. 'Don't touch them, Tommy!' He lowered his hand guiltily.

'Suit yourself.' Beppe ducked through the old door and began to climb the rickety wooden staircase that wound around the inside of the bell tower. 'Get ready to run when the old priest comes.' His voice sounded distant and muffled. Maria turned back to the pictures and was soon absorbed by the strange images. Each scene was different but one particular figure was in all of them. An old man, completely bald, but with a long grey beard that hung almost to his feet. She didn't know who he was.

'How do you like our saint?'

Maria jumped as a man's voice broke the silence just behind her left shoulder. She spun around quickly to see Father Romano standing and smiling at her in his black robes and hat. Her eyes darted to the door of the bell tower. Why hadn't the bell rung yet? The priest seemed to read her thoughts. 'Yes, I thought young Beppe might be in high spirits after his little victory in the donkey race. I took the precaution of tying back the bell rope. We shall see how long it takes him to loosen it.' Maria grinned at him.

'Who is he?' she asked, pointing at the pictures.

'The old man? It's our very own Saint Arnaldo.'

'The one the town's named after?'

'The very one,' said the priest nodding. 'He lived here hundreds of years ago, further up in the hills. See?' He pointed to a scene where the old saint stood outside a cave. He was crying and Maria couldn't help giggling because the artist had painted giant teardrops flooding out of Saint Arnaldo's eyes like two fountains.

'He doesn't look very happy.'

'No. He was a miserable sort. It is said that when he first came to these parts he cried for a year and a day and during that time he neither ate nor slept. When he had cried all his tears he got up from where he had been lying and there was a spring bubbling up from the ground. It's still there to this day. We call it the Well of Tears.'

Maria looked at Father Romano suspiciously but his face was giving nothing away. 'It's a salt water spring then,' she observed. A smile flickered about the edge of the priest's mouth but he said nothing. He just raised an eyebrow as if he didn't understand. 'If the well really is Saint Arnaldo's tears it would be salty.'

'I don't know,' said the priest. 'Maybe you should go and find out.'

She wandered further along the aisle and looked at the other scenes. There was one of the saint wearing nothing but a loincloth and bandages. Blood was seeping through from a wound from his side. Another one showed the saint with a book in one hand and a sword in the other. A bright light shone out of his face and he was in the act of killing a creature that appeared to be a cross between a snake and a lion. A third showed him with his hand raised towards a witch-like woman who cowered before him. She was dressed in white with a tumbling mass of wild red hair and there was blood dripping from her mouth.

'Is he for real?'

'Oh yes,' the priest murmured. 'He is real. I can show you if you like.' Maria felt a sudden stab of fear.

'What do you mean, "show me"?'

'He is still here in the church.' He made a gesture towards the back of the building and Maria turned slowly, half afraid of what might be there. A saint that had been dead for hundreds of years had to be a skeleton or worse. The whole idea was pretty disgusting and yet . . .

'OK,' she said. Her voice was barely a whisper.

Father Romano pulled out a bunch of keys from inside his cassock. It was a heavy iron ring and the keys were mostly long and dark and ancient looking. He made his way to the back of the church where a small low door was set in the wall. Maria took a quick glance to see that Tommy was all right and then followed him. The lock was well oiled and with barely a sound the door to the crypt swung open to reveal nothing but a deep black hole. There were steps leading down but they became invisible beyond the third one. Some candles were burning in a nearby alcove. The priest took one and signalled for Maria to do the same. Then it was down into the vaulted burial chamber that lay beneath the church.

'Is everybody buried here?' Maria asked as they picked their way carefully down the steep stone steps.

'No, no. We don't bury anybody here. Everyone is buried in the graveyard.' Maria felt relieved to hear this but then the priest continued. 'After many years the ground needs using again so when a grave is dug we bring any bones we find in here.' Maria gulped. She wished she hadn't asked.

It was every bit as bad as she had expected. The candles cast a dull light that seemed to get swallowed up quickly by the blackness. When they flickered strange shadows leapt about, seeming to animate the dark corners and fill them with unknown terrors. She stole a glance at the recesses in the walls and with a shudder regretted it. One was piled high with skulls in neat geometric rows. Another contained only long straight thighbones. It was very organised but weird. Bits of people, categorised and neatly filed away. She turned back only to brush her face against a cobweb which made her let out a small shriek. She cast a longing glance back at the entrance but took a deep breath and carried on.

The crypt was very long, more like a tunnel than a room and they had to go past various dark openings in the walls. Father Romano kept on walking at a steady pace holding his candle out in front of him. From behind, his shape was silhouetted and unfortunately the curled brim of his hat looked extraordinarily like horns to Maria. She looked at the floor until she saw a rat scurrying along the edge of the wall. What did rats find to eat down here? She really didn't want to know the answer to that one. Eventually at the very end, the tunnel widened out into a circular room and here the priest stopped. They had come so far that Maria guessed they must be just below the altar.

'Here we are,' said the priest. He was standing in front of a raised stone platform on which an ornate coffin was laid. It was lidless and Father Romano was calmly holding his candle to illuminate who or whatever was in it. Maria hung back, not daring to go nearer. She felt her fear rising in her chest like a lump that would choke her.

'Is he just bones?' she whispered, not trusting her voice any louder.

'No. He is very well preserved.'

Good grief! That sounded worse. 'How?'

Father Romano shrugged. 'They say his holiness keeps him from decay but maybe the embalmer's art has helped. Who knows? Come, take a look. He won't hurt you.'

Reluctantly she edged forward. It would be stupid to come this far and no further. She kept her eyes lowered until she stood directly over the coffin then willed herself to look up. Nothing could have prepared her for what she saw. She gasped and felt suddenly light-headed. She instinctively reached for the coffin for support then recoiled as she realised what she was doing. Bones, rotting or shrivelled flesh – these she had been expecting, but not this. In the coffin lay an old man so perfect he might have been sleeping.

She shut her eyes tight as she fought to control the revulsion that was screaming inside her head. He couldn't be dead. He had to be alive. Any moment now he would open his eyes or sit up. It was a while before the shock passed and she was able to look at him again. He was quite bald as in the pictures but his beard was shorter and rested lightly on his chest. He was dressed in beautiful vestments – white linen embroidered with gold and silver stitches. His hands were folded over his stomach and his face was serene and gentle – very pale and smooth like an infant's. She noticed in particular his eyelashes which were dark and contrasted with his skin. 'Is he really dead?' she asked, knowing it was a stupid question.

Father Romano chuckled. 'But of course he is.' The old priest actually reached down and touched Saint Arnaldo on the forehead. 'He is as cold as clay.'

'It's horrible,' she said.

'Oh, I don't know,' he reflected. 'At least we keep him discreetly out of sight. Now in Sienna, they have just the head of Saint Caterina Benincasa. They keep it on a marble slab.'

'You're kidding.'

He was not. 'Come on,' he said. 'Let's go back up and see how Beppe is getting on.' Maria nodded. She was not sorry to go.

∞

Upstairs, she deposited her candle back in the alcove while the old man locked the crypt door. Its little flame seemed weak and lost in the church after the darkness it had been through. Together they walked up the centre aisle to where Tommy still stood. He was idly fiddling with a brass crucifix that he had managed to unscrew from its base. Maria felt the urge to touch someone warm and alive so she took her brother's hand and squeezed it tightly. Some muffled shouting was coming from the bell tower.

'Ah!' Father Romano seemed very satisfied with something as he returned the cross to where it belonged. 'That is probably young Beppe discovering that even when the rope is free, a bell won't ring without one of these.' He took a metal bell-clapper about eight inches long from inside his robes and held it up for the children to see. There were further sounds of thumping footsteps, then a rattling of a door handle and finally shouts and blows on the door. 'And if I'm not mistaken, that will be Beppe finding that the door to the tower is locked. Shall we go back to festival?' Maria grinned as she slipped her arm into the old man's and the three of them walked out into the sunshine.

The rest of the day was long and happy. After half an hour the priest went to let Beppe out of the tower only to find the bell rope dangling from the window and the prisoner long gone. They found him just as a performance was about to start on an outdoor stage set up in the centre of the square. It was an old traditional play that had been performed every year for as long as anyone could remember. Saint Arnaldo was in it and also the witch from the church painting. It was very funny with the witch played by an ugly man called Peppone in a white dress and red wig. Maria couldn't tell exactly what was going on but it seemed to involve eating babies and howling at the moon. The crowd booed and hissed the witch, and cheered when the hero entered played by none other than Uncle Giorgio in a bald wig and beard. He had his legs through a horse costume suspended from his shoulders and he mercilessly beat the witch about the head with a huge cardboard mallet. He was also holding a paintbrush and Maria kept expecting him to do something with it but he never did. She asked Beppe who just shrugged. It was a very old play so it may have meant something once. After the play was over the dead witch got up to take a bow and then everyone retired to eat the evening meal which was being prepared in the piazza.

There was a whole pig being spit-roasted on a huge fire. There were mounds of deep-fried crispy bread. There was pasta in tomato and tarragon sauce. There was unlimited red wine being siphoned out of great bell-jars. Beppe managed to get hold of some plastic cupfuls of this, which they drank while they thought no adults were watching. Then there was an enormous pudding that had a sort of hard chocolate base, with a squidgy chocolate filling and a crumbly chocolate topping. After her third helping Maria felt she had had enough but then decided there might just be room for one more little one.

It was late evening by the time the meal was over. The fire still burned and everyone sat around talking and laughing into the night. No one seemed inclined to put any children to bed but as the younger ones grew tired they would fall asleep where they were in an adult's lap. Tommy soon rested his head on his mum's shoulder but Maria was wide awake. The glass of wine she had drunk earlier had heightened her senses and the colours of the fire seemed more real and vibrant. A man had got out a guitar and was strumming quietly in the background until someone called for a song. He smiled and began singing in a low voice. An old song. Voices gradually fell quiet as people listened. It told a story which was simple and tragic. Two young lovers who could never marry because their families were enemies. They swore undying love for each other but the girl's father challenged the youth and slew him in a sword fight. The girl in her grief took her own life by throwing herself from a bridge. The strumming of the guitar and the low sonorous voice held Maria mesmerised. She seemed to be transported back to a time when love was stronger, when quarrels could be settled with the sword, when people lived shorter and blazed brighter. Then, the song came to an end. She blinked and came out of her reverie. The fire had burned low and she found she was suddenly very tired.

# Seven

'*You* are doing well, signor. It is still early of course, but your work shows definite promise. I must congratulate Verrocchio on having such an able assistant.'

Lorenzo de Medici stood behind Arnaldo and studied the portrait while the artist mixed his paints. He had recovered his breath after the fight but his feelings were still in turmoil. He had not wanted to share a drink with his enemy but dared not refuse. The half-drunk glass was even now on the table next to his brushes. He made no response to Medici's praise. Marietta was already at her post in the corner chair with her ever-present pile of sewing. A moment later Alessandra entered the room. She took her seat without a word as Arnaldo risked a quick glance at her. Her head was bowed so he could not see her face.

'Ah! Here is the fortunate girl herself. I am right in calling her fortunate, would you not agree, Signor Rossi?'

Arnaldo looked up at Medici. Was that just a courtesy question or was there some deeper significance? Medici wore a slight frown as he looked at his daughter. 'I . . . I don't know, signor.'

'Come now, don't be shy. Of course she is fortunate. Is she not to marry Signor Orsini? It is a good match. Very good. He has wealth. He has influence. His late wife, God rest her, did not give him a child so he has no heir.' Medici listed Orsini's merits as a husband to Arnaldo but his eyes remained fixed on Alessandra as if his words were for her benefit. 'Also he is my dear wife's cousin so family bonds are strengthened and wealth is not lost to strangers.' He walked over to his daughter and tilted her face upwards. 'Indeed she is most fortunate,' he said quietly. Arnaldo could see now why Alessandra had not come earlier. Her red eyes showed she had been crying but even now she looked lovely. Medici let go of her chin and she lowered her gaze immediately. Arnaldo felt a pang of pity for her. 'Make her beautiful, Signor Rossi. This picture must be worthy of such a union.'

'I will paint her as I see her,' Arnaldo said softly.

Medici turned and gave Arnaldo a penetrating stare, his dark eyes thoughtful as if he did not know how to take that last comment. 'Very good,' he said at last. 'Carry on.'

There was an uncomfortable silence when he had gone. Arnaldo stared resolutely at his paints and continued to mix them even though they were already smoothed to a fine paste. Finally he could delay no longer. 'If you are ready now, signorina . . . ?' She nodded but said nothing. 'I must begin on your dress today so

I will need you to hold your arm as before.' Alessandra turned listlessly to the left and raised her arm. The light from the window fell on the folds of her silk dress. The untrained eye would call it white but Arnaldo could see blues and greys in the shadow and yellow, almost gold, in the light. It would take all his art to capture it with his brushes.

His eyes rested slowly on Alessandra taking in every detail and planning how he would begin. He shifted his gaze to the portrait and then back to the girl again. A slight frown appeared on his forehead. Something about her pose was wrong. Her shoulders were bowed and her hand drooped. 'Signorina, your back is not as straight as it was and your arm needs to be a little higher.' She moved but it still wasn't perfect. Arnaldo's frown deepened. It had to be right before he could continue. 'No, no, signorina. It should be like this.' He stepped forward and unthinkingly placed his hand under her elbow to correct the position. Alessandra stiffened at his touch but did not snatch her arm away. Some of the fire returned to her eyes as she turned to face him.

'I will ask you to unhand me at once, signor.'

Arnaldo started guiltily and immediately pulled his hand away. His face flushed red. 'I . . . I am so sorry, signorina. I did not mean to offend. I only . . .' He tailed off in shame. He glanced at Marietta but she continued sewing with her head down. Arnaldo got the impression she was highly amused at the incident. Alessandra did not dignify his apology with an acceptance. She proudly drew herself up and assumed the perfect pose. Arnaldo returned to his brushes in silence. Could he do nothing right? At least he knew how to get the best out of her. He only had to make her angry. And that wasn't difficult, he mused as he filled his brush with white.

∞

Marietta watched Arnaldo's face closely as he worked. His brown eyes were half closed in concentration and he occasionally bit his lower lip. After twenty minutes he stood back and surveyed what he had done. 'Perhaps you would like to rest for a moment, signorina.' Alessandra lowered her arm and put her hands in her lap. Even the voice seemed familiar to Marietta. She did not know of course, but she had asked around those who remembered Francesco de Pazzi. Not many did – he came from Rome. But there was talk of a son – aged about ten years at the time.

She returned to her sewing and kept her face lowered as she idly said, 'It's strange, is it not, how no one goes by the name of Pazzi in Florence now.' Arnaldo, thankfully, was not painting else he would have made a bad stroke. His back was towards Marietta but, even so, he betrayed himself by the sudden tensing of his shoulders. Marietta's suspicions were all but confirmed. 'There must be many of that name who fear to use it.' Alessandra stared at her old nurse.

'What madness are you talking now?'

'You don't remember. You were just a girl of eight.'

'Remember what, pray?'

'The night your father came in with the wound on his neck. The day your Uncle Giuliano died.'

Alessandra's mind immediately went back seven years. She had only been a little girl. She remembered the shouts of alarm, the sound of footsteps hurrying, the sight of her father with the bloodied rag clutched to his neck. She saw again her mother begging him to be still so she could attend to him, the look of fury in her father's eyes as he raged around the room and swore eternal vengeance on his enemies. She and her brothers Piero and Giovanni had huddled together, unnoticed in a corner, watching terrified, not under-standing what was happening. 'Of course I remember,' she said quietly, 'but what has this to do with the name Pazzi?'

'It was a Pazzi who killed your uncle,' said Marietta.

Alessandra was silent at this revelation. Then she made an impatient noise in her throat. 'Why talk of this now? We should return to the painting.' She turned to resume her pose but still Marietta continued.

'I'm sure Signor *Rossi* will not mind.' She placed particular emphasis on the name.

Arnaldo felt sick in his stomach. What could he do? The old witch had him. She must know who he was. He had to get away. 'I think perhaps I have done enough for today,' he mumbled. His hands were shaking as he put his brush down on the table.

'Enough?' said Alessandra in surprise. 'You've done but twenty minutes. Come now, you should continue while the light is still good. You do not want to anger my father.'

Arnaldo went to pick up his brush but fumbled it. There was no way he could paint in this state. 'You should rest a little longer, signorina. I will mix some more paint.' He made a pretence of tipping some more powder on to his palette and began to mix, desperately trying to bring his panic under control.

'Very well,' Alessandra sighed. 'Come then, Marietta. Signor Rossi seems determined not to work. Tell us your story.'

The old nurse looked hard at Arnaldo. 'What do you say, signor? Do you want to hear my tale?'

Arnaldo did not. It was the last thing in the world he wanted to hear, but what could he say. Marietta with her knowledge had complete power over him now. 'If the signorina wishes it,' he said in a whisper.

Marietta put down her sewing and folded her hands in her lap. 'It was seven years ago . . .' she began.

# Eight

MARIA woke late the next morning. She wandered downstairs bleary-eyed, still in her pyjamas to find Nonna presiding over breakfast. 'Good morning, sleepyhead.' The old lady wiped her hands on her apron and pulled the girl towards her to give her a kiss.

'*Ciao!* Nonna.' She took her seat at the breakfast table and noticed that despite yesterday's feast there was another huge selection of food to tempt her. She helped herself to some bread and cheese and a slice of spicy sausage while Nonna placed a mug of steaming hot chocolate next to her. Her parents and Aunt Adriana were still at the table but Uncle Giorgio had already gone to work. Beppe and Tommy had gone off somewhere as well. She wondered briefly what sort of trouble those two might get up to together. Oh well. Not her problem. Her aunt and mum were talking – planning a shopping trip. Elisabetta always bought shoes when she visited her home town. And handbags. Often jewellery as well. And clothes of course. Her dad was finishing his coffee and reading a newspaper. One of the headlines read ORSINI PORTRAIT REMOVED FOR CLEANING.

'Are you going shopping too, Dad?'

'Not with your mother,' John said, looking up. 'She's already told me she'd find my company . . . inhibiting. I thought I'd have a wander around the piazza again. Maybe have a look in some of those antique shops. Might pick up a bargain.'

'There are some really old paintings in the church. I saw them yesterday.'

'Really? I must take a look then.'

'I'll come with you if you like. I can tell you all about Saint Arnaldo but you'll need the priest if you want to see him. He's locked in the crypt.'

'Who, Father Romano?'

'No! Saint Arnaldo.'

John made a face. 'I'll stick with the pictures,' he said.

There was still plenty of evidence of yesterday's celebrations in the town square when they arrived there later. Some men were busy taking apart the stage that the play had been performed on. Others were raking up the ashes from the fire and collecting the litter that the festival-goers had left behind them. Maria and her dad went into the first of the antique shops and started browsing among the piles of old pots, books, furniture and countless other treasures they had on offer. Maria was quite taken with a stuffed boar but John refused to even consider it. He was more interested in the paintings and spent some time casting his expert eye over the old oils and watercolours. Some were hung on the wall but others were just heaped up in piles in the corner or under tables. They were mostly nineteenth-century landscapes, none of them particularly good, and they soon moved on to the next shop.

They spent the rest of the morning in the same way, and after lunch in the sunshine outside a café they decided to do one more shop before heading off to the church. The bell over the door jangled as they entered and a man came out from a back room to stand behind the counter. He had black hair slicked back and stubble on his chin. The father and daughter chatted to each other in English as they looked through the artwork.

'What about this one?' Maria held up a dingy portrait of a woman in a silk dress with her hair piled up in an elaborate heap.

'Ugly,' was John's professional verdict.

'This one?' A lake scene with a man fishing from a rowing boat.

'Amateurish.'

She selected another, a rural scene with a peasant farmer leading a donkey. He could not find words to describe his contempt for this one but winced as if in pain. The shopkeeper's eyes flitted from father to daughter as they spoke, his English not quick enough to keep up with what they were saying. Maria had just about given up on the pile she was working through when she saw one more leaning against the wall. It was so dusty that she nearly missed it. She pulled it out and a huge dust cloud wafted into the room as she blew on it, making her cough. It was another landscape like the twenty or thirty her dad had already rejected, yellow under the layers of varnish that covered it. As far as she could see there was nothing special about it but as she held it in her hands she was filled with a vague sense of urgency.

'How about this one?' Her voice was uncertain. John glanced up from the early twentieth-century townscape he was inspecting.

'That is . . .' The word 'horrible' never reached his lips. Instead, a puzzled expression crossed his face. '. . . worth looking at,' he finished. He took the painting from his daughter and brought it nearer to the window to see it better. The frame was ornate gilt and slightly blackened with soot. He turned it over to look at the back and over again to resume looking at the front. The look of puzzlement deepened.

'Is it any good?' Maria asked in a low voice.

'It's awful,' said John bluntly.

'Oh!' Maria was confused. 'Why are you so interested in it then?'

'I don't know really. Feel the weight of it.'

Maria took the painting and weighed it in her hands. 'It's heavier than the others.'

'That's because it's painted on wooden board, not canvas.'

'How can you tell?'

'I've got a PhD in fine art.'

'Oh yeah. Is that unusual?'

'What, having a PhD?'

'No! Painting on board.'

'It is for a picture this age.'

They had been talking quietly but the shopkeeper could tell they were interested. 'Ees very nice, yes?' His broken English was hard to understand. 'Very old and valuable. I let you have it for tree hundred euros. Ees a bargain.'

John turned to the man and smiled disarmingly. Then in perfect Italian he said, 'It's a completely unremarkable, nineteenth-century, amateur oil painting but I quite like the frame.' The man's face fell. 'I'll give you fifty for it.'

The shopkeeper made an attempt to regain the advantage, this time in Italian. 'No, no, signor. It is very good. I sold one just like it last week for five hundred euros.'

'Then you ripped somebody off.' John looked at the name signed in the corner of the painting. 'Elenora Giannotti,' he read. 'Never heard of her.' Maria started in surprise. Giannotti. Where had she heard that name recently? The scowling shopkeeper eventually accepted seventy-five euros. He wrapped the painting in some brown paper which he tied up in string and handed over to John.

'*Grazie.*' John took the parcel and then they walked back out into the square. 'Right, let's go to the church then.'

∞

The church was quiet and empty save for one old woman dressed in black. She knelt in prayer by an altar where candles were burning. Her head was bowed so they couldn't see her face. They spoke in hushed voices so as not to disturb her. John didn't know anything about the life of Saint Arnaldo but he did know a lot about paintings. He explained that the pictures on the walls could last for hundreds of years – these were probably five hundred years old. It was to do with the way they were made. They were painted directly on to damp plaster and so the pigments soaked in and dried to become part of the wall itself. That way they could never flake off. Maria half listened but couldn't really take in what her dad was saying. Her mind was still on the picture they had just bought and her eyes kept wandering to the parcel he had clutched under his arm.

'Your mind's not really on this, is it?' John smiled at his daughter.

'No,' she admitted. 'I want another look at your painting.'

'OK. Let's go home then.'

They left the church and, as the door closed behind them, silence fell again. Some twenty minutes later the old lady finished her prayers and got up slowly, her joints protesting after being still for so long. She too stopped in front of the wall paintings. She briefly put out a hand, twisted with age, to touch the face of Saint Arnaldo. Then she muttered another blessing before turning to leave as well.

∞

Back at home John laid the parcel on the kitchen table. Nobody else was around. Maria found a pair of scissors in a drawer and snipped the string. Then she pulled off the paper and stood back to look at the painting. She wasn't quite sure what she was expecting but couldn't help feeling disappointed. Nothing had changed. It still looked like a grubby, boring, old painting. Her dad didn't feel much better.

'What have I done? It's horrible.'

'It might be better if we clean it.'

It was incredibly grimy, and even the bits that were cleaner showed it to be yellow with age. John wasn't hopeful. 'It'll take more than cleaning. Look at it. Clumsy brushwork, no sense of perspective, boring subject . . .' He tailed off, shaking his head but went to get his box of cleaning materials anyway. With a damp sponge he was able to clear the worst of the grime off. 'There,' he said after about twenty minutes. He studied the picture again with a critical eye. 'I think I prefer it *with* the dirt.'

Maria giggled. 'It's still really dull. Can't you make the colours brighter?'

'Not without taking the varnish off. That's what's gone yellow.'

'Can you do that?'

'Can I do that?' John pretended to look hurt. 'Of course I can. The question is, can I be bothered? I think we'd be better off, just hiding the thing before your mother sees it.'

'Please.' She looked imploringly at her dad who relented.

'Oh, all right. It'll be a good lesson in art restoration if nothing else. It takes a long time though. You'll soon get bored.'

Maria drew up a chair to watch her dad work. First he opened a window to let some air in. Then he fished out of his box the things he was going to need. Rags, cotton wool, cotton buds, a metal spatula and lastly a brown bottle with a skull and crossbones on the label. This was the cleaning solvent and he gently shook it before removing the cap. A strong smell of alcohol wafted into the room.

'This stuff will dissolve the varnish and then I can scrape it off. You have to be careful though, because if you leave it on too long it starts dissolving the paint as well.'

He started to work in the bottom left corner where Elenora Giannotti had signed her name. With a cotton bud he began applying the solvent, rubbing it in with gentle circular strokes. He worked at it until he had covered a small area and as he did it, the varnish began to bubble up. Then, when it was ready, he dabbed up the newly loosened varnish with a wad of cotton wool, lifting the more stubborn bits with the spatula. After forty minutes he had cleared about ten square centimetres. The colours were much fresher and more of the detail was visible.

'There. That will do for today.' Maria studied the cleaned section closely. John put the bottle down on the table and was about to put the cap back on when he heard the door open. It was Beppe and Tommy. 'Hello, you two. What've you been up to all day?'

'Nothing,' said Beppe innocently. John eyed him quizzically.

'I wonder if we mean the same thing by "nothing". Did Tommy break anything?'

'No,' Beppe said indignantly. 'Nothing important anyway.'

'Hmm.'

The door opened again. This time it was Nonna. '*Santa Tomata!*' she said clutching emotionally at her forehead. 'What are you doing in my kitchen. The smell, it is horrible.'

'Just clearing up,' said John quickly. He gathered up the soggy cotton wool and took the spatula away from Tommy.

The door went a third time and Elisabetta and Adriana staggered in, laden down with bags and parcels. 'What a day!' Elisabetta said. 'Maria darling, help me get the rest of the stuff in from the car.'

'You've got more?' John asked in disbelief.

'But of course,' said his wife. 'What is that?' She saw the painting and John winced as he anticipated her reaction. '*Mamma Mia!* Did you pay money for this? How much?'

'Seventy-five euros,' said Maria before her dad could stop her.

'Seventy-five!' Elisabetta's expression said it all.

'Yes,' said John defensively. 'I'm sorry if you don't

like it. Perhaps you wanted the money to buy yourself another shoe.' He looked meaningfully at the vast pile of shopping at her feet. She took the point.

'No, no. It's fine, darling, if you like it. Where shall we hang it?'

He was about to suggest the attic when something made him stop. There was suddenly a much stronger smell of solvent in the room. He spun around and there was Tommy standing guiltily by the bottle. It was lying on its side, the contents glugging out on to the table.

'My table!' screamed Nonna.

John quickly grabbed the bottle and turned it upright. Then he dabbed at the pool with his rags.

'It's on the painting!' Maria spoke shrilly and Tommy look frightened. Tears filled his eyes.

'Oh hell!' John muttered. The solvent had only touched one corner – the bit where he had already removed the varnish. He swabbed it with a huge wad of cotton wool.

'Is it all right?'

He removed the cotton wool, discarded it and applied a fresh wad. 'I think so.' Then a moment later. 'No.' He looked doleful as he pulled off the second swab. It came away covered in green paint. The corner of the painting was a smudgy mess. He gazed at it sadly for a few moments more. 'Well, it's no great loss to the world of art but I could've saved myself seventy-five euros. Don't cry, Tommy.' He put his arm around his son's shoulder. 'I'm not angry.'

Maria was staring intently at the spoiled picture. She took another wad of cotton wool and carefully wiped away the last of the dissolved paint and then looked up, wide-eyed.

'What is it?' John asked.

'I think there's a different picture underneath.'

# Nine

𝒜s Marietta spoke, Arnaldo found himself unwillingly dragged back seven years. Soon he didn't even notice her voice. He closed his eyes and the sights, the sounds were as vivid as if he were there now. The spring of 1478. They were frightening times; bewildering to a ten-year-old who understood nothing of power struggles, secret alliances, plots and conspiracies. But some things were only too clear. His father was dead. So were most of his family. Not only killed, but publicly shamed. Their wealth taken. Men of rank forbidden from marrying Pazzi girls. Their name wiped out – deliberately and methodically. Every paper burnt, every seal destroyed. Even the family crests and emblems had been chiselled out of the walls of his home. It was as if the Pazzi had never existed. He had survived because of his youth and the courage of his nurse. But he had not been too young to remember. Nor too young to swear his revenge.

It all happened in April of that year. The Medici finally went too far. After years of building power, they had imagined themselves strong enough to take on Rome and offended the Pope by refusing him a loan.

He wanted forty thousand ducats, a large sum but not beyond the Medici. The only trouble was, Pope Sixtus wanted the money to buy the Lordship of Imola – a town the Medici themselves were planning to control. So they hesitated and while they waited, the Pazzi family stepped in to make the loan. Then with the approval of the offended Pope they planned to challenge the Medici and bring them down for ever.

Lorenzo and his brother Giuliano were the chief targets. The Pazzi managed to gather around themselves resentful men who bore a grudge against the Medici. Salviati, Archbishop of Pisa whom Lorenzo had insulted. Bernardo Bandini who was so much in debt to the Pazzi that they all but owned him. Even Gian Battista da Montesecco, leader of a band of mercenary adventurers, who had been a personal friend of Lorenzo.

Their plan was laid. It was bold but so confident were they of success that they did not fear for the consequences. They chose their moment. Not secretly under the cover of darkness, but in full view of hundreds – on a Sunday morning, as the leading citizens of Florence assembled for High Mass in the cathedral. Two priests in the pay of the Pazzi had daggers concealed beneath their robes. They were to stab Lorenzo, while Bernardo and one other assassin would take Giuliano his brother. This second killer was called Francesco de Pazzi.

∞

'Do not wait for me,' cried Giuliano de Medici. Lorenzo stopped on the foot of the steps and turned to face his brother. The crowd streamed passed him, laughing and gossiping. Giuliano was still some distance away, limping from a recent illness. 'I am not alone.' Lorenzo shielded his eyes against the sun and saw that Francesco de Pazzi and Bernardo Bandini were lingering with his brother. He waved and turned to enter the church.

Giuliano stopped to catch his breath. 'I will not be long,' he panted to his companions.

'Do not distress yourself,' Francesco smiled. 'We have plenty of time. Here let me help you.' He slipped an arm around Giuliano's waist and helped him up the steps. Giuliano gave a grateful smile as Pazzi gently supported him. Pazzi caught Bandini's eye and nodded. That arm around the waist had told him all he needed to know. Giuliano had no armour under his tunic.

The inside of the church was cool despite the great crowd. The priests were already engaged in their service but there was still a buzz of conversation. Giuliano searched the crowd. There was Lorenzo up by the main altar. He would not join him there now. He leant against the doorpost and listened as the choir began to sing. As the moment for the blessing arrived, a tinkling bell brought the congregation to quiet. This was the signal the assassins had been waiting for.

Bandini was first into action. The mask of friendship slipped from his face and with a cry of 'Take that traitor!' he turned on Giuliano. He brought down his dagger with a wild blow on the bemused man's skull that split it open like butchered meat. Francesco de Pazzi also drew his weapon and attacked in such a frenzy that he plunged the knife in nineteen times. Only then did he realise that he had wounded himself in the thigh. Giuliano lay at their feet, his body a mangled mess and his life ebbing away with his blood as it spread across the tiled floor.

Screams of horror instantly filled the cathedral. In panic the congregation rose up and bolted for safety. The two murderous priests had drawn their daggers as well but Lorenzo was better prepared than his brother. With great strength he pushed them both off with a roar and took no more than a cut to his neck. Then he whipped off his cloak, wrapped it around his arm as a shield and quickly drew his sword.

The priests backed away, no match for the enraged man. But Bandini, having finished with Giuliano, was now running full pitch down the main aisle with his sword drawn. The people scattered as they parted to let him through and friends rushed to Lorenzo's side.

'This way, signor, be quick. You are not safe. There may be others.' Francesco Nori took Lorenzo's arm and urged him to move.

'Is Giuliano safe?' Blood was flowing freely from Lorenzo's wound down on to his tunic as his eyes searched for his brother.

'Hurry, my lord!'

Too late. Bandini was upon them. He lunged at

Lorenzo only to find his sword sink into the brave Francesco Nori. He fell dead instantly at his master's feet. Seconds later Lorenzo had been bundled into a side room where vestments and sacred vessels were kept and the heavy bronze doors were slammed shut. Lorenzo's face was white from shock and loss of blood. Strong hands settled him into a chair and one man, Antonio Ridolfi, impulsively lunged at Lorenzo as if to kiss him. Instead he put his lips to his neck and sucked the wound, spitting the blood on the floor. A poisoned blade could kill even when the wound was slight.

'Where is Giuliano? Is Giuliano safe? Somebody find my brother. Why does he not come?' Lorenzo kept up a constant mumbling as his wound was treated. None of his companions would answer him, or even catch his eye. Finally he pushed his attendants away and cried out, 'Why do you not answer? You!' He pointed to a young friend, Sigismondo della Stufa. 'Find out where my brother is.'

There was a spiral stairway in the room that led to a loft above that the choir used. Reluctantly the man climbed, knowing what he would find and fearful of being the one to bring the news. The view of the inside of the cathedral showed it to be almost deserted now. 'What do you see?' cried Lorenzo.

'I see my lord's brother lying in a pool of blood and I see Francesco de Pazzi's dagger still in his body.'

Medici became still at this news. A cold fury came into his eyes that made his companions draw back, afraid. 'Pazzi will pay for this,' he said at length. His voice was low and dripped with hate. 'Ten thousand times he will pay. He and all his kin.' He got up, pushed open the doors and strode out into the church.

∞

Outside, civil war appeared to be breaking out. Crowds of Pazzi supporters led by old Jacopo de Pazzi himself were massing with cries of 'Liberty! Liberty! Down with the Medici!' But there were more who cried, 'Medici lives! Long live the Medici!' As yet the exchanges were limited to shouts and taunts but if a blow were to be struck then that might be the flame that would light a roaring furnace. Lorenzo de Medici strode through the crowded streets, unaware of his fearsome appearance. Congealed blood splattered his face and clothes and the look in his eyes was enough to make brave men cower. There was a madness about him as he made his way to the Pazzi home. Fresh blood on the steps betrayed Francesco's presence inside. The sight of it seemed to incite him to even greater fury. He threw himself at the door and hammered on it, screaming for his enemy to come out and meet his destruction. There was no answer. In his frustration, he cast his eyes about and saw a low stone pillar at the foot of the steps. He seized hold of it and in his rage he managed to lift it a few inches before his friends rushed to help him. Together, six of them battered at the door which splintered in seconds and swung open. Lorenzo staggered in and the trail of blood took him right to the place where Francesco de Pazzi lay in his bed. His courage had deserted him in the cathedral and he was clutching a rag to his still bleeding thigh. Without a word Medici strode across the room and struck him hard on the face with the back of his hand. Then taking a fistful of Pazzi's hair he pulled up his head to expose the soft flesh of his neck. The veins throbbed as the terrified man's heart pumped wildly. Then there was a swish of metal as Medici pulled out his sword.

The boy of ten watched through his fingers from where he crouched behind a trunk, a silent scream stuck somewhere in his chest. Numbly he saw his father pleading for his life while his tormentor held the blade to his throat. He shut his eyes and covered his ears but nothing could block out the cries of fear that mingled with the curses of the bloodstained Medici. Then just as he was sure the fatal thrust would come, Lorenzo lowered his weapon and pushed his father roughly face-down on to the floor. He called to his men who stooped to grab Francesco, pulled him to his feet and bundled him through the doorway. All too soon the screams grew faint and then silent.

Arnaldo never saw his father again. The young nurse found him there twenty minutes later and led him, dazed, out of a side passage and quickly through the streets to her mother's home. Hastily dressed in poorer clothes he went unnoticed as the turmoil raged else- where in the city. A full three weeks he stayed inside, never daring to go out, barely speaking or eating in his shock and grief. With the shutters closed, he shrank back with fear at every footfall that sounded outside their door. In his darkened hideaway he was spared the sight of his father's naked body hanging from the second floor of the Palazzo della Signoria. There it stayed until the crows had picked the bones clean as a warning to any who were foolish enough to oppose the Medici. Arnaldo, meanwhile, was smuggled out of the city and taken to relatives in Rome. A while later he was apprenticed to Verrocchio under a new name and returned to Florence.

Forget your past, he was told. Forget your name. Forget you ever had a father.

But some things can never be forgotten.

# *Ten*

MARIA was desperate to see more of the hidden picture. Her dad let go of Tommy and leant forward to study the damaged area with his daughter. 'I think you're right,' he said. 'Look, there's another layer of varnish and the brushwork underneath is quite different. Can't tell much more than that at the moment.' He reached for his bottle of solvent but Nonna was having none of it.

'No! Not in my kitchen. Take that horrible thing away.' John stopped, poised in the act of wetting a cotton bud. Then he nodded reluctantly and began to collect his things together. 'You can put it in the basement. *Santa Mozzarella!* What a mess.'

Tommy was still sniffing and looking forlorn. Elisabetta put her arm around him and he buried his face in her blouse. 'Never mind, darling.' She ran her fingers through his hair until his crying subsided. 'You're a clever boy. See, you've discovered a new painting.'

'Please, Nonna. Can't we do just a little more,' implored Maria.

'*Certemente no!* Beppe, help your aunt get her shopping in. The rest of you, clean up my kitchen.'

'Don't worry, Maria,' said her father. 'I can work on it tomorrow.' He put the last of the cleaning materials into his box and shut the lid. There was still a strong smell coming from the dark patch of solvent soaked into the table. 'I wouldn't get too excited. Artists often paint over work they're not happy with. If Elenora Giannotti wasn't satisfied with what's under there, then it must be *really* bad.'

Maria wasn't so sure. That name again – she knew it was important.

She was up early the next day and hurrying her dad to get to work even before he had finished his breakfast. 'OK, OK. I'm coming,' he laughed. He picked up his coffee and carried it down to the basement. It was crowded down there: Uncle Giorgio's tools, old furniture, dusty bottles of wine on their sides, a huge terracotta jar of olive oil. The painting was on a workbench, propped up against the wall next to a stripped-down car engine. There were small barred windows set high in the wall, level with the street. Occasionally pairs of feet would go past. It was a good place for watching shoes. The room was still gloomy so John switched on the light and then took a seat, contemplating the picture thoughtfully.

'Well, don't just sit there,' said Maria. 'Do something!'

The first task was to clean up the corner they had started on the previous day. John worked even more carefully than before, cautiously taking off the upper layers of varnish and paint but stopping short of removing the varnish of the mystery painting. It was painstaking work but Maria watched intently the whole time. She got into the habit of passing him things, anticipating what he was going to need next. When it was done he sat back, blinking and massaging his neck where he had been bent over his work. There was not much to see. Underneath the green there was more green. But the colour was paler and more luminescent – almost glowing. The brushwork was more delicate too.

'This is definitely not by the same artist,' said John, puzzled. 'It's much finer work. Why would anyone paint over something like this?'

Maria was bursting with impatience. 'If you do some more, you'll find out?'

'I don't know.' John seemed reluctant. 'I could do with a break and I'm going to need more solvent.' After Tommy's mishap there was only a centimetre or so left in the bottle. 'I'm wondering if I should let a professional finish it.'

'Aren't you a professional?'

'Not in picture restoration.'

'Oh. Are there any here?'

'I doubt it. We'd have to wait till we were back in Florence.'

Maria couldn't bear the thought of that. 'You can do it, Dad.' John smiled at his daughter's confidence in him. 'Will you?' Her voice was pleading.

'All right, just a bit more. Let's go and get some more solvent.'

'Where from?' Maria asked.

'The chemist should have some.'

'OK. Write down what it's called and I'll go and get it.' She left two minutes later at top speed with a piece of paper and a twenty-euro note in her pocket.

It was bright outside after the gloom of the basement and it took a moment for her eyes to adjust. Then she ran down the street towards the centre of town, took a left turn and hurried off towards the piazza where she had seen a chemist's the day before. She had to stop at a busy main road as cars and buses rumbled by. She fidgeted with impatience, urging the light to turn green. After what seemed like an age it changed and a car pulled up in front of her. She was just about to cross when she saw something that made her stop – her feet fixed her to the pavement.

On the corner of the other side of the road there was a girl standing in a doorway. Not just any girl – the girl she had seen in the crowd at the festival. Maria stared hard, her heart beating faster. She appeared to be waiting for something, looking distractedly down the street. Her long auburn hair was hanging loose and she was wearing a simple white slip like a nightdress. Her feet were bare.

Time passed unnoticed as Maria stood and watched the girl. All thought of hurrying to the shop vanished.

It was as if there were just the two of them alone in the street. She found herself longing for the girl to turn and look at her. Until then she was powerless to move. Then she did turn and Maria gasped almost in pain. The girl's eyes widened as she returned Maria's gaze and Maria found herself trembling, held under some spell. She tried to fight it but couldn't resist. The eyes seemed to command her and in obedience she stepped out into the road. Immediately there was a screech of brakes and horns blared. With a cry Maria stumbled back on to the pavement, the spell broken. The lights had changed again and already the traffic was speeding up. Trembling, she waited a second time, watching the girl whenever she could catch glimpses of her between the cars. Then a big truck trundled by and hid her completely from view. It wasn't for more than a moment, but when the truck had passed, the girl was gone. The doorway was empty.

'Well?' Her dad was using up the last of the cleaning solution when she returned with the new bottle.

'Here it is.' She handed it over. Her face was white and her hands were still shaking. Her dad noticed the change.

'You all right?' he asked.

'Yeah,' she said listlessly.

He put down his rag. 'No really, darling. Tell me what's up. You're shaking.' He laid a hand on her shoulder.

~ 87 ~

'It's nothing really,' she said, managing a weak smile. 'I just . . .' She wondered for a moment if she should tell him about the girl. Then she decided not to. It was just stupid. 'I wasn't watching where I was going. I nearly got hit by a car. Shook me up a bit.' He studied her face, searching to see if there was more. 'I'm all right now, Dad, honestly.' She smiled more brightly and held his gaze.

'OK,' he said. 'Lets get back to work. He broke the seal on the bottle and poured out some more fluid.

'Ah!' he said twenty minutes later. 'I think I'm getting something different now.' He soaked up some loosened paint with a wad of cotton wool and looked at the newly cleared area. Maria bent over to look too. In the bottom right-hand corner of the partly cleaned picture they could see a delicately painted garland of flowers. The significance of what they saw was not lost on either of them but it was Maria who spoke first.

'Giannotti! I know where I've heard that name.' Her eyes were bright with excitement and she grabbed her dad's arm. 'It was in that book we read with your students. It's the name of the family who had the White Lady when their house burnt down. This picture must be the White Lady.'

# *Eleven*

' . . . and since that day, no Pazzi has been seen in Florence.'

There was a long silence after Marietta finished her tale. Arnaldo felt faint and sick. To be told again that he was in the house of his father's killer was bad enough. To learn that his father was no better than the man who killed him was unbearable. He hadn't heard the Medici side of the story before. These must be lies. No. Arnaldo knew in his heart the words were true. How did the nurse know? Curse her! What was she going to do now? Nothing it seemed. She took up her needle again and it was Alessandra who spoke first.

'If the Pazzi are no more then it is as much as they deserve,' she said decisively. Her words were like a knife in Arnaldo's heart.

'Yes, your father is always right,' Marietta said. Her tone was offhand and Alessandra could not tell if it was meant as a statement or a question.

'What is that supposed to mean?' she asked angrily.

Marietta shrugged. 'What I say. What your father decides is always right. Your marriage to Signor Orsini for example –'

She was cut short as Alessandra stood up suddenly. The stool crashed to the floor as she turned on her nurse making Arnaldo jump. His nerves were already stretched to breaking point. The girl's eyes were cold with fury but her lip quivered as if she were close to tears. 'How dare you?' Her voice was nearly a sob. 'You forget who you are, Marietta. You are just a servant. My father owns you.' With that, she stormed out of the room, slamming the door as she went.

Arnaldo quickly began to pack away his brushes. There could be no more thought of painting today. He wanted to go away, far away. His hands trembled with emotion making him fumble with his brushes and spill them on the floor. He dared not look at the old nurse in the corner of the room or speak to her. He meant to leave before she had the chance to confront him. But Marietta had other ideas.

'And what did *you* think of my story, signor?'

Arnaldo continued with his paints, his head down. 'It was a hard tale,' he said sullenly.

'My master is a hard man, as I'm sure you know.' Her voice was strangely soft, kind even. Arnaldo stared at her, surprised, but she was still engrossed in her task.

'There is much that Marietta knows,' she said. 'Many years I have served this family and my eyes and ears are always open.' Now she too looked up. She seemed to be weighing him with her eyes. 'But I can keep my mouth closed.'

Arnaldo felt a sudden stir of hope. Did she mean to

keep this secret? 'And will you keep your mouth closed, signora?' His voice was thin and strained.

'That depends,' she said.

'Depends! On what?'

'On you, signor.'

∞

Alessandra rushed into her room and threw herself on to the bed, blinking back hot bitter tears. Her mind screamed with fury at the injustice of it all. She clutched at the bedclothes and screwed them up in her fists. Her breathing was hard and quick as she buried her face in the softness of the sheets, trying to fight back the feelings that were threatening to overwhelm her. Marietta was so cruel. Why did she do it? She had done her best to bury her emotions. She had put a hard shell around her heart but Marietta knew her too well. With just a word or a look she could prise her open like an oyster and expose all the pain that lay inside. In front of the painter as well, which was even more shameful.

Her body trembled with silent sobs but she did not cry for long. She forced herself to be strong and after only ten minutes she rolled over and sat up. She would not let the world know that she cared. Quickly, she crossed to her table where there was a mirror. The rippled glass showed that her skin was pale but her eyes were red and puffy. She took up a bottle of scented water and splashed some around her eyes trying to calm the swelling. Then she took off the gold headband which was lying crooked across her brow and pinned back some loose strands of hair. She would have liked to change out of the white dress but for that she would need Marietta to unlace her at the back. She was growing to hate that dress. Its whiteness reminded her of a shroud. Fitting in a way because what awaited her was surely just like death.

When she was satisfied with her appearance, she reached a finger under her sleeve and took hold of a ribbon that she found there. She pulled on it and soon a tiny silver key dangled from her fingertips. She reached up to tie it about her neck where it usually hung, but then she changed her mind. Lying on the table was a wooden box which she pulled towards herself. She ran her fingers over the top which was inlaid with silver and jewels. It had been a gift from her mother and in it she kept her most precious and secret things. She inserted the little key into the lock and turned it with a quiet click. The lid lifted silently to reveal a chamber lined with red cloth. It still gave off a rich woody smell and she took a deep breath, enjoying the fragrance. After glancing quickly at the door she began to take out the contents of the box. There was a lock from the first cut of her baby hair tied up with crimson thread, a gold necklace, a tiny portrait of her mother, no more than a few centimetres wide but beautifully detailed. There were letters from friends, a pressed flower, picked from the fields of their country home where they stayed in the heat of the summer, a few coins. Each item represented a particular memory from her life so far. In a way, the whole of her childhood was held in this box. Her fingers lingered lovingly as she touched each one. Soon this life would be left behind for ever.

Finally she came to the last item which had not been kept there long. It was a small bottle of glass so dark that the liquid contents looked grim and murky. The cork stopper was sealed with black wax. It was an infusion of hemlock. It had not been easy to obtain the little bottle that now lay in her palm. It had required deceit and cunning. After weeks of practice she had mastered a fair imitation of her father's signature. Then she had written out an order to the apothecary and given it to a servant explaining that her brother Piero could not sleep at night because of his cough. The hemlock would relax his chest. The servant had been suspicious, she could tell, but he had not questioned her. A little hemlock was medicine, too much was poison. She gripped the bottle tight in her hand wondering if she would have the courage to use it.

A sudden noise made her jump. She quickly replaced the bottle and snapped the lid of the box shut before anyone could discover her. Then she listened but realised with relief that the noise was only the scraping of the door in the room she had been in. The painter must be leaving. Poor thing. She was not making it easy for him. Without quite knowing why, she got up and went to the doorway to look. There he was at the far end of the passage. Why didn't he leave? He looked as if he might go back into the room where

Marietta still sat. Then he seemed to think better of it and turned away.

She stood back quickly with a swish of her dress but he must have seen her. She waited behind the door feeling foolish. Why was she hiding? She wasn't a girl any more. She would soon be the mistress of her own home. Slowly, she stepped out again to face the painter. He still hadn't gone but was staring right at her. She opened her mouth to speak, meaning to apologise for her behaviour and Marietta's. But the words didn't come. There was such a look of pain on his face. There were even tears in his eyes. What could Marietta have been saying to him? Without thinking she took a step towards him with her hand held out.

'Signor! Are you not well?'

Then she stopped herself. This was not seemly behaviour. Alone in the house with a young man. They stood facing each other for a moment, embarrassed. He looked at her so strangely that she found herself blushing. He tried to speak but then all of a sudden he turned and rushed away down the stone steps. Alessandra's heart was beating quickly. That had been the strangest thing. She stayed there breathing hard until the door began to creak open again. Then she turned and fled into her room. She did not want to face Marietta now.

∞

Arnaldo raced through the streets of the city, not caring where he went. Images rushed through his mind as quickly as his feet carried him. The memory of

Marietta's story was still fresh and the scene played itself over and over again. Lorenzo de Medici standing over his father, his sword at his neck. Except sometimes the two became confused and instead of his father, he saw Medici with a blade at his throat. And always the face of Alessandra would appear. He could not forget the look on her face as she stepped towards him outside her room. When she looked at him kindly he felt as if he could forget the past.

His feet eventually brought him to the cathedral where all the trouble had begun – where the blood had been spilled. He entered through the great double doors at the west end. Inside it was cool and peaceful. Priests went about their duties marked only by the swish of their robes and the light footfall of their sandalled feet. How different from that day seven years before. He took a seat and leant his head against a marble pillar. If only things could have been different. If the Pazzi had not risen against the Medici, then he would now be the son of a leading noble and she would be the daughter of one. They would be of the same rank. An alliance between the two families, cemented by marriage, would have been quite possible. The thought was soothing. Now that the danger had passed he felt exhausted. With his head still resting against the cool stone he fell into a deep sleep.

It was much later when he made his way back to the workshop. Dusk was falling and he was ravenously hungry but, strangely, more hopeful. Marietta knew who he was yet she seemed willing to keep the secret. There must be little love lost between her and Medici. And Alessandra? His head told him he had no reason to hope, but his heart was not listening.

Inside he found Verrocchio and a few others seated with the remains of a meal at the table. 'Arnaldo! We began to worry about you.' They made room for him on the bench and eagerly he took a small loaf, bit into it and then started to fill his plate with meat. 'How does the portrait progress?' Arnaldo's mouth was full of food which allowed him to give a vague shrug rather than an honest answer. It wasn't progressing very fast, through no fault of his own of course. 'We do well with ours.'

Arnaldo swallowed his mouthful. '"We", signor?'

'Yes,' explained Verrocchio. 'I am letting Leonardo work on Orsini. He has new ideas on perspective he wants to try.'

'More new ideas? Master are you sure –'

'Yes, yes,' interrupted Verrocchio. 'Do not worry yourself. I will insist he finishes what he starts. Besides, he is so much quicker than me. If only he applied himself consistently I'm sure there is nothing he couldn't achieve. I fear the student has become greater than the master.' There were murmurs of dissent from all around the table.

'You are hard on yourself, master,' one man observed. 'Leonardo is a fine artist but his head is full of dreams.'

'Yes,' agreed another laughing. 'Last week I had to pull him from the Arno, half drowned. He had inflated bladders attached to his feet which he said would let him walk on water as Our Lord did.' The rest of the table laughed with him.

'You might mock him,' said Verrocchio over the noise, 'but not one of you can match him. In any of the arts.' Arnaldo frowned slightly at this. 'No, not even you, Arnaldo.' The young painter said nothing but his face showed his feelings. 'Aha! I see you do not agree. We shall have a contest then. You will paint Alessandra and Leonardo will paint Orsini. Then side by side we will be able to see who is the master. Agreed?'

'Agreed,' grinned Arnaldo. 'And I will win easily for I have the fairer subject. Where is Leonardo now? Working?'

'No, he is with the boys.'

∞

Arnaldo found them in the dormitory where the young apprentices slept. As well as learning drawing, painting, sculpture and metalwork, Leonardo had taken it upon himself to complete the boys' wider education with lessons in arithmetic, geometry, rhetoric, music and astronomy. Tonight they were answering riddles which their teacher believed not only imparted wisdom but also encouraged deductive thinking. Or would if they were capable of thinking.

'No! Don't be absurd. Giovanni, leave Filippo alone and pay attention. The answer is a statue. *Eyes I have, yet see not. Ears yet hear not. No word my mouth speaks. My flesh it is cold.* The answer is obvious.'

'I thought you said the answer was a statue,' said Antonio innocently. The other boys hooted with laughter and Arnaldo had to turn aside to hide his smile.

'It is *obvious* that the answer is a *statue*,' said Leonardo irritably.

'My answer was just as good,' said Tomaso sulkily.

'A blind, deaf and dumb man who has no coat?' He rolled his eyes heavenwards as if appealing for patience. 'Here, let us try one more. If you get it right then you can stay up a little longer.' Immediately all the boys sat up straight and attentive. *'Runs over fields and woods all day. Under the bed at night sits not alone. With long tongue hanging out. Awaiting a bone.'* There was silence as the boys pondered on these words. Leonardo smiled with satisfaction. At last they appeared to be thinking.

'Cat,' said a boy finally.

'What?'

'Cat?' he said more hesitantly.

Leonardo clutched his head in despair. 'Cat! When did you ever see a cat running with its tongue out, looking for a bone? You buffoon! Why didn't you say dog?'

'It seemed too easy.'

'Dog,' said Alessandro hoping it wasn't too late.

'Wrong!' cried Leonardo.

'But I thought –'

'No, you didn't. You never do. None of you. That's

the problem. The answer is a shoe. Now into bed.' The boys groaned in protest but Leonardo would not be moved. Reluctantly they began to undress for bed.

'I see the boys make good progress, Leonardo,' said Arnaldo.

The artist shook his head sadly. 'Aristotle says that all boys are blank slates on to which we can write knowledge and character. I fear these boys are still as blank as the day they were born.'

'Tell us a story, signor,' said Giovanni.

'When you are all in bed.' Moments later they were sitting up ready. All five of them in one enormous bed, three at one end, two at the other.

'Tell us the one about the Merchant and the Friar.'

'No. Make it the one about the Priest and the Painter.'

Leonardo held up his hand for silence. 'I will tell you the story of the Goldfinch.'

'I don't know that one, signor.'

'That is because I have never told it before. Now listen. The boys fell quiet as their teacher began to tell his tale.

*The goldfinch flew about the forest seeking food for her young. When she returned to her nest with a little worm in her beak, she found her children were gone. Someone had stolen them while she was away. Anxiously she began to search for them everywhere, crying and calling. The whole forest resounded with her cries, but no one replied for nobody could tell her where her children might be. Night and day, without eating or sleeping, the goldfinch sought her little ones, searching every tree and looking in every nest. One day when she was close to despair, a chaffinch came to her: 'I think I saw your children at the farmer's house.' Thanking the other bird, the goldfinch went off with new hope in her heart, and soon arrived at the farm. She perched on the roof, but there was no one there. She flew down into the yard but again she saw no one. Then raising her head, she saw a cage hanging outside the window with her children prisoners inside it. When they saw their mother clinging to the bars of the cage, the young birds began to cheep and hop about excitedly, begging her to let them out. She tried to break the bars of their prison, with her beak and claws, but in vain. So, with a great cry of grief, she flew away. The next day the goldfinch returned to the cage where her children were trapped. She gazed at them for a long time with love and sorrow mingled in her heart. Then she fed them through the bars for the last time and waited as one by one they fell into a deep sleep. The deepest sleep. She had bought them a poisonous herb, and the little birds had died. 'Better death,' said the goldfinch, 'than the loss of freedom.'*

There was a thoughtful silence after Leonardo had finished speaking. Better death than the loss of freedom. Arnaldo thought of Alessandra and her approaching marriage and hoped she did not share that feeling. He looked at the faces of the boys to see how this sad tale had affected them.

'That wasn't funny at all,' observed Filippo.

'Not as good as the Merchant and the Friar,' agreed Tomaso.

'And I still don't see how a shoe is waiting for a bone,' grumbled Alessandro.

Leonardo threw up his hands in disgust. 'Impossible! All of you.' He flounced out of the room, leaving Arnaldo to blow out the candles.

# Twelve

MARIA and her dad stared hard at the painting.

'No,' said John eventually. 'It can't be.'

'Why not?' demanded Maria. She was certain it was the White Lady.

'Because . . . well, because it's just too incredible, that's why. Why would anyone paint over a Renaissance masterpiece? It must be a different painting. Or maybe a copy of the White Lady.'

'Does it look like a copy?'

John was silent. That was the strange thing. While he couldn't believe he actually had a genuine fifteenth-century painting in his hands, that is what it appeared to be. 'I don't know,' he said.

'You're the one with a PhD in fine art,' Maria reminded him.

John smiled. 'OK. It doesn't look like a copy. But I can only see one small corner.' He reached for his bottle of solvent but then hesitated. 'You know, if this *is* genuinely by a Renaissance artist I really should let an expert restore it. It'd be unbelievably valuable.'

'How much?' Maria asked immediately.

'To the art world, unmeasurable.'

'Yeah. But how much money?'

John raised an eyebrow. 'Money isn't the only thing, Maria.'

'I know, I know. Just tell me, can't you?'

John thought for a moment. 'Well, if it's by Verrocchio like the Orsini portrait, then maybe ten, even fifteen.'

'Thousand?'

'Million,' said John.

Maria gulped. 'Pounds or euros.'

'Pounds.'

'Wow!' That seemed to be the only word.

'But if it's by Leonardo da Vinci, then that would be entirely different.'

'More?' Maria asked in a whisper.

John nodded. 'Much more. You see, Leonardo never completed more than a handful of portraits. He was forever coming up with new ideas and abandoning projects only half done. The few that he finished are all in art galleries and they never come on the open market. If one did then there wouldn't be a guide price. Every major gallery and art dealer in the world would be desperate to acquire it. Who knows how much it would go for? Fifty million? A hundred? Two hundred?'

Maria felt light-headed. Two hundred million pounds. It was almost meaningless. You could say it but you couldn't imagine it. 'Seventy-five euros was a bargain then.'

John chuckled. 'Certainly was.' He looked at the

painting with a longing, almost hungry expression. He was desperate to see more of it but he knew he shouldn't continue.

'What are you going to do, Dad?'

John wavered for a moment longer. 'Just a bit more,' he said, giving in. He picked up the cleaning fluid and dipped his cotton bud. Maria stood up decisively. 'Where are you off to?' he asked.

'I'm going back to that shop. See if that man's got any more paintings by Elenora Giannotti.'

'Good idea. Here take my wallet.'

Her mind raced as she hurried to the piazza. The painting was an incredible discovery but why had it been covered up in the first place? The only reason she could come up with was that somebody – Elenora Giannotti presumably – wanted to hide it so it wouldn't be discovered. But that only raised the question of why she would want it hidden. To prevent it being stolen? That didn't make sense. Painting over it was pretty much the same as having it stolen – either way you didn't have the picture to look at.

She felt a sudden knot of fear in her stomach as she found herself at the crossing where she had seen the girl. She glanced warily into the doorway where she had been standing. The door was closed hiding whatever was within. Gritting her teeth, she hurried by. She had a sudden bad feeling about the whole thing. The book had said that accidents seemed to follow the portrait through its history. The shipwreck of John Taverner, Elisabetta della Porta's suicide, the fire that destroyed the Giannotti home. It was as if there was a curse on it. And this morning she'd had a distinct feeling that that girl had wanted her dead.

Her thoughts were broken as she entered the piazza. Beppe came hurtling around a corner with Tommy following as fast as he could. Beppe was laughing in delight with Tommy looking bemused. She groaned inwardly. If they wanted trouble and accidents they didn't need a cursed painting – they had Beppe and Tommy.

'What have you two been doing?' she demanded.

'Nothing.'

'Yeah, right. And is your nothing going to cost anything?'

'No! Nobody knows it was us.' Beppe glanced behind quickly, down the alley they had just come from. 'Why don't we go somewhere else?' he suggested quickly.

'Where?'

'Anywhere but here.'

'I was going back to the shop where we got that painting but I really don't think it'd be a good idea to take you two. It's got old valuable stuff and the shop-keeper is grumpy.'

There was a sound of shouting in the distance. Beppe's eyes opened wide with anxiety. 'Good, let's go now.' He grabbed Tommy's hand and dragged him off to the far corner of the square. Maria followed in despair.

'Which one?' Beppe asked urgently as they stood outside the row of antique shops.

'This one.' She looked up at the sign over the door which she hadn't paid much attention to the day before. It said *Silvio Zappini*. That must be the name of the man they bought the painting from. 'Why don't you – ?' Too late. Beppe and Tommy were already inside so she had to hurry after them.

'Stand there and don't touch *anything*!' she said in a low fierce voice. Tommy nodded. Silvio Zappini, if that was his name, scowled suspiciously at the three of them from behind the counter.

'You three got any money?' he asked. 'This is a shop, not a museum.'

'I'm looking for my dad,' said Maria.

The man shrugged and held out his hand to indicate the empty shop. 'He's not here.'

'No, I mean I'm looking for stuff for my dad.'

He grunted as if he wasn't impressed by the amount of money her dad was willing to part with. 'He likes his picture?'

'Yes, thank you.'

'No, he doesn't but it's all right. It's got another one underneath,' said Beppe, looking up from the pile of old coins he was rummaging through.

'What?'

'Nothing,' said Maria smiling brightly. 'Shut up, will you,' she hissed at Beppe. Signor Zappini stared hard at her and she turned away. She started looking through a pile of paintings, painfully aware of the shopkeeper's gaze on the back of her neck. He must be suspicious now and she didn't want anybody finding out they had a painting possibly worth millions in their basement.

One by one she went through all the paintings. She occasionally glanced up to check on Tommy but he was being remarkably good. There was a display of old costume jewellery on a cloth-covered table by him. He was standing mesmerised by the shiny metal and glass but he wasn't touching it at all. Even Beppe wasn't restless. He had found some collectable football cards and he was thumbing through them. 'Franco Baresi ... Gigi Riva ... Dino Zoff.' He mumbled the names of legendary players from the past. She began to relax.

'Anything your dad wants in particular?' Silvio Zappini was growing impatient.

'Not really.' She had done all the pictures now and hadn't found any by Elenora Giannotti. Disappointed, she started looking at other stuff. In the corner where she had found the painting was an old wooden box full of dusty books. It was blackened along one side as if it had been in a fire and the books were grimy with dark coloured dust. She picked one up and glanced through it. It was old and looked boring and left her fingertips black. She tried another and found it similar. She was about to give up when she noticed the name pencilled in the inside cover. Giannotti. Her heart beating faster, she looked though a few more and found another one with the name.

'How much for these books,' she asked.

They emerged from the shop ten minutes later with

Maria carrying the box of books. 'What do you want those for?' Beppe wanted to know. He glanced around to see if he was still being followed.

'I like reading,' said Maria. 'What did you want to go and tell that man we'd found another picture under the one we bought for?'

'Why shouldn't I?' he said defensively.

Maria stopped and thought. Beppe didn't know about the White Lady so he could hardly be expected to keep it a secret. 'Never mind,' she said. 'Well done, Tommy.' She turned to smile at her brother. 'You didn't break anything. You didn't even touch –' Her smile froze. Tommy was clutching a shiny brooch in his hand.

Nervously Maria pushed the shop door open again. The chimes sounded and Signor Zappini came through from the back room. He scowled when he saw who it was.

'Well?'

'I . . . I'm very sorry . . .' Her voice faltered. 'My brother, he doesn't know what he's doing really.'

Zappini's frown deepened. 'He doesn't know what he is doing. So what is he doing?'

Reluctantly she held out the brooch. 'He picked this up while we were in the shop. It's not broken or any-thing but –' She stopped as she saw Zappini reaching for his phone. 'What are you doing?'

'I'm calling the police,' he said shortly.

'The police! But . . . he hasn't done anything.'

Zappini wasn't impressed. 'He's a thief. And you and that boy. I know how it works. One of you distracts me while the others help themselves.'

'No! Don't please. He doesn't know what he's doing. I'm bringing it back, aren't I?'

'And how much else has he taken, eh? You can tell it to the police. I've had enough of kids thinking they can take what they like. Breaking things and not paying for them.' He jabbed a button angrily with his finger.

'Stop! Please. It's not like that. I'll pay for the brooch but please don't call the police. He doesn't mean any trouble.'

Zappini stopped, his finger poised over the next button. 'You'll pay for it?' Maria nodded anxiously. Slowly Zappini hung up. 'Why didn't you say?' he said. 'We could have avoided this misunderstanding.' He took the piece of jewellery from her and his whole attitude changed. 'What have we here then?' She watched numbly as he turned it over in his hands, still shocked at what he had been about to do. 'Nice piece,' he said. 'Your brother has a good eye. 1970s. Genuine glass and silver plate. What shall we say? Two hundred euros?'

'What?' She stared in disbelief at the shopkeeper. He had to be joking. His cruel, mocking smile said he wasn't. 'No way! It's not worth twenty.'

Zappini shrugged. 'So should I call the police?'

She glared at him for a moment more then pulled out

the notes and slammed them down on the counter. Without a word, she picked up the brooch, turned and stormed out of the shop.

'A pleasure doing business with you,' said the shop-keeper. He looked at the money and then glanced at the door that Maria had just slammed. His hand hovered over the till but then he changed his mind. He picked up the notes and thoughtfully pushed them into his wallet instead.

'You'd better look after that,' said Maria, thrusting the brooch into Tommy's hands. Then she picked up the box of books and set off back to the house fuming at Zappini. She was glad that he had sold them a priceless masterpiece for only seventy-five euros. He didn't deserve any more. Beppe shrugged and followed after her with Tommy. She didn't say a word until they were almost home. Then her anger dissolved into fear. Something was wrong. She could hear Nonna's shouts through the open doorway from halfway down the street. 'Come on,' she said to the boys. 'Something's up.' They quickened their pace and hurried in to see what the problem was. Nonna was on the phone gabbling away to someone while Aunt Adriana sat at the table, white faced and shaking. Her mother looked anxious but in control.

'Maria,' she said urgently. 'Where is your dad? I've been calling for him but he doesn't come.'

'He's in the basement,' she said, confused. Surely he

could hear all the noise that was going on.

'Run and fetch him quickly,' she said.

'Why? What's wrong?'

'Hurry! We have to get to the hospital. It's your Uncle Giorgio. There's been an accident at work.'

Maria's heart seemed to miss a beat at her mother's words. Her face paled and she dumped her dirty box of books on the table. Fear clawed inside her. It was the painting. It had got her uncle and now her dad was down in the basement alone with it. Why didn't he answer?

# Thirteen

THE next few weeks were the happiest of Arnaldo's life. Each day the portrait grew under his skilful hand. He was inspired. The gentle rolling countryside, park-like with its scattered trees beneath a blue sky, became so real that you half expected the branches to stir in the breeze, or the wispy clouds to float quietly by. Alessandra filled the foreground as she filled his heart. From her slender waist up to her auburn hair which hung in a neat braid about her neck, she drew the eye and held it like a magnet. There were still many layers of paint to come so the subtle skin tones, the folds of the dress were not yet perfect. But even so, Arnaldo had captured all her grace, all her simple elegance. He poured his soul into his work and went home each evening, exhausted and exhilarated. It had to be the finest portrait ever painted.

Lorenzo seemed to think so. He took to spending more and more time in the room watching Arnaldo work, often dismissing Marietta on some invented errand so he had an excuse to stay. Arnaldo did not welcome him. His presence made him uncomfortable. He could not gaze so intently at Alessandra with her father breathing down his neck. Once he came and stood right next to him and leant in close to look at the brushwork. Arnaldo's jaw tightened as Lorenzo's face hovered inches from his own, the scar on Medici's neck mocking him. This man lived while his father lay dead. Worse still, Medici laid a hand on Arnaldo's shoulder as he congratulated him. He couldn't help but flinch. He wanted to push the hand away but he forced himself to stay calm. Soon Medici retired to the far side of the room unaware of the feelings that raged inside the painter. But it became easier. Medici would usually sit silently, completely absorbed by what he was seeing so that Arnaldo could almost forget he was there.

Alessandra remained always distant. That moment in the corridor when she had spoken seemed a far-off memory. She did not speak now – not when her father was there and seldom when he was absent. Arnaldo ached as he looked at her. It was as if there was a deep chasm between them. She sat just a few feet away yet he couldn't get near her. She grew more cold and remote every day. She never looked at the portrait despite Lorenzo urging her that she should. She did not appear to be interested. Or perhaps she didn't want to be reminded of her marriage.

The impending wedding was the dark cloud in Arnaldo's life. While he painted he managed to forget, but it loomed ever closer. The day when Alessandra would be possessed by another man, placed out of his reach for ever. In three weeks' time Orsini and his entourage would arrive from Rome. Arnaldo remembered him dimly from his days in that city. He was not a bad man. But he was so old. He thought of the hooked nose, the watery eyes, the heavy brow and the tufts of hair that grew from his ears. The idea of this misshapen old man holding the young and beautiful Alessandra made him shudder. The old man's breath drawing close to kiss those perfect lips. At night he would wake suddenly with a feverish urge to rush and rescue her from her fate. Then he would fall back on his pillow, cursing his powerlessness, and lie wakeful until the first flush of dawn gave him the excuse to get up. During these long lonely hours his thoughts would often turn to Medici himself. The more attached he became to Alessandra, the more confused he became about her father. Of course he hated him still. But how could he think on Alessandra as a wife without thinking on Medici as a father? It was after one such sleepless night that Lorenzo noticed how pale he looked.

'Signor, are you well?'

Arnaldo turned to Medici. 'Yes, of course.'

'No. Indeed you look tired. You are working too hard.' He came and stood next to him and together they studied the portrait. Arnaldo had just been working on the hair, adding layer after layer of different tones – deep reddish brown that gave it depth to hints of light yellow for its lustrous shine. It was very good and Lorenzo nodded with approval. Arnaldo wondered if he was going to rest his hand on his shoulder again. A small part of him hoped he would but he pushed that thought away. 'You do very well. But there is no hurry. You have been kept inside too long. Come, walk with me in the sunshine.' Arnaldo took another look at his work. It was true, he was feeling fatigued. A rest would be welcome.

'Very well, signor.' He put down his brush and together they walked outside.

It was early afternoon and the sun had warmed the stones of the courtyard. There was a lazy heat in the air, warm and relaxing. The young artist and his patron walked together up and down as they talked. Medici spoke of many things while Arnaldo listened dutifully. Whenever he had the chance he would glance up at the window of the room where he had been painting. On his first day here he had glimpsed a face at the very same window. He guessed it might have been Alessandra and he kept hoping to see her again, watching him, but it remained empty.

'You have a great future ahead of you, signor,' Medici was saying. Arnaldo murmured his thanks. 'There will be many commissions for your work once this portrait is seen. I will make certain of that. Who knows? Maybe you will even be called to Rome.'

'You are kind, signor, but Leonardo is considered the more skilful by my master.' Medici made a dismissive noise in his throat at da Vinci's name. 'He is back from Milan and is painting Signor Orsini. When we have finished, then we will see who is the best.'

Medici turned to face Arnaldo, smiling. It was a

look of almost fatherly pride. 'You have the will to succeed. I saw that when we fought with swords. That is good. Ambition is a powerful force, signor. It will drive you to ever greater heights.' He suddenly gripped him on the arm and spoke urgently. 'Never settle for less than you desire. Always strive until you achieve your purpose.'

His eyes burned fiercely and Arnaldo was taken aback. He had the sudden mad urge to take Medici at his word and ask for his daughter. Forget caution and secrecy. Lorenzo was so pleased with the painting, maybe he would consent to his daughter marrying the artist. 'Signor . . .' he began. Medici looked at him expectantly but then his courage left him. 'Sometimes,' he finished sadly, 'what we desire will always be out of our reach.'

Lorenzo gave a great roar of laughter and let go of Arnaldo. 'What's this? A philosopher as well as an artist. You have an old head on your shoulders. Come.' He slapped him on the back. 'Let us fence again. I can teach you a few tricks your father didn't.'

The mention of his father was like a sudden wound. He realised the warmth he had been feeling towards Medici and was bitterly ashamed. How could he think of forgetting his death? Images of his father came back to him, his cries as he was dragged from his home. Before him, Lorenzo was calling for two swords. He tossed one to Arnaldo who caught it neatly by the handle and then stared at it. 'Well done, signor. Have you read Filippo Vadi? You should. He is very good on sword handling. I have a copy you may borrow. Let us start with the middle guard.'

Feet apart, knees slightly bent, he held out his sword at waist height pointing upward towards his opponent's neck and face. Arnaldo did the same but mechanically. He barely noticed Medici's words. 'Good. Bend your knees just a little more. It will give you readiness to move quickly. From this position we can use the eight basic cuts. First we have the vertical downstroke.' He demonstrated with a swish of his blade that whistled inches from Arnaldo's face. Arnaldo did not flinch and got an approving smile from Medici. 'Now you, signor.'

Arnaldo's sword moved almost without him knowing. The cut was quick and decisive and when it was done Medici found himself staring at a neat slit down the front of his tunic. His skin was unmarked. 'That was either the finest stroke I have ever seen,' he observed, 'or the luckiest. What will my wife say when she sees my clothes in rags, signor?'

Arnaldo stared too. Even now he did not know what he had been intending. To wound Medici? To frighten him? Whatever his intentions had been, he grudgingly had to admire his opponent. The man's nerves were of steel.

'Let us continue a little *less* enthusiastically,' Medici said. He demonstrated each of the moves and Arnaldo carefully repeated each stroke, the sun glinting off his blade as it turned and twisted. 'Excellent, signor! My tunic remains in one piece still. Now you attack me with each of those in turn and I will demonstrate the corresponding defensive move.' He stepped back and held up his weapon. Arnaldo faced him, shifting his weight from foot to foot as he eyed up his opponent. Then he moved quickly with a horizontal sweep from left to right. It met Medici's blade and was blocked. The older man raised an eyebrow. 'I thought we were starting with the vertical cut, signor.'

'I thought we would make it more . . . interesting,' Arnaldo replied. His voice was strange, as if someone else were saying the words and he was only watching.

'Indeed? Then you will not object if *I* try something a little different.' Without warning he lunged at Arnaldo who was ready for him and deflected the blow safely.

'Not at all, signor.'

Soon the sound of clashing blades resounded around the courtyard as the two of them fought, half playfully, half seriously. Alessandra and Marietta heard them in their room and the old nurse heaved herself out of the chair to hurry to the window and watch. 'They are fighting again.' She sounded slightly anxious.

'I guessed as much,' said Alessandra.

'He handles a sword well, your artist. There are not many who can match the master.'

Alessandra frowned. 'He is not *my* artist. He is my father's. I have no interest in painting. Or the painter.' Nevertheless, she too got up and watched at the window. She stayed there long after Marietta had tired and returned to her seat. He was so young. And he moved gracefully. She liked the way his hair fell over his eyes as he leant forward. And the way he swept it back with his free hand. He smiled as he managed to pull off a clever sword trick that fooled her father and his whole face seemed to light up. She nearly smiled too. Then suddenly she gave a small cry and her hand flew to her mouth.

'What? What is it?' cried Marietta. But Alessandra was already gone. Her footsteps were echoing on the steps outside the door. Marietta pulled herself up and ran to the window. What had the stupid boy done? She looked out of the window on the scene below but Medici still stood with his sword in his hand. It was the painter's weapon that lay on the flagstones while he clutched his left arm. His teeth were gritted with pain. Moments later Alessandra almost tumbled into the courtyard. Medici turned quickly and spoke to her as he took the artist's arm. Alessandra's voice then drifted up from below, urgent and frightened.

'Fetch water and bandages, Marietta. Arn . . . the artist! He is hurt.' The nurse quickly did as she was told while Medici led Arnaldo into the house.

'It is nothing, I assure you,' Arnaldo insisted. His face was pale.

'I commend your bravery, signor, but what will Verrocchio say when I return his artist weak from loss of blood, eh? He will think the painting must be very bad. Come, we must tend to your wound.'

Alessandra hovered behind unnoticed as Arnaldo was taken to a downstairs room and seated on a couch.

Gently Lorenzo unbuttoned Arnaldo's shirt and pulled it over his head as the artist winced with pain. Then despite his protests he was lain back to wait. His bare chest rose and fell quickly with his breathing and there was a trail of blood flowing down his left arm. Alessandra watched anxiously from the corner. For a few moments Medici strode around the room, agitated. 'Where can she be?' he said as Marietta failed to return. Suddenly he quit the room altogether and went in search of her. Arnaldo and Alessandra were left alone. A fact that Marietta did not miss as she entered a minute later. She raised one eyebrow knowingly but all she said was, 'Here you are. I've been upstairs, I've been down. Run and fetch water Marietta, they say. They do not think to tell Marietta details like where the water is wanted.' Grumbling, she placed the bowl by the couch, slopping some on the floor.

Arnaldo's eyes widened suspiciously. 'What are you going to do?'

'What am I going to do? I'm going to stop you bleeding all over the furniture. What do you think I'm going to do?'

'No, really . . .' Arnaldo struggled to move away but the nurse had already dipped a rag into the water and was pressing it on the wound. 'Ouch!'

Marietta tutted impatiently. 'Lie still, can't you.'

'Please. I would rather do it myself.'

'Don't be stupid.'

'I'm not being . . .'

Quietly, Alessandra came and stood behind her

nurse and Arnaldo was suddenly very still. She laid a hand on her shoulder. 'Enough, Marietta. Let me do it,' she said. The nurse turned to object but then she saw the look of tenderness on the girl's face. It was a long time since she had seen anything but coldness there. Slowly she stood back and let Alessandra take over.

She took the rag from Marietta's hand and knelt beside the couch. Gently she began to sponge away the blood from the wound. It hurt just the same as when Marietta had cleaned it but now Arnaldo didn't make a sound. Alessandra kept her eyes lowered so that he could not see her face but he watched in wonder as her slender white fingers moved softly over his skin. Her touch was gentle and kind. Too soon the wound was clean – a thin pink line across the light brown of his upper arm. It wasn't deep. Carefully she applied a wad of folded cloth and then deftly wrapped a bandage around to hold it in place. It was done but Arnaldo wished he could have been wounded ten times. A hundred times. Alessandra stood up, not daring to look at anyone. Then a noise from the passage outside disturbed the moment.

'Marietta! Where in heaven's name are you?'

The nurse snatched the cloth from Alessandra's hand and pushed her quickly away. Not a moment too soon. The door burst open and Medici strode in. 'Marietta! Where have you been?'

The nurse shrugged. 'Here, signor. See I have already cleaned the wound.'

Medici looked to Arnaldo and saw that his arm was

~ 121 ~

already bandaged. He relaxed a little. 'I see. Good. How does it feel, signor?' Arnaldo did not answer. He had a dazed look on his face and Medici became anxious again. 'Signor? Are you well?'

Arnaldo suddenly became aware that he was being questioned. 'Yes, fine,' he said quickly. 'It feels very good.' He hurriedly swung his feet round to sit up and reached for his shirt.

## Fourteen

'DAD!' cried Maria as she raced down the stairs. 'Dad! Are you all right?' She was relieved to see he was still there absorbed in his task. He looked fine but he didn't seem to hear her until she stood right next to him.

'What? Oh, hello, darling. Any luck?' He turned back to the painting as soon as he had acknowledged her.

'No, well yes, in a way, but that's not important. You've got to come. Didn't you hear Mum?' John made no response as he gently prised up a stubborn piece of varnish with his spatula. 'Dad! Are you listening? You've got to come quickly. Uncle Giorgio's been hurt.'

John looked round again, confused. 'Hurt? How? What happened?'

'I don't know. An accident at work.' The sounds of Nonna's wailing still drifted down from upstairs.

'Where is he now?'

'At the hospital I think.'

'OK. I'll be right there. Just let me finish this bit.'

'What?' Maria was shocked. How could her dad carry

on with his painting when Uncle Giorgio needed them? 'Didn't you hear what I just said? Uncle Giorgio is in hospital.'

'Yes, yes, I heard but . . .' He paused to dab up some loose paint with a cotton wad. 'If he's in hospital, the doctors will be doing all they can for him won't they? We won't be any help.'

'Dad!'

'Maria, please!' He spoke a bit sharply. 'I'm worried too but I've just painted some solvent on. I can't leave it now. By the time I get back it will have eaten its way right through to the board.'

Maria bit her lip. He had a point, she supposed. She couldn't resist a glance at the painting and saw that a slender hand holding the garland of flowers had been exposed. It would be a crime to ruin it but what if her uncle was really badly hurt? What if he was . . . dying? Aunt Adriana should be with him. She didn't dare nag her dad again. She just waited in agitation while he swabbed up the rest of the solvent and made sure the portrait was completely dry.

'There,' he said after what seemed like for ever but was actually only a few minutes. 'It's done. Let's go.' He got up and headed for the door. Maria felt awkward, almost shy of him. He still didn't seem to be hurrying. At the foot of the stairs he couldn't resist a longing glance back at the painting.

'It's not going anywhere, Dad,' she said nervously. 'It'll still be here when you get back.' John nodded and mounted the stairs.

An uneasy calm settled after the adults left for the hospital. The kitchen seemed lonely without Nonna. Maria was supposedly in charge of Tommy and Beppe, but in practice this meant the boys went off somewhere leaving her on her own feeling anxious but powerless to do anything. Beppe did not seem too troubled by the news of his father. Maria was worried about him though, and almost as concerned for her own dad. In all the time she could remember she had never known him do anything deliberately unkind or selfish but he appeared quite unconcerned at the news of Uncle Giorgio's accident. He seemed more interested in the painting. She went down to the basement to look at the portrait. Even from the small cleared section she could tell it was going to be beautiful. The flowers seemed to float down from the gentle fingers that caressed them. The colours were as bright and fresh as if they were newly done. She gazed at it for she didn't know how long and then suddenly couldn't bear to look at it any more. She turned away and found an old sheet to cover it up.

Upstairs in the kitchen she took a deep breath. She had felt stifled in the basement and not just because of the closeness of the room. She got herself a drink of juice from the refrigerator and sat down at the table meaning to look through the box of books she had bought at the antique shop. They were very dirty and after blowing a cloud of sooty dust off the first one she decided Nonna wouldn't appreciate that. She got up again to find a duster but then there was a knock at the front door. Not knowing who to expect she made her way through the hall to answer it. She was surprised and not pleased to find Silvio Zappini standing on the front step.

'What do you want?' she demanded, all her anger at him resurfacing quickly. 'I paid you for the brooch, didn't I?'

'Hey!' The man held up his hands defensively. 'Not so fierce. I only knocked at your door.' He gave an oily smile which showed he had a gold tooth.

Maria tried to be calm but her anxiety was making her even more short-tempered. 'Sorry,' she muttered. Then she had another thought. 'How do you know where I live?' She didn't like the idea of this man following her.

'The boy you were with,' said Zappini with a shrug. 'Everybody knows him.'

This made sense. Beppe was what you might call notorious. But she still didn't trust the man. 'OK. What do you want?'

He looked suddenly uncomfortable. 'I . . . I wanted to say sorry for being so angry earlier. In my shop,' he added as if Maria might have forgotten. She was taken aback. This was not what she was expecting. 'I have trouble with the kids you understand and business has not been so good. But I should not have lost my temper.' He struggled with himself for a moment. 'Here, I want to return this to you.' He took some notes out of his wallet and pushed them quickly into her hand. Maria was astounded. There were a hundred euros. She didn't say anything and the man misunderstood her silence. 'OK, OK. Here, have this as well.' He gave her another fifty.

'Thank you,' she eventually managed. She pushed the money into her jeans pocket before he could change his mind. Zappini watched it disappear wistfully.

'It's nothing, really,' he said through clenched teeth. They both stood there awkwardly, Maria not knowing what to say and wondering what he would do next. 'That picture,' he said at last. Maria was immediately on her guard again. So this was what the visit was all about. She said nothing. 'Your dad likes it?'

'He's happy with what he paid for it,' she said.

Silvio Zappini looked injured. 'Yes. I'm sure he is,' he said bitterly. 'The boy, he said something about another picture . . . ?' He looked hopefully at her.

'Did he?' she said unhelpfully.

'I think so.' Maria stared at him, not speaking. He held her gaze for a moment and then looked down, defeated. 'Perhaps I am mistaken,' he said. 'Is your dad in? I could speak to him.'

'No, I'm sorry.'

'Oh!' He sounded disappointed. 'I would like to see that painting again.'

'Not possible, I'm afraid.'

'No. Of course.' He half turned as if to go but then asked suddenly, 'Where is it?' He took her by surprise and she unintentionally glanced down at the basement windows that were at their feet. If he noticed he didn't show it.

'Inside,' she said recovering quickly.

'Inside, yes, of course.' He looked thoughtful. 'Well goodbye, signorina and again I am very sorry to have troubled you.' He turned and walked away. Maria closed the door and made sure it was locked before returning to the kitchen.

She took her duster and one by one pulled the books out of the box and wiped them over. Somehow she felt grimy and unclean like the books – as if the memory of Zappini clung to her skin. They were all in Italian and covered a variety of subjects – some history, some nature books with photographic plates of plants and animals, quite a few art books which her dad might be interested in. One thing they had in common though, was their binding – dark boards with blue leather along the spine and the titles blocked in real gold. She got the idea they were all from the same library, maybe from a great country house. There were sheets of newspaper between the books dated 1873. Perhaps nobody had looked at them since then. It was a shame because some of them were quite lovely. She soon became absorbed turning the thick, creamy coloured pages. The black grime was confined to the edges leaving the insides clean and fresh.

When she had gone through about ten volumes she came upon one that looked promising. Its title was very long. *The Ancient Art of Florence: Being a Catalogue of the Works of the Great Masters Held by the Chief Fami-*

*lies of Tuscany.* Eagerly she opened it. The title page informed her it was printed in 1871 and that it was a limited edition of five hundred copies available only to subscribers. Then there was a list of the names of people who had bought the book – all five hundred of them. She ran her eye down the list which thankfully was in alphabetical order. Yes! There it was. Giannotti. Perhaps it would have information on the family and the works of art they held. She flicked through the pages. Mostly it was just writing. Lists of titles with a brief description of the piece and information such as who painted it, how old it was, its size and so on. Occasionally though there were photographic plates of the more important works of art. Impatiently she searched until she found what she was looking for – the Giannotti family. They had several pages of their own. What a waste, she thought. It must have all been destroyed in that fire. She ran her finger down the titles on the left-hand side of the page as she read them. There it was – The White Lady.

It was just a short entry.

*Late fifteenth century. Oils on board. 26 inches x 17 inches. Young lady, unknown model, in white dress holding flower garland in raised left hand. Artist unknown, after School of Verrocchio. See plate xiv opposite page 87.*

She read through the entry four or five times until she could almost remember it word for word. Twenty-six inches by seventeen. What was that? About sixty centimetres by forty. That was about the right size.

Perhaps she should go and find a ruler and measure the picture. It was while she was musing on this that the meaning of the last words in the entry finally sank in. Plate fourteen. There must be a photograph of the portrait here in this book. Quickly she thumbed through the pages, looking for the picture. Page eighty-two, eighty-three, four, five . . . She turned over the last page and gasped with horror at what she saw, her hand clutched to her mouth in disgust.

There was the portrait, or what was left of it. Someone had taken a pen, one of those old-fashioned ones with the sharp iron nibs, and scribbled all over the girl's face. Not childish scribbles but vicious, hate-filled scratches. Back and forth the pen had gone, digging deep into the photo and the pages beneath. The ink had run out after the first few strokes, the marks becoming no more than ugly gashes as if cut with a knife. Maria closed the book trembling. She felt troubled, as if she had just witnessed the actions of a seriously disturbed mind.

## Fifteen

'LEONARDO was instructing the boys in drawing when
Arnaldo found them. Each had a board resting on his
knees and they sat in a semicircle around their subject.
'You must forget what you know,' he said. 'It will
deceive you. Draw only what you see. Not what you
think you see.' They looked at him uncertainly but
picked up their charcoal and began to draw. An indus-
trious hush settled on the room – the only sounds, the
soft whisper of pencil on paper. Arnaldo felt an anxious
knot tighten in his stomach as he watched. He glanced
around as if someone might be there and then spoke in
a low hiss.

'What are you doing?'

Leonardo looked up from his notebook where he
was annotating a diagram of a man wearing a set of
wood and canvas wings. 'Arnaldo! I did not see you
enter.'

'What are you doing?' he asked more urgently.

'I'm teaching the boys, of course.'

They were ranged around a portrait of the Virgin
cradling her child. It was beautifully and delicately
drawn, softened and blurred like smoke so the lines

blended into shadows smoothly and naturally. There was such tender love on the face turned towards the infant. He rested at peace, safe in her arms, his cheek against her breast. It was the perfect image of the perfect mother. There was only one problem with it.

'The picture, it is upside down, signor.'

'Yes. I find it helps. You see –'

'But –' Arnaldo ran his fingers through his hair nervously. 'You cannot turn our Lord and his mother on their heads. It is disrespectful.'

'I mean no disrespect,' said Leonardo. His face was a mixture of surprise and innocence.

'It is what the heretics do. People have been burned for less.'

'Heresy? But it isn't really the Madonna,' Leonardo explained. 'It is a girl I met in the market and her brat. I paid her half a florin to sit for me. She'd have done a lot more than sit for that much, believe me. And the child! I had to lace its milk with wine before it stopped its squawking –'

Arnaldo clutched his hands to his head in despair. 'Stop! Please. People will hear you. The boys have ears and tongues you know. You must not talk like this.'

'Like what?'

'As if –' Arnaldo stared helplessly at his friend. He wanted to say *as if the world were a fair place. Where everyone let reason be their guide. Where superstition and tradition did not numb people's intelligence and make them behave like dumb beasts.* But Leonardo's eyes were wide and curious. He was not like other men. Arnaldo knew he would not understand. And even if he could be made to realise, it would be a crime to disillusion him – like corrupting a child. He reached out and touched his hand. 'Please, Leonardo. You must be careful. People talk. The monk has been preaching again in the piazza. If they were to learn you did things like this then I do not know what the consequences would be.' Leonardo stared back blankly. Arnaldo sighed. 'Why is Our Lady upside down, signor?'

'Ah! This is an idea of mine.' He was immediately his old self. 'It helps the boys to see things as they really are.'

Arnaldo looked at him doubtfully. 'And does it work?'

'See for yourself.' Leonardo waved a hand in the direction of the young apprentices and Arnaldo went and stood and looked over Giovanni's shoulder.

'May I?' The boy offered him his half-finished drawing. Arnaldo took it and was amazed to see a very fair copy of the original. Not perfect but much better than he would have expected from one so young. 'Very good,' he said returning it thoughtfully. The boy himself could hardly believe what he had achieved. All around there were murmurs of surprise as the others turned their own work the right way up. 'I am impressed, Leonardo. Is this how you intend to work on the Orsini portrait? Ask him to stand on his head?'

'Alas, no,' the inventor sighed. 'There are limitations in the application of this idea. I did devise this in Milan, which I thought might allow people to pose upside down.' He flicked through the pages of his book and sadly showed Arnaldo an elaborate drawing of pulleys and harnesses attached to a wooden frame. 'But it proved unworkable. The subjects complained of dizziness and in the finished picture their hair hung upwards.'

'Never mind. Do you still make good progress with the portrait?'

'Yes, indeed. I will show you.' He stood up and led Arnaldo past the boys to another room where there were papers scattered everywhere. There was also a large amount of cheap cotton cloth bundled in a heap.

'What is all this for? Are you making a tent?'

'I am.'

'Why?' laughed Arnaldo. 'Are you not happy at Ver-rocchio's?'

'It is a design I have been meaning to test for some time. If a man has a tent twelve arm-lengths' wide and twelve high, he can throw himself down from a great height without hurting himself.'

'Really? And you are going to throw yourself from a great height?'

'I might. Or one of the boys. Here is the portrait.' Leonardo was standing in front of the Orsini painting, where it was mounted on an easel. 'I have been experimenting with the effect of space and how it affects colouring. You notice these trees in the distance. As well as making them smaller, I have painted them bluer and less distinct. It gives the impression that they are further away.' Arnaldo's eyes carefully absorbed everything Leonardo had done. The painting was all but finished and it looked exquisite. The landscape with its rolling green countryside drew the eye inwards towards the horizon. There was such a sense of depth. The sunlight was diffused through the clouds giving the whole scene a gentle luminosity. It would be a hard task to judge between the two portraits. The figure of Orsini sat in the foreground from the waist upwards, holding the garland of flowers in his outstretched hand. But there was an eerie hole where his face would eventually go.

'You are nearly finished.'

'I have a little more to do.'

'I will sit for you if you like.'

'Are you not going to the Palazzo Medici today?'

'Later. The signorina is busy this morning having her dress fitted for the wedding.'

There came a sound of bumping and muffled shouts and laughter from the next room where the apprentices were. 'Well, as the boys seem to be behaving themselves, I might do a little work,' Leonardo said. 'Thank you, Arnaldo.'

He had his paints already mixed on the palette. The red tunic was draped over the stool so Arnaldo removed his shirt and pulled it over his head. His arm was still bandaged. Then he sat down and arranged himself in the correct pose. A subtle change came over Leonardo as he prepared to work. He took up two brushes, one in each hand. He paused momentarily and then all of a sudden began to make swift steady strokes as his eyes darted around the portrait. With his left hand he added some dark shadow to the folds of the clothes, with his right he touched up the clouds with a bluish grey. It was extraordinary to watch. Arnaldo had once seem him draw a picture of a sleeping cat with one hand while making notes on irrigation with the other and carrying out a completely unconnected conversation at the same time. Genius. Some called it witchcraft.

Arnaldo let his mind wander as Leonardo worked. His thoughts turned as always to Alessandra and he was strangely content to be modelling for the portrait of her husband. It meant part of him would be in the painting that would always be paired with hers. He relived his dream again, imagining that things had been different – that he actually was posing for his own wedding portrait. It was a beautiful thought. Slowly an idea dawned on him. It crept in almost without his noticing but once there it took hold. It gripped him and he could not be free of it. He shifted in his seat wondering how it might be achieved. He couldn't do it unaided. He would have to ask for help.

'Leonardo,' he said quietly. 'I wonder if you might do something for me.'

∞

There was a smile about his lips as Arnaldo made his way to the Palazzo Medici. Leonardo had agreed to help him. It was a foolish plan and would achieve nothing in the end. But it would bring him happiness.

He was still smiling as the great doors were opened to admit him by Medici himself.

'Greetings, signor. How is your arm? You are looking well.'

Arnaldo shrugged. 'It is fine. Indeed I am very happy. The sun is shining, I am young . . .'

'And in love by the look of things.'

All the colour drained from Arnaldo's face. What did Medici know? 'Signor . . . ?' He fell silent, embarrassed and fearful. Medici studied him thoughtfully and then let out a great roar of laughter.

'I believe you *are* in love. But this is magnificent.' He seemed genuinely pleased. Arnaldo felt his fear lessen as he realised that Medici did not suspect the full truth. 'Well, who is the fortunate girl?'

'I . . . cannot say,' mumbled Arnaldo. 'I have not spoken to her father.'

'But you have spoken to the girl.'

'I have yet to find the courage.'

Medici frowned. 'You must speak, signor. Is the girl supposed to guess what's in your heart? Your intentions are pure I trust.'

'Oh, yes.' Arnaldo hesitated. 'It is just that I am only a poor artist.' He looked into Medici's eyes, searching for a clue to what he might be thinking. 'Her father is rich. I do not know what he will say.'

'And you never will if you do not speak. You are poor now,' Medici admitted. 'But what a future you have. You will not always be an artist's assistant. Soon you will be your own man. And with your skill, fame and riches must surely follow. You should go to the girl's father,' he urged. Arnaldo's heart began to thump. Was this an invitation? He found he couldn't talk. 'Come, tell me who the girl is. I can be discreet. If I know the father perhaps I can speak on your behalf. I am not without influence.'

Slowly Arnaldo shook his head. 'I thank you, signor, but please do not ask me.'

Medici relented. 'Very well. I will not press you, but if ever you need help, on this or any matter, please come to me first.' He laid a hand on Arnaldo's shoulder. 'I like you, young man. I like you very much. I could help you.'

Arnaldo nodded, not trusting his voice.

They turned and began to make their way through to the courtyard. 'At least you can tell me something about the girl, eh? Have you known her long?'

'Less than a month,' Arnaldo said softly.

'So short a time?' Medici raised his eyebrows in surprise. 'She must be remarkable to have won your heart so soon. What spell does she weave? Is it her beauty?' Arnaldo blushed slightly. 'Ah! So she *is* beautiful. I suppose an artist like you could never love ugliness. I thank heaven my own wife is no artist.' He laughed cheerfully. 'But, tell me, is she as beautiful as my own Alessandra?'

'Signor . . . You ask me a difficult question. How should I answer?'

'Truthfully of course. You have nothing to fear.'

'Then I would have to say that they are equal in beauty.'

'Good answer!' Lorenzo was delighted. 'You have defended the honour of your own lady and not offended your host.' They had reached the foot of the stairs now. 'My daughter awaits you, signor, but do not go without taking leave of me. I would like to practise our swordplay some more if your wound allows it.'

'Gladly, signor.'

Medici bid him farewell and Arnaldo let out a sigh of relief. He climbed the stairs thinking deeply. He was shaken by how near Medici had come to finding him out. True, he spoke highly of him but what would he think if he knew it was his own daughter he desired? He felt a quick pang of guilt. The very man he had sworn to kill was fast becoming the man he most wanted to impress.

The door was already ajar when he reached the top of the stairs. He was so lost in his thoughts that he neglected to knock before entering. He pushed it open a little further and then froze, his hand still on the latch. Alessandra had been trying on her wedding robe and now Marietta was helping her back into the white dress which was still unlaced, the ribbons fluttering loose. He could see the graceful curve of her spine under smooth white skin. The way her shoulders moved as she slid her arms into the sleeves. Colour flooded his cheeks as he watched the old nurse lace up the dress and pull it tight. Then he came to his senses and began to back out of the room before he was discovered. But too late. They turned towards him. Alessandra gave a slight gasp when she saw him standing in the doorway. Arnaldo trembled as they looked straight into each other's eyes for a moment. Then she lowered her gaze and quickly went to take her seat.

'Why don't you knock?' Marietta rounded on him. There was a determined look in her eye and she rolled up her sleeves as if she were prepared to defend her mistress's honour against any threat. 'How long have you been skulking there, eh? You might have managed to get your shirt off last time you were here but that doesn't mean . . .'

'Marietta! Please!' Alessandra interrupted her nurse giving Arnaldo a chance to defend himself.

'I . . . I just arrived. Please believe me. Signor Medici has just this moment bid me come up as he assured me that you were ready. I . . . I am so sorry, signorina.' He looked to Alessandra desperately. She gave a slight nod.

'It is nothing. Marietta, we should continue.'

The nurse gave one last glare at Arnaldo to let him know that she would be watching him. Arnaldo's cheeks still burned with shame as he went to take up his brushes. He wished the floor would swallow him up. He wished he could speak – say something natural as if everything were normal. But he could not. He was horrified at what he had done. Alessandra had been very gracious but surely she despised him now. All his earlier happiness left him and he worked with a heavy heart.

The painting was almost complete and Arnaldo was working more slowly, delaying the time when he would have to finish. Today he was adding some shading to the folds of the dress. He glanced up to observe how the creases fell and was startled to find Alessandra looking at him. She turned her head quickly back into position but then surprised him again by speaking.

'You do not smile today, signor. Does your wound trouble you?'

Arnaldo was stunned. She never spoke unless absolutely necessary. 'My arm is fine,' he assured her. 'I wanted to thank you for . . . your help.'

Alessandra coloured slightly at the memory and could not look at him. She did not see Marietta's quiet smile.

'It was nothing.'

'I am sorry if I am not cheerful, signorina,' Arnaldo continued.

'Do not be. We cannot always be joyful. I rarely smile.'

'I had not noticed.'

Marietta snorted scornfully.

'Thank you,' said Alessandra, ignoring the servant. 'But you need not lie on my account. What reason have I to smile?' Arnaldo did not know how to answer. Marietta stopped her sewing and stared at Alessandra. 'And why do you not smile today? Is the portrait not good?'

'Have you not seen it?' Arnaldo asked.

She looked down. 'I have not.'

'It is good. I believe it is the best I have ever painted. Or ever will,' he added.

She seemed surprised. 'You mean you will never paint again?'

'No, I mean I do not believe I will ever be inspired to paint this well again.'

She turned and gave him a long curious stare. Arnaldo's heart sank. Had he gone too far? She did not seem angry at his words though, only sad. Then she bit her lip and quickly looked away. Arnaldo could not be sure but he thought there were tears in her eyes. He dared not speak again, but his heart ached as he longed to comfort her.

## Sixteen

'JOHN! Please! Slow down!' Elisabetta's eyes were wide with fear as the truck trundled towards them its horn blaring. John slammed on the brakes and swerved back into his own lane.

'Sorry,' he muttered. 'Thought there'd be space.'

'*Santa Marmellata!*' cried Nonna. 'Isn't one accident enough in one day. What are you in such a hurry for?'

'I said I'm sorry.' John's voice was irritable. 'If you'd rather drive just let me know.'

'Certainly I'll drive. Pull over.'

John didn't pull over but he did slow down a bit. The car fell into an uneasy silence.

Giorgio was not as badly hurt as they feared but he did have to stay in hospital, at least overnight. Aunt Adriana was with him now. It could have been so much worse. Nonna had already heaped her thanks on Caterina of Alexandria, patron saint of mechanics, with a promise to light fourteen candles next time she was at Mass. A chain had snapped while Giorgio had been hoisting an engine out of a car and the block had landed on his ankle. If he had not been momentarily distracted and turned away, it would have been his head. The seriousness of the near miss left them all feeling subdued.

John's behaviour was also making Elisabetta feel uncomfortable. He had been impatient to leave the hospital and now he was driving faster than she liked. Much faster. She glanced at him anxiously. His eyes were slightly feverish. John never got angry and she didn't like it. What could be wrong with him? The car's speed began to creep up again.

There was a green light ahead and John accelerated wanting to catch it. But he was just too late. It turned red and he had to brake sharply as a bus ponderously crossed the junction. He muttered a curse and got a sharp telling-off from Nonna. Firstly because of his language. Secondly because she'd been thrown forwards against the front seats. A girl in white with flowing auburn hair stood on the pavement but nobody in the car noticed her. John's eyes were fixed firmly on the lights, his fingers drumming on the steering wheel. As soon as they changed he was away. The girl watched them go with deep brown eyes, staring without moving.

A lorry pulled out in front of them and John blew his horn angrily. Then he drove right up close to its bumper waiting for a space in the oncoming traffic. It loomed over them casting a shadow and belching black exhaust fumes. Elisabetta put her head in her hands so she didn't have to watch. Even Nonna was quiet now. He seemed driven by some unnatural obsession and it was frightening. Soon they would be home and she was murmuring prayers that they would get there safely.

But the saints were not listening this time. John finally managed to overtake the truck and accelerated to race along a straight stretch of road and then applied the brake as he turned a corner. With an eerie sense of having been here before he found a little old lady, dressed in black, standing right in the middle of the road. He swore terribly and slammed his foot down hard, spinning the wheel in his hands. But with a horrible thump the wing of the car clipped the old lady before coming to a halt halfway on the pavement.

For a moment there was stunned silence. Then Nonna began shrieking in the back seat. Elisabetta turned very white. Her breathing was shallow as if she was close to panic. John let go of the steering wheel trembling. 'Why is that woman always standing in the middle of the road?' he said, staring at his hands as if they didn't belong to him. The anger seemed to have left him and if anything he seemed confused now. Slowly he opened the door and got out.

There was chaos in the street. A crowd had already gathered and there were shouts and cries of horror at what they had just witnessed. Someone was calling an ambulance on his mobile. A couple of people stooped by the body of the woman where she lay face-down on the road. She must have been thrown about five metres by the impact. She looked so small and frail. Tentatively a man felt for a pulse on her neck but she groaned and stirred slightly before he could locate it. 'She's alive,' he said, relieved. 'Don't move her,' somebody warned. 'She may have a spine injury.'

People were beginning to stare at John but it was a while before he even noticed. He was trying to piece together what had just happened. He finally became aware of the attention he was getting. 'I'm sorry,' he said defensively. 'What could I do? She was standing in the middle of the road.' He threw up his hands in frustration. Nobody answered. They turned away, muttering among themselves.

Within minutes the orange-striped ambulance had arrived and with it the police. The old woman was checked carefully and then eased over gently on to a stretcher. A nasty graze scarred the side of her face and her frightened eyes darted around as they fitted an oxygen mask over her mouth. Then they lifted her into the back of the ambulance, cocooned in blankets and set off for the hospital, blue light flashing, siren wailing.

The police meanwhile were asking questions, taking names and addresses of witnesses and writing them in their notebooks. One man was photographing the scene from every angle. Another was measuring positions and recording everything on a form. One lane of the street was blocked so traffic needed directing. John was being interrogated closely by a frowning officer. What was his speed? Had his attention been on his driving or had he been distracted? Had he indicated clearly his intention to turn? Were his brakes working properly? He answered as best he could but the truth was he couldn't quite remember what he had been doing. It was as if another John had been driving. The policeman wrote down everything he said, never smiling. Then he conferred with some other officers before turning back to face John.

'I am sorry, signor, I must now ask you to come with us to the station.'

John felt a sudden knot tighten in his stomach. 'What? Why? What have I done?' He began to panic at the thought of not going home. He had to get back to the painting. It was like it was calling him.

'You have been in a car accident, signor.'

'But I couldn't help it. She was standing right in the road around a blind corner. She does it all the time. I nearly hit her last week.'

'Really?' The policeman seemed interested by this new piece of information and wrote it down in his book. John cursed silently. It might have been better not to mention that.

'Are you arresting me?' he asked anxiously.

'No, signor. Not unless you refuse to come with me. But I should warn you, dangerous driving is a serious offence and if . . .' The officer looked uncomfortable and made the sign of the horns quickly so that his words would not tempt fate. 'If the old lady should . . . die, then the charge could be manslaughter which carries a prison sentence.'

John paled at these words. He was about to speak angrily but then thought better of it. He bit his lip and turned away. Elisabetta listened numbly as he leant over the car window to explain the situation.

'OK, officer. I'm ready.' Dejectedly, he got into the police car and was taken away. After a while, Elisabetta moved over to the driver's seat and shakily drove off.

Bit by bit the crowd dispersed and soon the scene had returned to normal. Only one person lingered. She had watched the whole thing. A girl dressed in white.

∞

It was evening before John returned. He had spent two hours being interviewed, making statements, having his breath analysed for alcohol. He looked pale and was not in a good mood when he entered the kitchen. Everyone looked up expectantly as he took his place at the meal table. He poured himself a generous glass of wine, took a long drink and then refilled his glass.

'Well?' Elisabetta asked cautiously.

He helped himself to a piece of bread. 'They are going to make more investigations before deciding if they're going to press charges.'

Elisabetta nodded. They would have to wait. 'Is the old lady all right?'

John shrugged. 'I don't know. I've been at the police station.'

'I thought they might have told you.'

'Well, they didn't!' he snapped. Elisabetta bit her lip. She was obviously close to tears. John saw he had upset her and he leaned over to take her hand. Maria was shocked to see how much older he looked. 'I'm sorry,' he said in a flat voice. 'I've had a bad day. I think I need to get to bed.' He stood up, nodded to everyone else and left the room.

'*He's* had a bad day?' said Nonna in disbelief. 'He wasn't a passenger in that car.'

## Seventeen

ARNALDO sat with his right hand raised, his face half turned. With only an occasional glance in his direction, Leonardo worked with two brushes to complete the Orsini portrait. He made one last deft stroke and then stood back to survey what he had done.

'That is enough for today,' he said, satisfied. Arnaldo lowered his arm gratefully and came to join him. His heart swelled when he saw what Leonardo had achieved and for a moment he could only look in wonder.

'It is . . . perfect,' he said.

'You like it?'

'I do. I foolishly told Master Verrocchio that I was your equal, no, your better. Now I am not so sure.'

'Ah! I wish the Duke of Milan thought as you do.'

Reluctantly Arnaldo pulled his gaze away from the portrait. 'Do things not go well for you there, Leonardo?'

'I survive. The duke has commissioned one or two things from me but I see lesser men promoted while I am passed by.'

'Then why do you not stay with us in Florence? Verrocchio is not as young as he was. One day someone will have to take over here. There is enough work to last us for years.'

'True, there is work here, but not for me.'

'What do you mean?'

'Medici.' Leonardo scowled as he said the name.

'What of him?'

'He does not like me. Why, I do not know. But while he holds power in Florence then Leonardo must seek fame and fortune elsewhere.'

'Surely not!' exclaimed Arnaldo. 'Medici is . . . he is kind to me. He has promised to help me in any way he can.'

Leonardo raised an eyebrow. 'Really. Then you are a most fortunate young man.'

Arnaldo blushed. 'What do you mean?'

'I mean that all the Medici are true to their word. Once their opinion is formed, nothing will change it. They are the most loyal of friends, the most deadly of enemies.'

'It is true,' said Arnaldo. 'I have experienced that . . . loyalty.' He thought of his dead father and then of Lorenzo's open smile. How quickly would that friendship turn to hate if he knew who he was? He looked again at Leonardo and was surprised to see him so dispirited. Usually his love of life and work was infectious. He laid a hand on his shoulder. 'Be patient, my friend. Your day will come.'

'You think so?'

'I am sure of it. One day you will be the most celebrated artist the world has ever known.'

'Ha! Now I know you jest.' He looked pleased nevertheless.

∞

Arnaldo was thoughtful as he made his way to the Palazzo Medici. He couldn't forget Leonardo's comments. Friend or enemy he thought as Lorenzo held out his hand.

'Good day, Signor Rossi. Have you spoken to your sweetheart's father yet.'

'Not yet, signor.'

'There is an old proverb, is there not, that flowers can fade before they are picked. If you are not careful her love will have died.'

'That is a sorry proverb,' Arnaldo smiled. 'For all flowers must fade but love need not.'

'I only urge you to hurry,' laughed Lorenzo. 'Let he who would be happy, seize the moment, for tomorrow may never come.'

'And I thank you for your counsel.'

'Will you stay and fight awhile?'

'I should continue with the portrait.'

'But it is nearly completed. How many more sittings will you require?'

Arnaldo's heart sank but he maintained a cheerful face. 'Not many, signor. Maybe I will finish today.'

'Excellent! Though I will miss your visits.'

'As will I,' admitted Arnaldo regretfully.

'Then let us fight one last time.' He called for swords and tossed one to Arnaldo.

'I believe I have mastered that trick you taught me, signor,' Arnaldo said, cutting the air with a practice swing. 'The one for disarming your opponent.'

'Then no more talk. Show me,' cried Lorenzo. Without further warning he rushed at Arnaldo and they met in a clash of metal.

∞

'Do not hurry yourself, Alessandra,' said Marietta, shaking her head. She was standing at the upstairs window. 'They are fighting again.'

Alessandra came and watched with her old nurse. Arnaldo bettered Medici with a clever move and, laughing, her father congratulated him with a slap on the back. 'My father is fond of Signor Rossi,' she observed. 'He treats him as a son.'

'He does. And what about you?'

Alessandra sighed. 'I suppose he loves me too. He only does what he thinks is best but I fear . . .' she tailed off. 'You know my feelings,' she finished.

'I was not thinking of your father. I wondered how *you* felt about Signor Rossi.'

There was a flash of irritation in Alessandra's eyes. 'Why should I have an opinion on Signor Rossi?'

'I don't know,' shrugged Marietta. 'You seemed eager to talk with him yesterday. Heaven knows you have little enough to say these days. There must be something about him to stir you to talk.'

'I was merely being polite.'

'Of course. And you were being polite when you

pushed me out of the way so you could bandage his arm. How did you like him without his shirt?'

'Marietta! That is enough!' The nurse said no more but Alessandra still felt obliged to defend herself. 'Signor Rossi is a pleasant young man, a little awkward sometimes. I saw that he was not smiling and thought it kind to put him at his ease.'

'So, he is pleasant and shy. You have noticed his smile and you wanted to show him kindness. It sounds to me as if you *do* have an opinion of him.'

'What are you suggesting, Marietta?'

'Nothing.'

'Good.'

There was silence. Alessandra tapped her foot impatiently. Marietta clearly had something to say but she wasn't going to give her the satisfaction of asking her to speak her mind.

'I have seen the way he looks at you though,' she said at last. If Alessandra had been in the habit of smiling she would have smiled now. It was good to know that she could be more strong-willed than her nurse.

'He looks at me because he is painting my likeness. He could hardly paint me if he did not.'

'It is more than that.'

Alessandra turned and stared hard at Marietta. 'What do you mean?'

'You think I don't know when I see love in a young man's eyes. I wasn't always old and fat you know.'

Alessandra did not answer but her face softened.

Then the pain returned. 'You are cruel, Marietta. Why do you taunt me with this when you know I am to marry Signor Orsini?' She turned away.

'I speak because there is still time,' said Marietta, suddenly urgent. 'In two weeks it will be too late.'

'It is already too late. My fate is sealed.'

She would say nothing more, but took her seat, waiting for Arnaldo. Marietta also sat down and sadly picked up her sewing. She and Alessandra often argued but she loved her as if she were her own. She would risk anything for her, but she seemed defeated already. Resigned to a life of misery.

Later there came a knock at the door. 'You may enter,' Alessandra said dully.

There was another knock. '*Santa Maria!* Are you deaf?' cried Marietta. 'You can come in. We have our clothes on today.' Arnaldo pushed on the stiff and creaking door and cautiously stuck his head into the room.

Alessandra studied the young artist as he mixed his paints. Was it true what Marietta said? She had not meant to encourage him if it was. He stole a quick glance at her but looked away again as soon as their eyes met. A dull blush began to creep up his cheeks as he worked on, aware that she was watching him. Was it just shyness or something more? The more she looked at him the more troubled her heart became. She had thought herself safe but once again Marietta had opened a chink in her defences. She found all her bottled-up feelings begin to rise to the surface, unsettling her. He straightened up.

'When you are ready, signorina,' he said quietly. She nodded and lifted her arm but she was trembling. 'Are you well?' he asked, his face full of concern.

'Yes,' she said in a whisper.

'Your arm, it is not quite right.' She raised it some more and sat up a little straighter but then slumped again. 'I will come back,' said Arnaldo. 'You are not yourself.'

'No, please stay,' she said quickly, turning to him. She realised at once she had sounded too eager. 'You must complete the painting. There is so little time.'

He looked at her curiously. 'It is nearly finished,' he assured her. 'There is very little left to do. I can return tomorrow.'

'Oh! If it is nearly done, we may as well finish it today.' She turned back into the correct pose and raised her hand again.

'Your arm is still not right, signorina.'

'Show me,' she said softly, not daring to look at him. For a moment he did not move. Then his shadow fell across her face as he came and stood in front of her.

'Like this,' he said. He gently put his hand under hers and moved it slightly. She closed her eyes as she felt his warm skin against her own. His hands were strong and slightly rough, with pigments ingrained in his nails. Her fingers twitched – she instinctively wanted to take his hand and hold it. Then she mastered her feelings and he let go. He had held her just a moment longer than necessary.

'Thank you, signor,' she said.

'You are welcome.'

In a dream he returned to his easel while Marietta smiled from where she sat watching in the corner. Maybe there was hope.

# Eighteen

THINGS were better in the morning. John was still very quiet but Maria assumed this was because he was worried about the old lady and the police investigation. Aunt Adriana was on the telephone, talking quietly as the others ate their breakfast. She eventually hung up and joined them at the table. 'He's all right,' she said shyly. 'The doctor says he can come home this afternoon.'

'*Grazie a Dio!*' cried Nonna. She was missing out the saints now and going straight to the top.

'That's wonderful,' agreed Elisabetta.

There was the sound of a scraping chair. Everyone turned in time to see John disappearing into the basement. Elisabetta watched him go, worried, and Nonna shook her head as she went into the hall to fetch a broom.

'What is so exciting about that painting?' frowned Elisabetta. 'Why does he want to spend all his days down there? He is supposed to be on holiday.'

'It's the White Lady,' said Maria, also looking at the doorway where her father had just gone. 'It goes with the one painted by Verrocchio in the Uffizi. It might be worth millions of pounds.'

'Really? A painting by Andrea del Verrocchio?' She looked suddenly more interested. A Renaissance painting would buy a lot of shoes.

'No, not definitely Verrocchio. It could be by Leonardo da Vinci.'

'Leonardo!' Elisabetta was incredulous. 'But . . . but that's impossible. It would . . . How much did you say it would be worth?'

'Lots.'

'But why would anyone paint over such a thing? It would be madness.'

Maria thought about the mutilated picture in the book she had found the day before. Maybe madness wasn't far from the truth. Then again, perhaps there was a good reason for getting rid of the painting. Already they had had Uncle Giorgio's accident, her dad's strange behaviour, the car crash, not to mention the elusive girl who looked exactly like the girl in the portrait. She didn't say any of this to her mum. She just shrugged. 'I dunno.'

Just then Beppe and Tommy came into the kitchen and headed straight for the hall. They met Nonna coming back in. 'Just a minute,' she challenged them, blocking the doorway. Beppe stopped reluctantly. 'Where are you two off to?'

'Nowhere.'

'Nowhere, eh? Well, you might as well stay in then.'

Beppe's face fell. 'All right. We're going up to Arnaldo's Spring. There are some men there. We wanted to watch them.'

'Men? What sort of men?'

Beppe shrugged. 'Men with beards and spades.'

'Sounds like archaeologists,' said Elisabetta.

'Sounds more like the Seven Dwarfs to me,' said Maria.

'Well, whoever they are, you are not going up there on your own. When I think of the trouble you make wherever you go, Beppe. Your mother has enough to worry about with your father in hospital. No. Unless Maria wants to go with you, you will have to stay in.' Nonna held her broom like a guard's spear and glared at him.

Beppe turned and looked pleadingly at his cousin. A day out minding Beppe and Tommy. Hmm! She could think of things she'd rather do. Like having a tooth out without anaesthetic. She was about to shake her head when something occurred to her. 'Is Arnaldo's Spring what Father Romano called "The Well of Tears"?'

Her mum nodded. 'Yes. It's very pretty. There's a stream that bubbles up from underground, and caves that Saint Arnaldo is supposed to have lived in. Your dad and I used to go there a lot.' Her face clouded as she remembered happier times.

'Is it true that it's Saint Arnaldo's tears?'

Elisabetta looked at her daughter strangely. 'It's a story, Maria.'

'Yeah. I know. OK. I'll go.'

'Yes!' cried Beppe.

∞

It was a long walk and all of it uphill. Maria didn't mind though. She walked slowly with her brother while Beppe raced on ahead, then lingered behind, then caught up again. They went through olive fields – neat rows of trees with silvery leaves and the unripe fruit still green and hard. Beppe found a lizard which he generously dropped down the back of Maria's T-shirt. She gave him a scornful look, fished it out and let it go. It darted under a rock with a wriggle of its tail. Only when he had turned away, disappointed, did she squirm with disgust. As they got further away from the town, so the fields disappeared and gave way to open countryside. Elegant cypress trees of dark green cast long shadows across their path. The ground became more rocky with outcrops of big boulders. When they stopped to rest they could turn around and look right across the valley. There was San Arnaldo below looking like a toy town and the winding track they had walked up.

Before long the path joined a stream which gurgled over a rocky bed in a series of small waterfalls. Maria guessed this was a sign that they were nearly there and sure enough, around the next bend they arrived at the source. It was beautiful, just as her mum had said. The spring bubbled up at the foot of a huge projection of rock and flowed into a deep pool. The water was sparkling clear and cascaded over a mossy stone to feed the stream. Maria glanced at her watch. Nearly midday. How long would it be before one of the boys fell in she wondered.

There was nobody there at the moment but there was plenty of evidence that there had been. A mud-splattered 4x4 was parked on a grassy ledge, its chunky tyres just right for off-road driving. There were some shovels and measuring sticks lying next to a freshly dug trench. There was a silver-coloured tripod that had a little yellow box with a glass window mounted on it. Tommy immediately wandered over to this and to his delight found that the box rotated and if he pressed a button a red light shone out of the glass.

'Tommy, don't fiddle with that.' Maria looked around slightly anxious. Where were the men in charge of all this stuff? She wished they were here. They'd soon tell the boys not to mess around with the equipment but they'd never listen to her. It was typical. You take Tommy for a two-hour walk into the middle of nowhere and there was still something fragile and horribly expensive he could break. The red light turned out to be a laser and now he was shining it at the rock face making the tiny point of light dance along the surface. 'Careful, Tommy, you might blind someone if it . . .' She stopped herself. When you start-ed warning people about putting things in eyes there was no hope for you.

Hoping the men would be back soon, Maria went to look into the trench. It was less than a metre deep and there was a big pile of loose soil and stones piled up at one end. It was a very neat trench. The edges were marked out with orange string and the sides were cut straight and even. The bottom was flat and there was no debris lying on it. Everything was scraped clean. At one end there were some large squarish stones that crossed the ditch in a straight line. Further along was a black stain on the soil as if there had been a fire. Apart from a few holes and small pits there was not much else to see. She looked up. Tommy was still playing with the tripod thing. Beppe was by the pool, dropping stones in and listening to the plop. There were some flowers scattered by the water's edge that she hadn't noticed before. Offerings to the saint, she supposed. She cast her eyes around and saw an opening in the rock that might be the entrance to a cave. She was about to ask Beppe about this when a man suddenly emerged from it. 'Hey!' he cried when he saw the children. There was a loud splash. Maria looked at her watch again. Just over seventeen minutes. Longer than she had expected.

There were three men altogether and only one of them had a beard. He was wearing a checked shirt and seemed to be in charge of the excavation. The other two were younger and wore T-shirts. All of them had muddy boots and thick woolly socks on and they appeared to be friendly. One of them had found a blanket for Beppe who now sat huddled and shivering with it pulled around him. Another one showed Tommy how they used the laser instrument which was called a theodolite and was used for measuring stuff. Tommy was shy and refused to touch it while the man was watching. The third archaeologist showed Maria around the site and was happy to answer her questions.

'Did Saint Arnaldo really live here?' she wanted to know.

The man shrugged. 'Somebody did. See that?' He pointed to the stones in the foot of the trench. 'That's part of a wall, or what's left of it. And those holes are where wooden posts would have gone that held up the roof.'

'Yeah, but he was supposed to live in the cave.' She glanced up at the dark entrance and noticed that Tommy had become bored of surveying and was now scrabbling through the soil heap. The other man was still with him so she assumed he was OK.

'You could live in the cave,' the young man admitted. 'But it's cold and damp.'

'But he was a saint,' she said turning back to him. 'Saints were into that sort of thing. It makes them holy.'

He laughed. 'Maybe he wasn't so holy. Somebody built a house and lit a nice warm fire to cook their food on. No, I think Saint Arnaldo lived in this lovely house. Or perhaps he didn't live here at all. Maybe this was just a shepherd's hut. I don't know.'

Beppe began to moan about the cold. The sun was out but they were high up and the wind was sharp. 'We ought to go,' said Maria. 'It's a two-hour walk home. Thanks for showing us everything.' The young man smiled and told her it was nothing. She turned to her brother who immediately put his hands behind his back and looked guilty. 'What have you done?' she asked, automatically looking to see what he had broken. He shook his head and said nothing.

'It's all right,' the archaeologist assured her. 'He's done nothing.'

Maria was not so sure. 'You've found something, haven't you?' Another shake of the head. 'Show me your hands.' He held them out. They were dirty but empty. 'What's in your pockets then?' He pulled his pockets inside out. A lot of stuff did fall out but nothing that he could have found there. 'Hey! That's my watch.' She stooped to pick it up and then helped him collect the rest. 'OK,' she conceded. 'Maybe you haven't done anything. Which has to be a first.'

She looked at him suspiciously for a moment more and then called to Beppe who stood up miserably. The bearded man said he could borrow the blanket so he set off squelchily down the slope with it wrapped around him. Maria followed and, as soon as his sister's back was turned, Tommy opened his mouth and let a small object fall into his hand. It sat there, a bit spitty but gleaming in the sunshine.

'Tommy, hurry up,' his sister called. Quickly he slipped the thing into his pocket and trotted after her smiling. It was not every day you found half a gold coin.

# Nineteen

ARNALDO made his way slowly to the Palazzo Medici for the last time. He had finished the painting on his previous visit – the day when he had held Alessandra's hand. That had been a week ago and now the paint would be dry enough to move the portrait back to Verrocchio's workshop for varnishing and framing. Orsini had been delayed in Rome and so Leonardo had not yet been able to add his face to the other portrait. Verrocchio fretted and grumbled that there would never be time but this did not concern Arnaldo. He liked it the way it was.

He wondered what would happen today at the palazzo. Would Medici be there to greet him? Perhaps they would drink wine together and discuss further commissions. But maybe he was too busy with the wedding arrangements and then it would be left to Marietta or some other servant to usher him quickly in and out like any other tradesman. Where would Alessandra be? Would he have a chance to speak with her? What would they find to say if he did?

With all these questions filling his mind, he walked the busy streets unaware of what went on around him.

It wasn't until he reached the Piazza del Duomo at the foot of the Santa Maria del Fiore that he noticed that something out of the ordinary was happening. He stopped and looked around, wondering what was going on. The square was as crowded as ever, busier in fact, but the people did not move about their daily tasks. Porters had laid their loads on the floor. Goods went unsold on the market stalls. Carts were stopped, the horses standing and vainly nosing the hard trodden ground for any blade of grass that might be growing there. All around, the people stood and stared, upwards at the great cathedral.

It was a glorious sight of course. The huge octagonal dome that dwarfed every other building in the city has been designed by Brunelleschi and completed fifty years ago. They had said it could never be done – the expanse would be too wide – but it had been done with eight huge stone ribs. Only the Pantheon built by the Romans of old was bigger. Inside, the vaulted roof was so high and open that it reminded you of heaven and if you wished to go to the very pinnacle, then you would have to climb four hundred and sixty-three steps. Almost as tall was Giotto's Campanile, the square tower at the other end of the cathedral with its long gothic windows. The whole effect was dazzling. The sun had risen over the distant hills and gleamed on the marble facade – stone of white, black, green and pink, all inlaid in geometric patterns. But all this did not explain why people were gazing at it now. It was not as if it was any different from yesterday.

Most of the attention seemed to be on the Campanile at the west end. Fingers pointed that way as people huddled together nodding and muttering. Arnaldo searched to find what they looked at, shielding his eyes against the sun and squinting. Nothing looked unusual until finally he saw it. A man stood on the very edge of the parapet. Eighty metres up and looking over the brink at the crowded square below.

'Who is it? Is he going to jump?'

Arnaldo seized a man standing nearby but he couldn't tell him. Apparently the figure had been there for the last half an hour. First the priests had pleaded with him to come down. Then soldiers had been dispatched to retrieve him, but they had found the door to the roof locked. They did not want to force it for fear of panicking the man into jumping. All they could do was wait and see what would happen.

The crowd was hushed and tense apart from a small group of boys who were playfully fighting each other, pushing and shoving and shouting. They laughed loudly as one of them fell backwards and sat down hard in the dust. Arnaldo was distracted and glanced their way briefly. Then he looked again. They were the apprentices from Verrocchio's workshop.

'Antonio? Tomaso? What are you doing here?' The boys started guiltily, all their laughter leaving them instantly. 'Why aren't you back at the workshop? Does Master Verrocchio know you are here?' They hung their heads, not answering. The fallen boy got up and slowly brushed himself down. 'Well?' Arnaldo demanded. 'Are you going to tell me?' Finally, after being nudged forward by his companions, Giovanni spoke up.

'We came to watch Signor da Vinci.'

'Leonardo? Why? Where is he?'

The boy pointed to the top of the Campanile.

∞

At the top of the tower Leonardo da Vinci was busy. The cotton tent was laid out behind him, eight metres square and rising to a point eight metres high in the shape of a pyramid. The base was made rigid with a framework of wood and Leonardo had it raised up to allow the breeze to blow in and gently fill the fabric. It fluttered and billowed as it filled out and began to slide across the roof tiles until it reached the end of the ropes that secured it at each corner. There it stopped and tugged and bobbed like a giant kite. The other ends of the rope were attached to a padded harness that Leonardo was wearing around his chest. Now he braced himself against its pull while he made small adjustments – tweaking and tightening ropes as he waited for a good moment to jump. He wanted the breeze to drop a little so that he would not drift too far and end up crashing on to rooftops.

Nothing could go wrong, he was sure of it. He had done the calculations carefully and was confident that the drag of the tent would be sufficient to slow his fall and allow him to drift to earth like a leaf falling from the tree in autumn. He looked down. A lot of people were looking back up at him. Tiny, they were like ants. Leonardo was very fond of ants. They were well organised and disciplined. He was glad the people had come to watch him. Leonardo – the first man to fly since Icarus. Perhaps now he would gain the recognition he deserved. Just then the wind dropped. Perfect. With a tug of the ropes to give the tent lift, Leonardo stepped out over the edge.

∞

'He's jumped!'

The crowd below gave a collective gasp of horror. There were loud screams, people covered their eyes and several women fainted. But just as quickly the terror passed to be replaced by wonder and confusion. The man did not plummet instantly to his death on the hard stones below. He fell slowly like a feather borne up by the wind. And above him was . . . was what? A cloud? Who was this miracle worker?

'It is an angel!' cried one.

'No! It is Our Lord himself!' Savonarola the monk with unkempt hair and a fiery light in his eyes began to quote from The Book of Revelation. '*And I looked, and behold a white cloud, and upon the cloud one sat like unto the son of man, having on his head a golden crown, and in his hand a sharp sickle.* He comes to judge us! Beware Citizens of Florence. Your sins are secret no more!'

There were murmurs of dismay and many of the devout fell to their knees with prayers for mercy. Even the less devout began to look a bit nervous. Still the figure descended as rapt faces turned upwards. But slowly the looks of fear turned to bewilderment. As the man drew nearer it was clear that something was not quite right.

'If it is Our Lord,' said one of the bolder spectators, 'he's wearing very dirty britches.'

'I can't see a sickle either,' said another.

There was a moment's more deliberation. Then people began to think that, whoever the mystery man was, it would be wiser not to be standing where he landed. In a panic, they got off their knees and scattered just as Leonardo landed gently among them. 'That seemed to work quite –' he began, only to be enveloped in a jumble of billowing cloth.

Hesitantly at first, the crowd came forward to help him out. They took the cloth and hauled it over his head. Then they stared in amazement at the man who had achieved the impossible. It's Leonardo, they murmured. The artist, he works with Verrocchio. I thought he had gone to Milan. They have plague there. It's just a cloth tent. How did he do that? I don't like it. I don't trust him. He's left-handed you know. They say he cuts up the dead. The mutterings of discontent spread slowly across the crowd. People had been frightened, which they did not like. They had also been made to look foolish, which they liked even less. Anxiously, Arnaldo tried to get near his friend and lead him to safety but Leonardo remained oblivious to the way things were turning against him. He slipped out of the rope harness and then stood, nodding and waving amiably.

'A very smooth descent, I think. Perhaps a little unstable. Possibly a vent cut in the top would reduce swing. I must try that again, only the door is locked now. I am down here, the key is up there . . .' His voice died away as he became lost in his own thoughts. He was not to be allowed to reflect for long though.

'Men of Florence!'

Savonarola was the angriest of all. In front of everyone he had confidently predicted the return of the Son of God and he had been shown to be dramatically wrong. He stood now on a barrel with his hands outstretched as he glowered over the watching crowd.

'Men of Florence. There stands among us one who defies all that is natural and Godly.' His voice began low and intense and it sent tremors of fear through the listening crowd. 'Did not Satan himself tempt Our Lord to do this very thing? Did he not take him to the highest point of the temple and tell him to cast himself off so that angels might bear him safely to the ground? This man!' His voice rose and his pointing finger was dramatic but hardly necessary. 'This shameful man, with brazen cunning and by dark arts, does the very thing which Our Lord refused to do.' There was a murmur of agreement from the people. They turned and glared darkly at Leonardo who finally became aware of the hostility that was brewing.

'No! Indeed,' he protested. 'You are wrong, good friar. Not by dark arts at all. It is simply –'

'Silence, devil!' Savonarola was not going to be proved wrong twice in one day. Arnaldo desperately struggled through the crush to get to his friend. Leonardo was such an innocent. He assumed that people would listen to him and understand and it would all be all right. But people weren't like that. Sometimes they didn't want to be reasonable. 'Do not let him speak!' cried the monk. 'He will bewitch you with his voice. He has the power of Satan in him.' Finally Arnaldo reached him and grabbed him by the arm.

'We have to get out of here, Leonardo. This crowd will burn you if they keep listening to him.'

'No, if they would just listen to *me*. There is a perfectly natural explanation for what has happened. I can show them the calculations.'

Arnaldo dragged his friend away as the crowd began to stir and close menacingly. 'They don't want to see your calculations, Leonardo. They want to see the colour of your blood.'

Leonardo looked puzzled but did not resist as Arnaldo hurried him away. The voice of Savonarola floated after them as they ran into a narrow side street. 'Sinners! Unnatural, God-hating sons of Beelzebub! You will burn! If not in this life then in the fires of eternity. You, who dare . . .' His words faded as their steps carried them away from the angry mob. Finally they stopped and gratefully Arnaldo leant back against a wall in a deserted alley to catch his breath.

'It's red,' said Leonardo. 'What other colour could it be?'

# Twenty

UNCLE Giorgio was still in his green hospital pyjamas when they came to pick him up. Sitting up in bed, his left leg bandaged to the knee, he greeted them cheerfully with a big grin on his face. Aunt Adriana squeezed his hand and gave him a kiss. Then she stooped to pick up all the things he had managed to scatter around the floor and began putting them in a suitcase. Nonna started to grumble, insisting that her boy was wasting away, that hospital food was always bad and that there was never enough of it. Had the nurses been looking after him properly? She had seen them as they passed. Mere girls they were. What could they know? They still needed mothers themselves.

'I'm fine, mamma,' Giorgio insisted, leaning over to receive her hug.

When the doctors had signed the release forms and a nurse had packaged up some medication, they were free to go. A young man in a blue uniform came and helped Giorgio into a chair and then wheeled him out into the corridor. They passed other wards, kitchens, equipment stores. Some old people were sat around a television set, their eyes fixed dully on the flickering image. Giorgio nodded and waved to the nurses while Nonna clicked her tongue in disapproval. At the end of the passageway was a set of double doors that led into a reception area from which they could get a lift to the exit. Even before they opened the doors they could hear that there was trouble on the other side. An alarm bell was blaring, voices were raised, there were hurrying footsteps.

'*Santa Cioccolata!* What a noise. Don't they know there are sick people in here?'

Once through the doors all they could see was a huddle of white coats and uniforms crowding around someone they couldn't see. They could hear her though. A high-pitched voice was shrieking and gabbling too quickly to be understood, while doctors and nurses shouted to each other over the top. A red light was winking on and off. One medic had a syringe held over his head, clearly waiting for an opportunity to sedate whoever it was at the centre, doing his best not to inject his colleagues by mistake. An assortment of patients and visitors watched with interest. They seemed to get the person under control for a moment and down came the needle. Then they lost it again. One of the doctors reeled back clutching his stomach as if he had been kicked. The ranks parted, the patient broke free and staggered out of the group.

Elisabetta put her hand to her mouth as she gasped with surprise. It was the old lady that had been in the car accident the day before. She was wearing a white nightdress that was too big and hung on her like a sack.

Her face was scarred, her hair was dishevelled and there was real fear in her eyes. With a cry she lurched towards them and hung on to Elisabetta, imploring her to protect her. Elisabetta instinctively put her arm around her and as she held her there, the doctor managed to jab the hypodermic into the old woman's arm. With a look of outrage she stopped her crying, turned on the man and slapped him hard across the face.

At the sound of the smack everybody stopped in surprise. There was quiet apart from the alarm bell and soon that was silenced too. The doctor put a hand to his face where a red weal was already rising. For a sick old woman she packed quite a punch. She glared at him, her dark eyes glinting. Then they seemed to mist over and she staggered back into the arms of Elisabetta.

'Who is this little woman?' Giorgio asked incredulously.

'We don't know who she is,' said Elisabetta as she supported the lady who was now mumbling incoherently. 'We ran her over yesterday.'

'You ran her over? *Porco Zio!* I hope the car is all right.'

Some nurses came and helped the old lady into a chair and a doctor took her pulse. 'She seems calm now,' a nurse said.

'Calm! It should have knocked her out.' The doctor couldn't believe it. 'Look at her. She's as stubborn as a donkey.' The old woman's head lolled around and her eyes went in and out of focus. But she did not give in and fall asleep.

'What was that all about?'

The doctor turned and faced Elisabetta. 'Are you a relative?' he asked hopefully.

'No,' she admitted. 'But my husband did run her down so I feel a little responsible.'

He looked hesitant. He shouldn't really discuss patients with just anybody but this old lady was clearly a problem to them. 'She insists on leaving,' he said eventually. 'Crazy old woman.'

'Leaving? Is she well enough?'

'She's not too bad. Only bruising and cuts. Old people, they are like infants. They do not tense up when they fall.'

'But where will she go? Where is her family?'

The doctor shrugged. 'That's the problem. We don't know. She wasn't carrying anything to identify her, and either she doesn't know or she won't tell us who she is.' He frowned. He suspected she was refusing to talk.

'But you can't just turn her out with nowhere to go.'

'Who's turning her out? What do you think that wrestling match was all about?' He shook his head and signalled to the nurses to help her back into the ward. They gently lifted her out of the chair but as soon she was on her feet she began to struggle again. She grabbed hold of Elisabetta's hand and hung on, whimpering miserably. They tried to pull her away.

'Enough!' cried Elisabetta. 'Can't you see she is unhappy? She can come home with us.'

∞

Late that afternoon, tired, hungry and in one case wet, three children trooped into the kitchen. Elisabetta and Nonna were preparing the evening meal. 'What happened to you? Get your muddy feet off my floor.' Nonna quickly pulled out an old newspaper and spread it on the floor. She made Beppe stand on it while he took off his wet things. Slop! Muddy water spread across the stone tiles as he dropped them in a heap. 'No! Not there. Put your clothes in here.' She pulled an old bucket out from a cupboard. 'Where did you get this disgusting thing?' She held the archaeologists' blanket out at arm's length as if she suspected fleas.

'Who's that?' Beppe asked.

Maria turned at his words and was surprised to see the old woman dressed in black sitting on a chair in the corner. She was by the stove for warmth with a rug over her knees. Her eyes were bright and alert, taking in everything that was happening. 'Is she the lady that got knocked down? It's the same lady we saw on the way here.'

'That's right,' said Elisabetta. 'We found her at the hospital. She wouldn't stay but she didn't have anywhere to go.'

'Who is she? I mean where does she come from? Has she got a name?'

Elisabetta sighed. 'We asked her all that. She won't say anything. She might still be shocked.'

Tommy gazed at her open-mouthed. He was usually shy of strangers but for some reason he was fascinated by this old lady. He came and stood right in front of her, staring.

'Tommy, come away,' said his mother. 'You mustn't upset her.'

He didn't move and the old lady returned his gaze with her own piercing stare. Who would look away first? 'Hello,' Tommy said.

'He can speak!' cried Beppe.

'Shh!' Maria dug her elbow into his ribs.

The old lady did not reply. 'I'm Tommy.' Still she didn't say anything. Tommy seemed to be thinking hard. Then he suddenly turned and rushed out of the room. There was an awkward pause.

'Where's Dad?' asked Maria.

Elisabetta's face darkened. 'Have a guess.'

'Still in the basement?'

She nodded. 'He hasn't come out all day, I think. He's driving me crazy. It's hard when you lose your husband to another woman, but when the woman is only a painting . . .' She went back to chopping tomatoes despondently. Pasta was already beginning to boil in a big pot on the stove.

'Does he know that the old lady is here?'

'Yes, he does,' said Nonna crossly as she mopped up the damp patch at Beppe's feet.

'Does she know that he was the one who —?'

She was cut off by a sharp look from her mother. 'Hush,' she said in a low voice. 'Just because someone is old and doesn't speak, doesn't mean they don't hear and understand.'

Maria nodded guiltily. She glanced at the old lady, who was still watching intently everything that was going on, and wondered how much she knew. 'I'll go and see Dad,' she said.

Nervously she took the steps down to the basement. What sort of mood would she find her dad in? He was hunched over his work and he either didn't hear her approach or ignored her. He had a bright lamp fixed to the bench now, powered by a cable that ran across the floor to the wall. She could see that he had taken the picture out of the frame to work on it right up to the edges. She came and stood by him and for a few moments all she could do was gaze at the painting. The whole of the arm was uncovered now – slender and elegant in a close-fitting white sleeve. It was beautiful. She watched as her dad finished soaking up some loose paint before speaking.

'Hello, Dad,' she said softly.

He looked up, surprised to see her there. 'Hello,' he said. His face was pale and lined with tiredness. He tipped some more fluid on his cotton bud and began working on the next section.

'Shouldn't you take a break, Dad?'

'I suppose I should. Is it lunchtime yet?'

'Lunchtime! It's nearly six o'clock. Haven't you had anything to eat today?'

John looked confused. 'I don't remember.'

'Aren't you hungry?'

'Not really,' he said listlessly.

'Dad, I really think you should stop now. The old lady you ran over is upstairs. She's come to stay.'

John frowned. 'I didn't run her over. The car barely touched her.'

Maria didn't want to argue. 'Please come,' she said.

'OK,' he muttered. 'When I've finished this bit.'

She glanced over the surface of the workbench while he worked. There was the discarded frame with its backboard now loose. Some old papers were lying by it. 'What's this?' she asked, picking the sheets up.

'Hm? Oh those. I don't know. They were between the painting and the board. I haven't had a chance to look at them yet.'

Maria unfolded them to get a better look. They were yellow with age and covered in old loopy handwriting. She glanced at her dad. He was not paying her any attention so she carefully slipped them into her pocket. A few minutes later he had finished and reluctantly he stood up.

'Well,' said Nonna. 'Look who's come out of his hole.' John scowled at his mother-in-law.

'Hello, darling,' said Elisabetta. She came and put her arms around his neck and looked into his face, concerned. 'You look tired.'

'I'm all right,' he said listlessly and pulled away.

Elisabetta's smile was brittle. 'Someone's come to stay,' she said looking towards the corner. The old woman was glaring at John malevolently as if she knew very well who he was. John turned and took a half step towards her but then stopped. He gave her an embarrassed nod.

'I'm pleased to see you're up and about again,' he said. The old woman said nothing. He looked longingly at the basement door. He really did not want to be here. The lid of the pasta pot was rattling as the water bubbled up inside so John took the handle to drain it.

'Damn!' He let go immediately and the pot fell back with a clang. Water slopped out and hissed and spat as it hit the heat. Everyone turned in alarm and saw John holding his hand out as if in pain.

'Quick! Put it under the tap.' Elisabetta grabbed her husband's arm and pulled him towards the sink. Nonna shook her head and used an oven cloth to rescue the upset pan.

'The handle is hot,' she said unnecessarily. The old woman gave a quiet look of satisfaction.

Bit by bit calm returned and soon the only sound was of the running water where John still tried to soothe his burn.

Just then Tommy came back. He came and stood in front of the old woman again but it was a while before anyone else noticed him. He was holding out his hand and in it was the shiny silver brooch they had bought from Silvio Zappini. Elisabetta gasped. Tommy never gave any of his treasures away. He usually had a tantrum if one went missing. Yet here he was, offering a gift to the old lady. She reached out her old and twisted hand and took the jewellery from him. She held it up close to her face.

'Thank you, little boy.' Her voice was soft and lilting. 'It is beautiful.'

# Twenty-One

Ιτ was much later in the day when Arnaldo eventually reached the Palazzo Medici. He had left Leonardo at Verrocchio's workshop but that would not be the end of it. They knew who he was and where he lived. Florence was a great city – forty thousand souls lived and breathed within its walls – but someone like Leonardo da Vinci could not stay hidden for long. It might not be too bad for him. He had not broken any laws. And he had damaged nothing more than pride. It all depended on the mood of the people.

As Arnaldo knocked on the door, he made up his mind to ask Medici to protect Leonardo. It was a bold move. Lorenzo had insisted that he wanted to help him, but would that extend to assisting his friends? Leonardo himself had admitted that Medici had little love for him. The door opened. It was Marietta who told him he was late and that Medici was no longer at home. Arnaldo bit his lip anxiously. His request would have to wait but there might not be time.

He was shown to the room and then left to collect his things together. He sighed. So this was how his last visit was to be. He was just a passing craftsman. His task was finished here and he no longer belonged. He cursed himself for not arriving earlier as planned. Maybe things would have been different then. He frowned as he saw that there were repairs finally being made to the doorway. There were tools lying on the floor – a hammer, a saw, some chisels – and a fine layer of dust lay over the contents of the room. He hurried to the portrait but thankfully someone had had the presence of mind to drape a sheet over it. He pulled it off and there was Alessandra looking as radiant as ever.

'Beautiful,' he murmured wistfully.

As he stood and gazed he became aware that there was somebody else in the room. Marietta, no doubt, come to hurry him along. He looked up. It was Alessandra herself dressed in a green silk dress. She didn't wear the circlet of gold around her head today but Arnaldo noticed that there was a ribbon around her neck with something small and silver glinting against her skin. She stood perfectly still with her hands clasped in front of her. How long had she been waiting? he wondered. He glanced at the doorway. Surely Marietta or some other servant should be present.

'Is everything satisfactory, signor?' she asked when she saw him look up.

'Yes, thank you, signorina. I was just going to wrap the portrait and then I will be going.'

'My father regrets that he is not here to bid you farewell and to thank you for your work.'

'It is I who am sorry. I was delayed.'

'He asks me to assure you that you will meet again. He has many ideas he wishes to discuss.'

Arnaldo nodded. He couldn't help a thrill of pleasure at her words. And then a pang of guilt. A month before he had wanted to kill Medici. Now he was planning to serve him. Such was the power of Lorenzo the Magnificent. He pushed this troublesome thought away. 'I would like to visit again,' he said. 'I have enjoyed my times here.'

She let her eyes fall. 'As have I, signor. I am only sorry that I have not been better company. You have been patient and courteous and I thank you.'

'Indeed, you are mistaken. You have been all the companion I have wanted,' he said. He hesitated, gathering the courage to say more. 'It saddens me that when I come again, you will not be here. Or that if you are here, it will be as a visitor yourself and I will have to address you as "signora". You will no longer be a child.' He stopped. He wanted to go on but wondered if he had already said too much. She looked up at him but there was no anger at his words, only sadness.

'I too wish things might have been different. If only our fathers had not been who they are.' Arnaldo stiffened, his old fear returning. Alessandra saw him tense and nodded. 'Marietta has told me who you are – Signor de Pazzi.'

Arnaldo felt a sudden clammy fear spread across his chest. What had the old woman done? Who else had she told? She said she could keep her mouth closed.

'Signorina . . . I . . . d–does your father know?'

She shook her head. 'You need not worry. Marietta has not told him. I do not intend to either.'

'You do not despise me?' he asked in disbelief.

'Not if you do not hate me.'

'No!' he protested. 'Never! I . . . I did wish your father ill. But that was before I met him. Before I met you.'

'He has that power,' she agreed. 'All who hear him, obey him. All who know him, love him.'

'You are wrong. It was *you* who won me over.'

She smiled. It was the first time he had seen her do so and it filled her face with the warmth of afternoon sunshine. In the portrait he had not been able to resist giving her just a hint of an upturned mouth, but it had had to come from his imagination. Here was the real thing and it made him feel suddenly weak. 'I would take your words as just flattery, signor,' she said. 'If I did not know your change of heart to be sincere. I remember the first day you came, you wore a dagger at your waist. You do not wear it now.'

'All thought of injuring your father has gone,' he admitted. 'I have found that it is hard to hold love and hate in the same heart.' He studied the floor as he spoke, not daring to look at her. He did not see the anguish in her face. When she spoke it was as if she struggled to get the words out.

'That sounded dangerously like a declaration of love, signor. You should remember that I am to be married.'

'To Signor Orsini,' he said despondently.

'To Signor Orsini. It is my father's decision and a prudent match.'

'Would anything persuade you to go against your father's will?' He looked up hopefully.

'Nothing.' Her voice was barely a whisper. 'Please do not try to tempt me.' They held each other's gaze for a moment until Arnaldo nodded in defeat.

'I am sorry to have unsettled you, signorina. It was not my intention. I wish you well in your future life.' Slowly he began to pack his things away and she found that she was trembling. She had been very close to giving in to him. What had stopped her?

Arnaldo was about to take the picture from its stand but then hesitated. 'Have you seen your likeness yet?' She shook her head. 'It is finished. Would you like to look before I take it?'

'I am sorry. I do not wish to see it. Though I am sure it is good.'

He frowned. 'I understand that you may think it a vain thing and beneath you, but it is to hang in your house in Rome. You cannot avoid seeing it for ever, I think. Unless you intend to keep your eyes closed the whole time.'

She smiled again but a sad one this time. 'That would save me from looking upon my husband. Would it please you if I looked at the portrait?'

'It would.'

'Then for your sake I will.'

Arnaldo stood to one side and held up his open

hand towards the painting. Hesitantly she stepped forward and came to stand beside him. Her silk dress rustled as she moved and as she drew near he could see there were gold threads embroidered around the neck. The piece of glinting metal on the ribbon about her neck was not a jewel but a tiny key. He could feel the warmth from her body as they stood almost touching. He could smell the scented oil she used to dress her hair. Her presence near him made him suddenly fearful. However the world judged him, he realised that hers was the only opinion that mattered. For a long time she simply looked while he waited anxiously. Then she closed her eyes and took a deep breath.

'You told my father once that you would paint me as you see me,' she said. 'Is this how you see me?'

'It is,' he said softly. Did she approve? Why didn't she say?

She nodded. Her cheeks were flushed faintly red. 'Then I was wrong. There *is* one who might persuade me to go against my father's will.' She turned to him impulsively and took his right hand in hers gazing at it in wonder. Then she looked him in the face. 'This is the hand that has won my heart,' she said intently. 'I believe I might do anything for the man who sees me the way you see me.'

There was a sound outside the door as if someone had stumbled and bumped into the wall. Arnaldo and Alessandra froze where they stood, his hand still in hers. They were both filled with a sudden dread that Medici had returned and was even now coming to see them. He was fond of Arnaldo but he should not find him alone with his unmarried daughter, holding her hand. Who knew what he might do in his anger? Alessandra quickly let go of Arnaldo and moved aside. Then she went to the door and put her ear to it, frowning. There was a quiet shuffling as if someone on the other side was trying to keep very still. If it was her father, why did he not enter? She slid her hand down to the latch, paused there for a moment, and then opened it suddenly. It moved smoothly and silently now.

'Marietta! What are you doing?' she hissed.

The servant had the decency to look a little ashamed. A little. 'What does it look like?' she asked.

'It looks as if you are listening at the door while I talk with Signor de . . .' She lowered her voice' . . . de Pazzi.'

'Then looks are not deceiving.' She stared at her mistress defiantly. 'Who are you going to tell? Your father?'

Alessandra knew that Marietta was right. There was no one she could tell. And if the servant chose to talk then she and Arnaldo would be in grave danger. 'What did you hear?' she asked.

Marietta gave a sly smile. 'Everything.'

'And what are you going to do?'

'All that I can to help you.'

# Twenty-Two

JOHN gazed at the portrait, his eyes unnaturally bright and animated. He ran his fingers lovingly over its surface. It was getting dark outside now. The lamp at his side created a patch of light in the wide, gloomy basement. At last he was alone with the painting. He had had to endure the evening meal even though he had no appetite. All those faces and pointless chatter. The accusing eyes of that evil old woman boring into the back of him. But it was over now. He was alone. Or was he? What was that noise? He glanced up sharply. Was that something moving in the corner? There was a face at the little window. No, it was gone. He waited, listening, watching. There was no further sound. He pulled the portrait protectively towards himself and reached for a large spanner that was lying on the bench. He tested its weight in his hand. The painting was his. No one was going to take it away from him. He picked up the bottle of solvent and returned to work. Just a bit more before bed. He would stop soon. Just a little more.

∞

In the morning, Maria came into the kitchen to find Nonna already there making breakfast. The old woman sat, bright eyed, by the stove. She was wearing the brooch that Tommy had given her, a flash of brilliant silver on her black dress.

'Morning,' she said.

Nonna leant over and gave her a kiss but the old lady was silent. She had been sitting there in the same chair when Maria had gone up to bed the night before. One by one the rest of the family joined them. Her mother had dark rings under her eyes as if she hadn't slept well.

'Where's Dad? Still sleeping?'

Elisabetta shook her head. 'He never came to bed. I went down three times. Always he said just a bit more, just a bit more. In the end I gave up.'

'What's wrong with the man?' said Nonna indignantly.

'Nothing, Mamma, please.'

'Nothing! A man stays out all night and his wife says nothing is wrong!' Nonna turned on her daughter, spoon in hand. 'Something *is* wrong! And what about his driving eh? That wasn't right.'

'Mamma!' Elisabetta glanced anxiously at the old lady and Nonna lowered her voice.

'I still say something is strange. What's he got down there? Another woman?'

Elisabetta smiled weakly. 'In a way. He's discovered a painting of a woman. It's old. Very old. Might be worth millions of euros. Who knows?'

'Millions?' Nonna fell quiet as if this had partly explained John's obsession. 'He should still come and have some breakfast. The painting isn't going to run away.'

'Would you go and see him, darling?' Elisabetta said wearily. 'I don't think I can face going down there again.' Maria nodded and headed for the basement door.

At the top of the stairs she could see her dad slumped over the workbench. Her heart began to beat faster. He was only sleeping she hoped. 'Dad!' He didn't move. She hurried down to him being careful to avoid the trailing lamp lead. 'Dad! Wake up.' She spoke more loudly but he still didn't move so she laid a hand on his shoulder. John jerked awake with an incoherent cry. His hand closed instinctively around the spanner and he rounded on Maria viciously.

'Mine!' he snarled. Maria shrieked and backed away. Her dad looked terrifying. There were red marks across one side of his face where he had lain against the bench. Bits of dirt and dust stuck to him. He held the spanner up in his clenched fist, his face twisted with anger.

'Dad! It's me. Maria.'

'It's mine!' he repeated, staring wildly. Then he seemed to come to his senses. He recognised her and slowly lowered his weapon. His eyes went dull.

'Dad?' Maria was almost crying. 'What are you doing? You've been here all night.'

'Got to keep working,' he mumbled. 'S'important.'

He rubbed his face in his hands and then ran his fingers through his hair. He blinked a few times before picking up the portrait and studying it in the daylight. Maria couldn't believe that he didn't apologise or make any attempt to comfort her. It was as if she wasn't there.

She hung back feeling hurt and a little scared at the same time. He must have been busy for most of the night because half the picture was uncovered now. A slender torso covered in white silk. Her right hand resting in her lap. Even without her face the White Lady was beautiful. Slowly Maria's curiosity got the better of her fear and she came and stood by her dad, enchanted by what she saw. She reached out and gently took hold of the portrait.

'Can I?' she asked. John tightened his grip possessively but then nodded reluctantly and let her take it. Eagerly she drank in the image. She had never seen anything so lovely. It was as if the painter had reached into her very soul. The painter. Her eyes darted to the bottom corner but it wasn't signed. 'Who is it by?' she asked. 'Verrocchio or Leonardo?'

John shook his head. 'Neither. I don't know the artist. There's nothing else like it.'

Maria couldn't tear her eyes away. Who was this unknown master who only ever completed one painting? Her dad gently tugged at the portrait, then more forcefully and Maria unwillingly handed it back. John laid it on the bench and reached for his bottle of solvent again. Maria remembered why she was there.

'Not now, Dad. You need breakfast.'

'Yeah. I could do with a coffee. Could you bring me one?'

'No. You need to stop.'

John scowled angrily at her. 'I'm fine.'

'You're not fine,' she said firmly. 'You haven't eaten or slept properly for days. And believe me, you really need a wash.' Her dad remained silent, sullen. 'Look at your hands, Dad. They're shaking. If you carry on like this you're going to spill fluid all over the painting. Come on.'

'All right,' he agreed grudgingly.

After breakfast John went upstairs to shave and have a shower. Nonna shook her head as he went. '*Santa Frittata!* He's got a problem.'

'Please don't, Mamma.' Elisabetta could feel things slipping out of control. 'He's been working very hard. He's under a lot of pressure at the university. This is a big discovery for him. It's important. Just think, a newly discovered Renaissance painting. It will make him famous.'

'If it doesn't kill him first,' Nonna muttered to herself as she cleared up the table. Maria felt a chill at her grandmother's words and looked at her closely to see if she was serious. The old woman watched everything from her chair, missing nothing. Tommy got down from the table and went and stood beside her. She smiled and leant over and whispered something in his ear. He grinned and nodded.

'What does she say?' his mum wanted to know. But Tommy wouldn't tell her. Elisabetta smiled weakly. They made a strange pair. 'Well, it seems she wants to talk only to you. Has she told you her name?' Tommy nodded. 'Are we allowed to know?' He glanced at the little old lady and then nodded again. Everyone had stopped by now and they all listened expectantly.

'*Donna Vecchia*,' he said softly.

Beppe let out a howl of laughter. '*Donna Vecchia!* That's not a name.' Tommy's face crumpled as if he were about to cry and Beppe got a clip around his ear from Nonna.

'Stupid boy,' she cried. 'See, you've made your cousin cry.'

'What did I do?' he said indignantly, rubbing the side of his head.

'Get out!'

'What?'

'Out!' Nonna advanced on Beppe threateningly and he disappeared upstairs, scowling. 'That boy! I swear he will be the death of me. Come here, Tommy. Never mind.' She gave her grandson a big hug. Her apron smelt nice – a mixture of soap powder and baking. 'If our visitor wants to be known as *old woman*, then that is what we shall call her.' Old Woman. It suited her.

'How old is she, Tommy?' Maria asked.

'Maria! Don't be so rude.'

The old woman didn't seem to mind though. She spoke up for the first time that day. 'I am fifteen years old,' she said dreamily. Everyone stared at her but she was lost in her own memories.

'Let's clear up the breakfast things,' said Nonna tactfully. 'Help me Maria.'

As she stood up from the breakfast table, Maria could feel something in her back pocket. It was the bundle of papers that had been concealed in the frame of the portrait. She had forgotten about those. She stacked a few things in the sink and then, excusing herself, hurried up to her room and unfolded them curiously. They might be just old sheets that the picture framer had used to line the board. They might be far more interesting. Perhaps they held clues that would help explain where the portrait came from and how it came to be painted over.

She glanced at the top sheet and frowned as she tried to make sense of it. It wasn't going to be easy. Not only was the handwriting old-fashioned, the author didn't seem that organised either. There were fragments of writing, unfinished sentences, single words. It was not even all the same way up and occasionally the writer had written a paragraph, rotated the page by ninety degrees and written another piece over it. The rest were the same. With increasing frustration she scanned them, hunting for anything that made sense. She was about to give them up as just random old notes when she found her first clue. The name Giannotti, scrawled in one corner. Yes! They must be important. She read on until she came upon something that made her stop with a stab of icy fear.

At the top of one sheet, the words *La Strega* had been written in uneven letters. The Witch. Underneath there was a strange warning.

> . . . *she did not die. Do not believe them. Arnaldo slew the witch they say but she did not die. I know for I have seen her. She is beautiful, yes so beautiful, but do not be deceived. She is evil. She will beguile you, entrance you, steal your life away until nothing remains but longing. Empty, unfulfilled craving. It can never be satisfied. I hate her. I hate her. She must die. I will kill her. I hate her. I will destroy the Lady in White.*

The last line was little more than jagged spikes of ink as if the writer was really losing control. Maria's heart thumped as she read those words. So this *was* about the painting. But what did it have to do with the story about Arnaldo and the witch? They both wore white, but the girl in the painting was beautiful. There was no denying that she cast a spell over people though. Did Arnaldo know the girl in the picture? Did he kill her? She shivered as she reread the words 'she did not die . . . I have seen her'. What about the girl in white that *she* had seen?

Frightened, she lay the sheets out on her bed. She would get to the bottom of this mystery. She would read every word until she understood the strange events of 1873.

## Twenty-Three

ᴇʟᴇɴᴏʀᴀ Giannotti dined alone. The food lay untasted
on the plate as she nervously fiddled with the cloth,
clenching and unclenching her fingers until it was
twisted and creased. Luciano was late again. Where did
he go these days? He was so seldom home. It did not
used to be like this, not when they first married. Then
he had been kind and attentive. But now he had grown
cold. There was no love in his eyes – no love for her at
least. The candle spluttered in a sudden draught and a
door slammed in the distance. He was home. At last.
She would go to him and confront him. She had to
know the truth even if it brought her pain.

He was in the great hall, taking off his travelling
cloak and handing it to a servant. He smiled to greet
her but it was fleeting. She tugged at her fingers anxiously, twisting her wedding ring.

'You are home, husband.' Her voice was thin and
strained.

'It would appear so.'

'I had expected you earlier.'

'Then you were disappointed, no doubt.' He turned
to go but she would not be ignored. Not this time.

With a cry she clung on to him, forcing him to turn back to her. The servant retreated quickly. There was anger in Luciano's eyes.

'What is it? Leave me, woman.'

'Not until you tell me where you have been.'

'What business is it of yours where I have been?' He struggled to disengage himself from her. 'It is a sorry day when a Giannotti has to keep account with his wife. I go where I please.'

'Who is she?'

'Hands off me I say. Who is who?'

'The woman you see.'

He stopped and stared at her. Then he let out a great laugh. 'Is that what you are thinking?' Her look of pain turned to one of confusion. 'Foolish woman. There is no-one else. If you must know I have been negotiating the purchase of a painting.' The light of desire in his eyes brought her no comfort. 'It is the finest piece I have ever seen. It will crown my collection.' He took her hand and spoke more tenderly. 'Come, do not worry yourself. When you see the White Lady you shall love her as much as I.'

Elenora Giannotti slept alone. Except sleep would not come. With a sigh she reached out to her husband's side of their bed and found it empty still. She sat up. The fire had burned low to red embers. She rose and slipped a robe about her shoulders. Then, stooping, she lit a candle from the glowing coals. Half-past two, the mantel clock said. Luciano slept little now and ate less. He was a shadow of his former self. His once strong frame was wasting away. His fair skin had become lined and wrinkled. Only his eyes stayed bright but with a fierce unnatural light. Like paper in the flames he was being consumed and it seemed to her that he was burning brightest just before he would be extinguished for ever.

Wearily, warily she made her way down the unlit corridors, the stuttering candle in her hand. She knew where he would be. With her. How she hated her. The witch. She had stolen her husband with her beauty and her cunning. She knew exactly how she would find him. He would be as he was every night. Staring at her portrait unable to take his eyes off her captivating beauty. Each night she pleaded with him but her pleas fell on deaf ears. He could not or would not hear her. Or if she did manage to penetrate the wall around his heart he would turn on her with such ferocity that she would flee back to her bedchamber. There she would fall on her bed, crying until sleep came to relieve her of her pain. But even then she was tormented. The White Lady was in her dreams. And not only in sleep but also her waking dreams. She had seen her, she was sure of it. First, in the marketplace. The young woman in the white dress had peered at her from the crowd. Then at the theatre. In the box opposite she had been standing, staring. She had turned away in despair but when she looked again she was gone.

Fearfully, she laid her hand on the door. How would

she find Luciano tonight? She opened the door and with a scream let her candle fall to the floor. Its light was snuffed out but not before she had time to see her husband slumped, lifeless on the floor. Above him the White Lady mocked them with her smile.

Elenora Giannotti lived alone. No, not quite alone. *She* was still with her. She hated her but could not be rid of her. More than once she had tried. She had seized the portrait intent on casting it into fire only to be held back by some unknown power. Another time she had taken a heavy brass candlestick and rushed at her, screaming, only to freeze with the weapon poised above her head and then collapse, crying.

It wasn't just the portrait either. She saw the girl more and more now. In the street. In the park. Everywhere. Indeed, her waking and sleeping life became so confused that they were indistinguishable. Sleeping she walked, waking she dreamed. Less and less she ate and weaker she grew. Her servants watched her waste away, powerless to help her. Until one day when she struck upon a plan.

The old servant Sara was preparing the breakfast when Elenora entered the room. '*Santa Maria!*' she exclaimed before she could stop herself. The mistress of the house was up early, washed and smartly dressed. She was thin and pale but her eyes were clear and she spoke calmly and easily.

'I am going out for the day, Sara.'

'Yes, signora.'

'I am taking a trip into the hills to do some painting.' She was carrying a large bag that could hold a canvas, and a box of paints. 'I used to paint often before my husband . . .' Her voice faltered for the first time and a pang of grief flashed across her features. 'It will do me good to get out,' she said more brightly. 'Life must go on, Sara.'

'Yes, signora. I will pack you some food.'

'Thank you. That would be kind.'

'*Grazie a Dio!*' said Sara when she was gone. 'The mistress has returned.'

In the hills, Elenora found a suitable spot and set up her easel. Then she slid the board out of the bag and placed the White Lady on it. 'Take a last look at the world, my lady,' she murmured. 'I cannot kill you but I can bury you.' She dipped her brush and with great pleasure made a broad stroke of blue across the young woman's face. 'See no more,' she said. 'Trouble me no more,' she prayed.

Each day for a week Elenora returned to the same spot. Each day more of the White Lady was confined to darkness. As the new picture grew, so did the sense of peace in Elenora's heart. Until at last the White Lady was gone.

Gone. If only that were true. Yes, she was buried but she was still there. Elenora could feel her presence. She had a hold on her heart that could never be broken. She took to sitting for hours staring at the picture she had painted. She longed to peel back the paint and see her lovely face again. She grew to love the thing she hated. Or hate the thing she loved. She tasted despair, drank it to the bitter dregs and when she had drained the cup, knew that it had to end.

∞

Elenora Giannotti died alone. She knew she must die and she wanted to do in death that which she could not do in life. The White Lady would die with her. It was in the small hours of the morning when the servants awoke to the sound of flames and the choking taste of smoke. Gasping and coughing they staggered out into the night. Already townsfolk had gathered at the sight of the great blaze. Brave men ventured in to see what could be saved. A box of books, some of the silver, a few of the paintings but of Elenora there was no sign.

'Where is the mistress?' cried Sara. 'You must save her.'

They looked up to the second floor. There the fire blazed most fiercely. Her window was a square of brilliant yellow with the occasional falling of blackened timbers. As they watched there was a groaning crash and the whole of the floor collapsed. A huge bellow of smoke and dust and ash belched into the night sky and the sparks flew upwards.

'God rest her soul,' said the servant. A last rescuer emerged from the building, clutching a painting in his smoke-grimed hands. He placed it on the grass as he caught his breath in great gasps.

'Ah! You have saved the mistress's painting!' cried Sara. 'I am glad. It was her favourite.'

## *Twenty-Four*

MARIA's hand trembled as she laid the last sheet of paper on the bed. The writing of a mad woman surely. But then how much of it reflected what was happening now? Her dad's behaviour had gone beyond strange. And the girl in the white dress that *she* had seen. Was she just a girl who happened to look like the portrait? She pressed her palms into her eyes and she tried to get her head round what was happening to them. It was all too much. She decided to get out of the house. To go for a walk until her mind cleared a bit.

In the kitchen Tommy was sitting on the floor by the old woman's feet. She was telling him a story but how much he understood she could only guess. Part of the time the woman would speak modern Italian but then she would lapse into the local Tuscan dialect that Tommy didn't know. Perhaps he just liked the sound of her voice. It was a pleasant lilting sound, quite mesmerising if you stopped and let it seep into your mind. It was a sound as old as the hills where the stories were born. The story she told now was a folk tale about a bird searching for her children. The way she said it suggested she had learned it by heart. Probably she had learnt the exact words from her mother or grand-mother. Stories like that could be hundreds of years old and often told of events that really happened. The old woman stopped when she became aware of Maria and looked up suspiciously.

'Don't worry,' said Maria. 'I'm not staying.' She made her way through the hall to the front door.

Outside she got an unpleasant surprise. Silvio Zappini was kneeling on the pavement obviously trying to look through the low windows to the basement.

'Hey!'

He jumped at the sound of her voice and got up quickly.

'What are you doing?' she demanded while he brushed some dust off his trousers.

'Nothing. I was just tying my shoelace.'

'With your nose pressed up against our window?'

'No! Really I saw nothing. Your dad, what is he doing down there?'

'I thought you didn't see anything.'

The man shrugged. 'I might have seen a little but only because I happened to be kneeling down you understand.'

'Your shoes haven't got any laces.'

Zappini's face didn't waver. 'What about my shoes?'

'You said you were tying your lace.'

'No, I was looking for a euro that fell out of my pocket.'

'Oh really. Did you find it?'

'Sadly no. But if you find it you can keep it.' He smiled his gold-tooth smile.

'Thanks.' She glared at him and it was obvious that he was not going to get any more information out of her.

'Were you going somewhere?' he asked.

'Not until you have,' she replied. 'Shouldn't you be in your shop?'

'Just going to open up now,' he said gloomily. He turned to walk away and Maria watched him until he was safely out of sight.

When she was sure he wasn't coming back, she set off walking as well. She didn't like Silvio Zappini, or trust him, but she didn't think he was much of a threat. After all, her dad had bought the painting fairly and if he discovered it was worth a lot more than he paid for it, then that was just his good luck. Perhaps Zappini didn't see it that way. Probably he wanted a share of the profits. Who wouldn't? She didn't see what he could do about it though.

What she really wanted was someone to talk to. Her mum already had enough to cope with and she didn't want to scare her. It was a bit far-fetched as well. She could just imagine Beppe's reaction if he ever learnt that she was seeing people from paintings walking around. She stopped on a corner to wait for the traffic. A taxi went past, then a few cars and a truck. Finally a figure dressed in black robes and riding a tiny moped drove by, the engine stuttering and straining. The man noticed her and waved a cheerful *buongiorno*. Father

Romano. She smiled and waved back to the kindly priest and then he was gone in a cloud of exhaust fumes. Only as she watched him go did it occur to her. She could talk to him. Priests were supposed to listen to people's problems.

She was standing deliberating whether she should go when she happened to glance up. The girl was looking at her from a window in the building opposite. She gasped and her heart began to pound. This was the very corner where she had seen her before. She should have come a different way. But it was too late now. This time she made sure her feet stayed firmly on the pavement. Her breath was short as she stared, trying to read the girl's expression. She had no idea how long they looked into each other's eyes but then a bus came between them and when it had passed the girl was gone from the window. That settled it. She was definitely going to speak to Father Romano.

She set off walking quickly, her mind buzzing. She assumed the priest was heading back to the church and she hurried towards the piazza, anxious to talk and even more anxious to get away from the girl. More than once she looked over her shoulder to check if anyone was there – to see if she was being followed. She wasn't. But she still felt uneasy. Without realising, she quickened her pace and people looked at her curiously as she hurried by. She wouldn't look back again. It was childish but she told herself that if she didn't look then there couldn't be anything there. Thirty seconds later she could no longer bear it and took another glance. Nothing. Unless that was her just ducking into a doorway. She was almost panicking now. She couldn't get rid of the thought that the girl was somehow still there. Even though she couldn't see her. She began to run, not even thinking about which direction she was going. People cried out in surprise as she passed. They stood back quickly and were left staring after her, shaking their heads. Cars blew their horns as she rushed across roads without waiting. On she ran. On and on. Away from the girl.

She was drawing big lungfuls of breath as she hurtled around a corner. Then she stopped dead, frozen with terror. The girl was standing in front of her. She had to cover her mouth to stop herself from screaming. How could the girl be here? She was back there. Maria had been running. How could the girl get here so quickly? Nothing made sense. What was going on? The girl walked on, staring straight ahead. Maria pushed herself back against the wall, shrinking away. She wanted to screw her eyes tight shut and block her out but she couldn't. The girl's eyes were deep and lustrous brown. They seemed to draw Maria in and hold her. Any moment she would fall, tumble in, be lost for ever. Still the girl came. Almost whimpering Maria could feel a paralysing dread spread slowly across her body. It was like a dream. She wanted to run and to scream but couldn't move.

The girl did not look at her until she had almost passed. Then she turned and stared briefly. What was on her face? Was it amusement? Contempt? Maria buried her head in her hands and did not look up until she was sure the girl was gone.

∞

She was still shaking when she entered the church. Father Romano had his bike helmet under his arm and greeted her with surprise.

'I just saw a girl like you on the other side of town. Have you got a twin?'

Maria smiled weakly. 'I ran.'

'For the exercise?'

'I wanted to talk to you.'

The priest held his hands open in a friendly gesture. 'So here I am. What do you want to say.'

Maria hesitated. 'It's a bit embarrassing really.'

Father Romano nodded. 'I see. It is like that. Come with me.'

He led her over to some wooden cubicles at the side of the church and opened a door for her. She looked uncertain but then entered and sat down. The door closed. A moment later there was the sound of another door opening and closing and a priest-shaped shadow passed across a wicker mesh that was in the cubicle wall.

'There.' The voice of Father Romano came through the mesh but they couldn't see each other. It was just right for an embarrassing conversation. 'Now everything you say is between you, me and God. I am not allowed to tell another soul and God will probably keep quiet about it as well. He usually does.'

'Really?'

'Really.'

'How do I start?'

'I ask you how long it has been since your last confession.'

'That depends.'

'Depends on what?'

'On what confession is.'

The priest sighed. 'So you have never been to confession. This could take some time. Now you say, "Forgive me, Father, for I have sinned."'

'Have I?'

'Probably.'

'OK. If you say so.' She felt silly. 'Forgive me, Father, for I have sinned,' she muttered, grateful that no one could hear her.

'Good. And now you tell me what is on your mind.'

That still wasn't easy. There was so much to say and all of it sounded unlikely. Taken on its own, everything that had happened had a perfectly ordinary explanation. Only together did they seem to add up to something more sinister. 'Do you believe in curses?' she asked eventually.

If this surprised Father Romano, he showed no sign of it. 'I do. Why do you ask?'

'I think there's one on my family. And what about ghosts?'

'You have ghosts as well?'

'I don't know. I think I might.' She felt like a patient describing her symptoms to a doctor.

'When did all this begin? You did not seem troubled last time we spoke.'

'It's all because of a painting my dad bought.' Bit by bit the story came out. He listened carefully, asking questions whenever she fell quiet. When she had finished there was a long and thoughtful silence.

'You think I'm being stupid don't you?' Maria asked when he did not speak.

'No, not at all.' He stirred in his seat as he shifted his weight.

'So do you think there really might be a curse?'

'It is hard to say.' The priest seemed reluctant to commit himself. 'Perhaps I should come around and visit your family.'

'You wouldn't tell them what I told you?' said Maria panicking.

'Of course not. I could just call by and visit your sick friends and relatives. I could also ask your mother, why in thirteen years she has never taken you to confession. It is good you have told me this.'

Maria thanked him and let herself out of the cubicle feeling better. Father Romano stayed where he was thinking deeply for a while. Then he too got up and went to look at the frescoes of Saint Arnaldo, stopping in front of the one of the witch.

'So the White Lady is back,' he said to himself.

## Twenty-Five

'*I* STILL think I should go to your father?' said Arnaldo.

Alessandra shook her head. 'What would you say?'

'That I love his daughter.'

She smiled and then immediately looked sad. She took his hand. 'That would be noble and brave. It would also be the end of it.'

'You don't know that,' Arnaldo protested. 'Your father likes me. He has told me so. He also told me that if I love a girl then I should speak to her father before it is too late.'

'Ah! But he did not think it was his own daughter that you spoke of.' Arnaldo did not respond except to look a little sullen. 'My father's heart is set that I marry my mother's cousin. He is rich and powerful. You –'

'I am just a penniless artist,' finished Arnaldo bitterly. 'Too young to wed and with no means to support a wife.'

'*Santa Maria!* What a sad face.' Arnaldo shot an irritated look at Marietta. She carried on, not caring. 'She has told you she loves you, hasn't she? What do you want? The moon?'

'What should I do then?' retorted Arnaldo angrily.

The joy of hearing that Alessandra loved him was beginning to turn to doubt and frustration after nearly an hour of discussing what could be done. He had spent weeks dreaming of this moment but now realised he had had no thoughts beyond declaring his love. But that was not enough. Each minute they lingered here, increased the chances of Lorenzo returning and finding them.

'You must go away, both of you,' the old nurse said. Her face was serious and sad. 'My master will never allow you to marry. He is proud and will not move. You must escape and make your life together without his blessing. Go far away. Go where even the arm of the Medici cannot reach you.' Arnaldo and Alessandra listened to these words silently. They knew what she said was true but did they dare to do it? Arnaldo had little to give up but Alessandra had much. Marietta saw their troubled looks. 'Who knows?' she said. 'Maybe when your father's anger has cooled, he will forgive you and you can come back.'

'My father never forgives,' said Alessandra. There was ice-cold certainty in her voice. 'He is a Medici. What he says, he means for ever. If I go, I will never return.'

The servant nodded slowly in agreement. 'Then that is a decision you must make.' She sighed. If Alessandra were to leave, it would sadden her more than anybody.

Unknowingly Alessandra let Arnaldo's hand slip out of hers as she thought about the significance of Marietta's words. It would mean leaving her home and her family. She would never again see her brothers and sisters, her mother or father. Even Marietta who had nursed her since she was a baby. Arnaldo studied her face and felt a deep ache in his heart. How could he ask her to give up all that he saw around him? The fine palace, the feasts, the servants, the clothes, the jewels. What did he have to offer in return? Would she be willing to sacrifice all that for a life with him in a foreign land where she had neither name nor wealth? He wasn't sure that she would.

'I cannot ask you to do this,' he said in a low voice.

'Indeed you can,' Alessandra insisted.

'But to leave all this?' He held out a hand to the room with its luxurious rugs and tapestries. 'To go who knows where, taking nothing with you.'

'I will do it.'

Arnaldo felt a wave of gratitude at her words, but he had to know she meant them. He did not mean to lead her to a life of long regret after a hasty decision. 'Do you know what you are saying? You have always slept on a feather mattress. You have never been cold or hungry. Your father has never denied you anything.'

'Except my freedom,' she said defiantly. 'What do I care for feather mattresses or for fine clothes. My father would send me off to Rome to be the wife of an old man. Yes, I would live in a palace but it would be my prison. No, my tomb.' Her eyes glinted angrily and her breathing quickened. 'See this,' she cried. She hurried to her box which was sitting on a low table beneath the window. She slipped the tiny key on its ribbon from around her neck and unlocked the beautifully inlaid box with a soft click. Then she took out the small dark bottle with its black cork sealed with wax. 'Do you know what this is?' She held it under his nose and he backed away, in awe of her anger. He could see now how like her father she was.

'I cannot know,' he said. 'Unless you tell me.'

'It is hemlock,' she said darkly. 'There is enough here to kill three grown men.'

Arnaldo's face paled and Marietta put her hand to her mouth to stifle a gasp. 'What do you intend to do with it?' he asked. His voice wavered as he spoke.

'I would drink it all rather than be Orsini's wife.' Her face showed that her words were true. 'So do not ask me what I am giving up if I become your wife. Ask me what I will gain. You offer me life where before I had only death. You offer me freedom instead of slavery, hope instead of despair.' These were the words that Arnaldo wanted to hear but her ferocity frightened him. Her eyes were bright and her lips parted slightly. 'Do you still doubt me?' she asked.

'No, but I want you to be sure. There can be no going back.'

Alessandra looked at him for a moment more and then returned to her box which was still lying open. She took out a gold florin which she held up for Arnaldo to see. It was newly minted and shone brightly in the sunshine that streamed through the window. 'I will give you an oath which cannot be broken. I call upon all the saints to witness that what I say is true.' She went to the doorway where the tools lay leaning against the wall.

She knelt down and placed the coin on the floor. 'This is my heart,' she declared. Then she took up the hammer and the largest chisel and with a single blow broke the coin into two. The ringing of metal on metal reverberated around the room and Arnaldo winced as if she had indeed wounded herself. The air seemed to cool suddenly and he watched transfixed as she picked up the two halves and rose to her feet. Her hair was dishevelled and her skin flushed red. He had never seen her like this before. He was used to her cold and aloof. Now it was as if she were on fire.

Her breathing was quick as she advanced as if in a trance. When she stood before him she held out her hand. One half of the coin lay on her slim white palm. 'Take it,' she said. Her voice was low and hypnotic and her eyes burned as she stared at Arnaldo. Hardly aware of what he was doing, he reached out and took the half-coin. Its newly broken edge felt sharp and jagged in his hand.

'I give you my heart,' she said. 'I will not rest, I will not know peace, I will not be whole until these two halves are joined again.' She closed his hand over the broken coin. Then with his hand still in hers she reached up and kissed him gently on the lips. 'I seal this vow with a kiss.'

'*Grazie a Dio!*' murmured Marietta. 'That was beautiful.'

Alessandra's eyes cleared and she seemed to become aware of her surroundings once more. She looked at Arnaldo expectantly.

'I will do all that you say,' he said softly. He touched his lips where he could still feel the warmth of hers. Then the moment was broken.

'Alessandra! Are you there? I have brought someone to see you.'

The three of them froze. Lorenzo de Medici was at the foot of the stairs.

## Twenty-Six

'JOHN! Are you there? It's time to eat. Please, won't you come upstairs now?'

Elisabetta's voice drifted down from the kitchen. John heard her but to him it was just irritating background noise, distracting him from what he had to do. He didn't answer. He had so nearly finished restoring the painting – just one corner to complete. But he could not work so fast now. Her face was uncovered and he found it hard to tear his eyes away from her. Her half smile was so beguiling that the minutes slipped by while he simply sat and stared. Her eyes followed him wherever he moved. He was ensnared. Blinking and shaking off her spell, he took up his bottle of fluid and forced himself to carry on. Maria came and stood at his shoulder. She spoke but what she said he didn't know. She sounded far off and muted as if speaking underwater.

'It's time to eat, Dad?' Maria sighed in desperation. Nothing she did got through to him now. She let her gaze rest on the face of the White Lady. She was young, but she could see why they called her Lady. She commanded attention. Her eyes were strong and proud as if she were used to being obeyed. She was certainly beautiful – perhaps the loveliest girl she had ever seen. But there was something terrible about her as well. As if she bore an awful burden which even death could not free her from. Maria shuddered and felt suddenly cold. 'Are you warm enough, Dad?' No answer. Sadly she left him and went back upstairs.

John worked on. Hour after hour, without any concept of time passing. The room grew dark so he switched on the powerful lamp at his side. The house grew quiet but that suited him well. He enjoyed the quiet tranquillity of the night. Alone. Occasionally he would glance around suspiciously, just to ensure he really was alone. Finally, in the small hours of the morning, it was done. The last blob of bubbling paint was dabbed up and every trace of the landscape painting by Elenora Giannotti was removed for good. The White Lady was free again.

John gazed with longing at the portrait before him. His eyes drank her in greedily, but rather than becoming satisfied his desire seemed to grow. The more he saw of the exquisite brushwork, the delicate lines, the more he craved. He reached out and gently ran his fingers over the surface of the painting. He could touch her but never reach her. She was trapped for ever in a layer of paint a few millimetres thick. John felt the first stabbing ache of despair. She was his but she could never be his.

Just then he heard a noise. He stiffened and turned quickly. He was right. He had definitely seen a face at the window this time. He turned back to the White Lady. She may never be his, but she was definitely not going to be anybody else's. He faced her for a few moments more then switched out the lamp. The room was flooded with darkness and he waited until his eyes adjusted to the low light that filtered in from outside. Then he pushed back his chair and stood up. Picking up the heavy spanner he withdrew to the corner. There he would wait and watch. Wait and watch. His eyes felt heavy and he began to nod. No! He snapped awake. He must remain vigilant. Must stay awake. Must . . . stay . . . awake.

At three in the morning Maria suddenly woke. She did not drift slowly out of unconsciousness – one moment she was fast asleep, the next she was wide awake. She lay very still, listening. Outside she could hear a cat miaowing. A moment later a car rumbled by. Other-wise everything was quiet and still. So what had woken her? She was sure something had. She rolled over and tried to get back to sleep but she was no longer tired. She decided to get up and go and find a drink of water.

The moon was bright. There was a sharp shaft of bluish light, lying across the hallway floor as she made her way downstairs. The boards creaked occasionally as she trod softly but the only other sound was her own breathing. She didn't bother with the kitchen light but found herself a glass, filled it from the tap and took a sip. Then she turned quietly to go back upstairs and stopped suddenly with a gasp. The glass nearly slipped from her fingers. Two bright eyes were staring at her from the corner. In a moment she saw it was only the old woman and she began to breathe more easily.

'You frightened me,' she said. There was no reply. 'Aren't you going to bed?' The old woman shook her head slowly. 'Can you sleep in that chair?' Why don't you sit in a more comfy one?'

'I do not sleep,' she said.

Maria had heard old people grumble about finding it hard to sleep before. But they usually still went to bed and dozed off eventually. Looking at this little old lady though, sitting on a hard chair, back ramrod straight, eyes wide open, she wondered. 'Not ever?'

'Never.' The word sounded final and slightly desperate. 'I haven't slept for . . . how long. Many years. Long years.' All the fight and fire seemed gone from her spirit and she looked nothing more than a frail, lonely old woman. Maria felt sorry for her.

'I can't sleep tonight either. I'll sit with you if you like.' The old woman didn't say anything which Maria took to mean she didn't mind. She pulled up another chair and sat down.

'How are your injuries?' she asked after a while.

'They do not trouble me.'

'Good.' There was another wordless wait. Maria began to regret offering to sit with her. She found the silence uncomfortable and felt the need to keep talking – even if it was a one-sided conversation. 'We were worried about you, you know. So many things seem to be going wrong. Uncle Giorgio had an accident at work. And my dad, he's . . . he's not himself at the moment. And I saw . . . something that freaked me out a bit.' She dried up. It was really hard talking to someone who made no response. Not a nod or a smile or even a flicker of understanding.

'What does "freaked me out" mean?' the old woman said suddenly.

'Sorry. I mean it scared me.' If Maria thought this was a sign that the woman was becoming more talkative, she was wrong. 'I'm beginning to think there's a curse.' She giggled self-consciously. She wished the old lady would say *something*. If she kept talking, pretty soon she was going to tell her everything. Not that it would matter much. She was not what you'd call a gossip. Suddenly it all came tumbling out. 'It all started when we got this painting, you see. My brother, Tommy, you like him, he spilt cleaning fluid on it and underneath was this other painting and my dad's been cleaning it. He's obsessed with it. Anyway he's just about finished it now. It's a really old painting of a girl dressed in white, holding flowers. It's sort of a lost masterpiece worth millions of pounds which ought to be a good thing but all this bad stuff is happening and I really think the girl in the picture might be to blame. I . . . I think I've seen her . . .' She tailed off again. There, it was out. She hoped she hadn't said too much. There was silence for what seemed like for ever.

'So you have found the White Lady,' the old woman said eventually.

'You've heard of it?' Maria turned towards her, excited.

She nodded. 'Of course. Many around here remember stories of her. But they do not speak of such things. They are afraid.' Her voice sounded bitter and scornful.

'Is there really a curse then?' Maria asked breathlessly.

'It is just a painting,' said the old woman. And she would not be drawn to say more.

In the stillness after this revelation, Maria became aware that there was movement down in the basement. She stirred. 'Is my dad still down there?' she asked.

'He hasn't come up.'

'Perhaps I should go and see him.'

'There was a noise down there, just before you came in.'

'What sort of noise?' Maria was suddenly anxious.

'A crash, like something falling and breaking.'

So that was what woke her. Maria got up and hurried to the basement doorway. It was dark down there. What was her dad doing, working in the dark? 'Dad?' No answer. More and more fearful she reached for the light switch. With a click the room was filled with light but she couldn't see anything. Not from this angle. 'Dad? Are you all right?' Slowly she put her foot on the first step, terrified of what she would find. The stone was cold on her bare feet. There was a draught blowing from somewhere. Perhaps a window was open. She glanced up. No, not open. Broken. Halfway down the steps she was able to see past the workbench. She stopped, horrified. No! It couldn't be true. It was horrible. She screwed up her eyes and let out a scream.

'What is it? What is this noise?' Nonna was at the top of the stairs in an enormous white nightgown. Behind her stood Elisabetta and Adriana. Even Giorgio was there hobbling with one bandaged foot. They all peered down anxiously. White faced and trembling, Maria turned to face them. She gulped and there were tears streaming down her face.

'What is it, Maria? What is wrong?'

Maria pointed. In the centre of the room Silvio Zappini lay face-down on the floor. There was blood seeping out from under his head. Over him stood John holding a heavy spanner in his hand.

## Twenty-Seven

'ALESSANDRA!' Lorenzo's footsteps sounded loud on the stairs as he made his way up. 'Are you there? I –' He stopped suddenly in the doorway as he saw the three of them standing awkwardly, none of them willing to catch his eye. His look narrowed suspiciously. Everything had the appearance of order. Rossi was here to collect the portrait. Alessandra was showing her usual courtesy and Marietta was present to maintain his daughter's honour. But he had interrupted something here, he was sure of it. He tried to dismiss his doubts. 'Signor Rossi,' he said stiffly. 'I had expected you earlier.'

'I . . . I apologise, signor. I was delayed.' His face flushed and he kept his gaze firmly on the floor.

'No matter. You are here now. Everything is satisfactory I hope?'

'Yes, signor. I am just now collecting my things. Your daughter has been kind enough to give your apologies.'

'Has she?' He turned on Alessandra and his face darkened further as he noticed her appearance. He made an irritated noise in his throat. 'Look at you, girl,' he hissed. 'Your skin is positively red. What have you been doing?' Alessandra swallowed and did not answer. Medici glanced anxiously at the door. 'Marietta, quickly do something with her hair.' The servant nodded a bow. She hurriedly took Alessandra by the shoulders and turned her to face her. Marietta's eyes were severe, warning her to be careful. And there was something else there as well, something Alessandra had never seen in her nurse before – fear. With expert fingers Marietta tucked away the loose strands, holding the pins lightly between her lips before refastening them. Alessandra closed her eyes and breathed deeply. The feel of her old nurse's firm and knowing touch was familiar and calming. She still clutched her half of the coin and it felt hot and heavy in her palm. It seemed to have a warmth of its own. She herself felt incredibly light as if the coin she held was the only thing anchoring her to the ground. So much so she was afraid to let it go. When she faced her father she was herself again. He took her by the chin and turned her head left and right as if he was inspecting a horse at market.

'That is better,' he said. 'Very well.' His good spirits seemed to return. 'I have someone to introduce to you. Alessandra, meet your husband.' He stepped to one side and held out a hand to the doorway where Signor Paolo Orsini now stood.

If Alessandra had been red, she now became pale. She felt a surge of fear and nausea rise in her throat as if she was going to be sick. She knew her intended spouse to be old but nothing could prepare her for the sight of the shrivelled man who was standing before her. His clothes were fine but his body was shrunken so they hung on him, crumpled and loose. His hair was grey and thin, just a few wisps lying across the mottled skin of his skull-like head. But his eyebrows were wild and bushy and hung down over his rheumy eyes like the branches of a willow reaching for water. Great tufts sprouted from his ears and from the mole on the side of his nose. The effort of climbing the stairs had tired him and he took wheezy breaths through his open mouth. His lips were very red and Alessandra shuddered as suddenly his tongue flicked out to moisten them. When he closed his mouth again the sagging flesh around his jaw folded loosely over toothless gums.

Medici saw her face change and frowned. He took her by the elbow and firmly ushered her forward. She took a deep breath and was strong again. She stepped toward Orsini and took his hand in hers and bowed her head. 'It is an honour to meet you at last, signor,' she said quietly. His hand felt twisted and knobbly under paper-thin skin, and standing this close to him she could detect a faint smell. Not unwashed, but still unpleasant. It was sickly and bitter, the smell of old age, of living flesh already decaying. She gripped the half-coin tighter in her other hand.

'What did she say?'

'She is honoured to meet you, signor.' Medici came and stood close by Orsini, speaking loudly and clearly.

~ 227 ~

'Is she? Whatever for?'

'This is Alessandra, my eldest daughter,' Medici explained. 'She is to be your wife.'

'Oh! Is it?' He studied her more closely, his eyes blinking and his jaw making moist munching noises.

Alessandra let go of his hand, straightened up and turned away, furious. Orsini did not appear to notice the insult but Medici did. He glowered at her but she returned his gaze boldly and defiantly. How could her father consider marrying her to this hideous old man? She could hardly love him as a grandfather, let alone as a husband. Medici did not speak but his look made it clear that he would later.

Arnaldo stood by, in turn fearful of Medici and appalled by Orsini. He was startled when Medici suddenly turned towards him. 'And this is Signor Rossi,' he said loudly in Orsini's ear. He led him across the room to where the portrait still sat on the easel. 'He has been painting Alessandra's likeness. We have commissioned a pair of them to celebrate your wedding. Signor Verrocchio has almost completed yours. It only requires you to sit while your face is completed.'

'Sit? I am good at sitting. Not much else I can do these days.' They came to stop in front of the painting and Orsini leaned in closely so that his forehead almost touched it. Arnaldo cringed and had to stop himself from pulling the old man away. The portrait was not varnished yet and still vulnerable to dirt and moisture. A slow change came over the old man as he studied the picture of Alessandra. He became calm and still and did not talk for some minutes. Medici's look of pleasure gradually turned to concern. Had the old man fallen asleep?

'Does the likeness please you, signor?' he asked. He put a hand on his shoulder, partly to rouse him from his stupor, partly to support him should he fall. Orsini came out of his reverie and turned, blinking to Medici.

'She's a damned pretty girl,' he said. 'Who did you say she is?'

∞

Arnaldo left the Palazzo Medici with the portrait of Alessandra safely wrapped in cloth and held tightly under one arm. The warmth of her hand was still fresh in his mind from her farewell. So was the look of pleading in her eyes, begging him to save her. He hadn't noticed the dark suspicion in Medici's face as he watched his daughter turn her back on her future husband to take leave of the artist. Marietta had seen it though. She showed Arnaldo to the door as Medici, Alessandra and Orsini retired to meet the rest of the family. In the shady passage before the main door, she stopped him and spoke in a low and urgent voice.

'You must make your plans quickly and make them well. My master is suspicious. Have you money?'

'Nothing,' he confessed.

She clicked her tongue impatiently. 'I will see what I can do. The steward has money, more than he should. There is much I know about his dealings that he would not to want to reach Medici's ears. He will buy my silence. You will need a horse, two if possible. And provisions. You must make haste, signor. The wedding is in little over a week. I will meet you this afternoon at the old market. Bring me news of what you have done.' With that she lowered her eyes and quickly withdrew.

Outside in the sunshine again, Arnaldo leant back against the palazzo wall and closed his eyes as he tried to gather his thoughts. As Marietta said, there was much to be done. Where would they go? How would he find horses? As yet he could not answer these questions but a slow smile spread across his face as he reflected that at least one thing was certain. Alessandra was his. How long he stayed there he could not tell. It might have been one minute; it might have been twenty. Only when he became aware that something out of the ordinary was going on did he open his eyes. There were the sounds of hurrying footsteps and excited voices. Everyone seemed to be heading the same way, towards the Piazza del Duomo by the great cathedral. Arnaldo looked up in that direction and his heart gave a jolt as he saw what all the excitement was about. A huge column of smoke was rising from the square, billowing great swirls of sooty grey into the clear blue sky. They were burning something, or someone. Leonardo! In a moment, Arnaldo was running with the rest of the crowd.

There was a huge crush of people around the fire and Arnaldo had to fight desperately to get to the front. Clutching the portrait tight to his chest he pushed and elbowed the spectators out of the way, ignoring their angry looks, taking their pushes and shoves without caring. What he would do when he arrived at the front he did not know. It would probably be too late. As he drew near he could hear the voice of Savonarola the monk rising above the sound of the flames. '. . . and so we will burn all works of the devil and all who dare to defy what is holy and good.' The crowd listened, seemingly mesmerised by the sight of the flames and the sound of the preacher's voice. His message was not unusual. There was always some mad priest ready to get up and call down the judgement of God. What was different now was that people seemed to be listening. He spoke with such passion that something quickened in the minds of the listeners, lighting the fire of his belief in their hearts too. As long as he spoke, he could persuade the people of anything. Almost that black was white or night was day or hot was cold. 'Who will bring me the man responsible for this wickedness?' Arnaldo had reached the front now and was relieved to see that the fire burnt nothing more than the strange tent that Leonardo had floated to earth under. His relief did not last for long though. Already the crowd was murmuring in response to Savonarola's challenge. Knots of men were forming and heading off together. It would not be long before Leonardo became fuel for the fire. In despair, Arnaldo set off for Verrocchio's workshop.

# Twenty-Eight

ELISABETTA was inconsolable as they took her husband away. Her shoulders heaved with great sobs while
she clung on to her mother. She couldn't bear to look
at John as they dragged him, kicking and shouting to
the waiting police van. Not that he spared her a glance
either. He had been quiet and subdued when the
police arrived. Just standing, gripping his spanner, staring dully. If he noticed their guns trained on him, he
didn't show it. They gently prised the spanner from his
unresisting fingers and clicked the handcuffs on him.
Their questions met with no response. It was like he
wasn't there. Then they tried to lead him away. That
was when he erupted into a fit of rage and terror. His
sudden change took them by surprise and he broke
half free of their grip, lunging forward with shackled
hands held out. He staggered towards the workbench
before being held back again, the angry cries of the
police officers failing to drown his anguished screams.
They were taking him away from her.

When they had gone, others remained. The blue
light of the police cars and ambulance swept around
the street, illuminating the crowds of curious neigh-

bours. Most of them were in their pyjamas or clothes hastily thrown on. Bursts of static and muffled voices occasionally emerged from the radios in the police cars. Medics carried Zappini out on a stretcher, only his pale face showing under the layers of orange blankets that covered him. There was a bandage around his head with a few drops of blood showing through. Uncle Giorgio scowled at the crowds. 'Well? What are you all looking at, eh?' They shifted uncomfortably and some turned to go indoors again. 'So we've had a bit of an incident here. So what?' He shook his fist angrily. 'Didn't you ever see a man arrested on suspicion of murder before. Go home before I make you, so help me.' A policeman laid a calming hand on his shoulder, but he shook it off irritably and hobbled indoors. '*Porco Zio!* What a night,' he muttered. The police officer waved the crowd away and reluctantly they dispersed.

Down in the basement Inspector Morelli and his team carefully went over the scene of the crime. There was a white chalk outline to show were Zappini had lain, not that it was really necessary with the pool of congealing blood already there. Bit by bit they observed and recorded all the details. One of the windows was smashed and two of the bars pulled away. The mortar they were set in was old and loose. Zappini must have entered that way if the old woman had been sat in the kitchen all the time as she claimed. A man was already dusting the window for fingerprints to confirm this. So it looked like Zappini had broken in, but that was no excuse for attempted murder. What happened after the entry was not so clear. There was a lamp lying smashed on the floor with its lead trailing to the socket on the far wall. Did Zappini trip or did that get knocked down in the struggle? Slowly, carefully the forensic experts went over everything looking for further clues. Suddenly one of them gave a small cry of excitement. Morelli turned to him sharply.

'Hey, Angelo! What is it?'

'It's here, boss. On the corner of the workbench.'

The detective shone his torch on the area and leant in close to look. There was just the faintest smear of blood and a few fragments of skin caught in the rough splintery wood. 'Good work! Get it to the lab straight away.' The junior officer nodded and with gloved hands and tweezers began to pick off the pieces of skin and drop them into a sealable plastic bag. His boss stood back and tried to visualise the possible sequence of events. If Zappini fell against the bench that might explain the head wound. But again, did he trip or was he pushed? He turned back to the bench. No guessing what he was after. It had to be that picture. He was no expert but he knew old and valuable when he saw it. His eyes narrowed as he surveyed the portrait. Something about it made him uneasy. He stared into the girl's eyes.

' . . . boss! Hey, boss!'

Morelli blinked and shook himself. His mind must have been wandering. 'What? What is it?' He glanced at his watch and then tapped it, confused. It must be running fast. They can't have been here that long already.

His young assistant was looking at him curiously. He was fresh out of training, hardly old enough to shave. 'We're just about finished here.'

'Good.' He tried to muster his thoughts and sound like he was in charge of the investigation. 'Got statements from everybody?'

'Not the wife. She's hysterical.'

The detective nodded. 'So would you be if your husband was a spanner murderer.'

'I don't have a husband.'

'Don't get fresh with me, boy. Let's move out of here. We can get the wife's statement tomorrow.' He turned back to the painting thoughtfully.

'Hey, boss! You coming or what?'

'Yeah, I'm coming.' He dragged himself away, taking a packet of cigarettes out of his pocket. Even when his back was turned he could feel her eyes boring into him.

After they were gone the family were left around the table staring at each other in despair. It was going to be a long time before any of them got to sleep again that night.

Father Romano called by the next morning. It was late but they were still in the kitchen trying to organise breakfast. '*Grazie!*' cried Nonna when she saw the priest. She put down her bread knife and gratefully kissed his hand.

'I see bad news travels fast,' scowled Uncle Giorgio.

'What?' protested Father Romano. 'I hear there are

sick people here. I came to visit.' He lifted his hat to the old woman in the corner who did not respond except to stare hard. Her eyes followed him around the room.

'And you heard about the trouble last night,' said Giorgio.

'Trouble?'

'My lunatic brother-in-law, he tried to kill a man.'

'Hush,' hissed Nonna. 'They will hear you.' She nodded towards the door. Elisabetta, Maria and Tommy had not come down yet.

'Hit him right on the head with a spanner,' continued Giorgio.

'We don't know he did,' Nonna retorted. 'Judge a man before you know the facts, why don't you?'

'Stupid woman! He was found holding the spanner next to a man lying in a pool of blood. I don't need to be Albert Einstein to work this one out.'

'What is all this?' cried Father Romano. 'Who is lying in a pool of blood?'

Just then Maria and Tommy entered the room and everything went suddenly quiet. Both children looked pale and frightened. Nonna glared at Giorgio before going to give them both a big hug. '*Bello bambinos*,' she murmured. 'Don't you worry. Everything is going to work out fine. I promise you.' She held them for a moment and when they separated there were tears in her eyes.

'Thanks for coming,' Maria said to Father Romano. Her voice was dull with despair. 'Things have got even worse now.'

'So I hear.'

'It's because of the White Lady, isn't it?'

The priest looked troubled but did not answer.

'What is this about the White Lady?' asked Nonna sharply.

'It's the painting in the basement,' said Maria. 'We bought it in Silvio Zappini's shop. You know, the one Dad's been cleaning. But ever since we got it things have gone wrong. Zappini must have been trying – Nonna! What's the matter?' Her grandmother had gone quite pale and sat down. She had a hand clutched to her mouth.

'Superstitious rubbish!' said Uncle Giorgio immediately.

'The White Lady is in my house.' Nonna spoke in a low moan. 'Why did nobody say? You told me it was just a painting.'

'It *is* just a painting,' Giorgio insisted angrily. 'A painting and some stupid old stories. It is nothing.'

'We are lost,' said Nonna, rocking back and forth gently. 'All of us.'

'We mustn't jump to conclusions,' the priest said half-heartedly.

'It explains everything,' said Nonna.

'It explains nothing,' Giorgio insisted angrily.

'Well, you all seem to know what you are talking about.' Maria glared at them, suddenly angry. She had enough of being scared. It was about time someone did something. 'Who is the White Lady?' No one seemed keen to answer her. 'Tell me,' she demanded. 'I want to know. It's my dad who's going to jail.'

Finally Father Romano sighed. 'It is like Giorgio says,' he said slowly. 'Only old stories. There was a painting. It has not been seen for over a hundred years. We thought it was destroyed.'

'Elenora Giannotti painted over it,' said Maria.

'So it wasn't burnt in the fire. I see.'

'But what about the stories? Who is the girl?'

'Nobody knows. The stories say she betrayed Saint Arnaldo. He nearly died because of her. They say she and the witch are the very same.'

'That is not true!'

Everybody turned in surprise to look at the old woman. Tommy was standing next to her and she was glaring angrily at them.

'Forgive me, signora.' The priest was apologetic. 'I did not mean to alarm you. But that is only what the stories say.'

'Not the stories where I come from,' she said severely. With that she shut her mouth tight and wouldn't say another thing.

## Twenty-Nine

'Even before he got to Verrocchio's workshop, Arnaldo could tell that there was trouble. The normally quiet street of Via de Agnolo was crowded and there were shouts and angry cries coming from around the doorway. He pushed his way through and soon his master's voice could be heard above the rest.

'. . . and I tell you he is not here.'

'Let us in then,' a voice cried. There was a sound of agreement from the crowd. 'It's him we want. We've no argument with you, old man.'

'No! You will not enter my house.' There was anger in Verrocchio's face and fear as well. He stood in the doorway alone, with only his thin old body barring the way to dozens of strong determined men. Some of them were armed. Arnaldo broke through and rushed to his side just as the crowd began to press forward menacingly.

'Get back,' he cried desperately. The front men paused momentarily but then burst into derisive laughter. Arnaldo racked his brains for a plan. He did not know if Leonardo was inside or if Verrocchio was lying to protect him, but they must not enter at any cost. 'Get back. You've no right to come in here.'

'And who's going to stop us, boy?'

'You're not justices. Where's your warrant?'

'Here's my warrant.' The biggest of the men stepped forward. He had one eyelid that drooped giving him a lopsided stare and he held up a vicious-looking knife. 'Want a closer inspection?' he sneered, thrusting the dagger towards Arnaldo's face. Arnaldo shrank back but held his ground.

'I work for Lorenzo de Medici.' He spoke boldly even though his stomach was churning with fear. 'My master and Leonardo da Vinci are also engaged by him. If you force your way in here, and if any harm comes to people or property then you will have to explain yourselves to him.' He glared at the man whose faced twitched as he slowly absorbed this idea. The knife wavered and was then lowered.

'Yeah, well,' he said gruffly. 'He better not do it again.' He turned back to the mob. 'Come on, let's go.' Bit by bit the crowd broke up and dispersed while Arnaldo stood defiantly and watched them leave. Only when the street was deserted again did he let out a sigh of relief and lean against the doorway for support. He felt weak and his hands were trembling.

'Is he here?' he asked eventually.

Verrocchio nodded. 'We need to get him away. They'll be back. And others.'

∞

Inside, Leonardo was busy shoving his things into a bag. 'Ignorant fools!' he muttered as he scooped up a pile of notebooks and thrust them deep inside. 'They speak of God, but they do not use the brains that God gave them.'

'They are gone, Leonardo.' Arnaldo and Verrocchio stood in the doorway to his room and watched him pack. 'But they will surely return. You should go while you can.'

'Don't worry. I'm going.' He picked up a pile of papers, considered them for a moment and then tossed them to one side.

'Where will you go?'

'Back to Milan. I will try my luck with the duke again.'

'But the plague −'

'Better the plague than the mob,' he said angrily, pushing the last of his belongings into the sack and pulling on the leather straps that buckled it. 'I flew today and all they can do is curse me as a devil.'

Slowly Verrocchio nodded. He laid a hand on his old student's shoulder and looked at him sadly. 'You will be missed,' he said. 'There is none like you. None!' he repeated and gripped him tighter.

Leonardo blinked as he rested his hand on Verrocchio's. 'You have been good to me. I will not forget my old master.'

'Not your master. Your friend.' They held each other for a moment before Verrocchio pulled himself away and turned to the desk where there was pen and paper.

'You will need a horse,' he said as he hastily began to scribble a note. 'Palaggio owes me money. He will give you use of a horse as payment of his debt.' He finished the letter and signed it with a flourish. 'Do you know where he lives?'

Leonardo shook his head.

'I'll go with him.' Arnaldo stepped forward quickly and took the letter from Verrocchio.

'Good. Come then, Leonardo. Let us get you some provisions for the journey. Have you enough money?' Their voices faded as Arnaldo was left alone in the room. He glanced around guiltily before carefully unfolding the letter and reading it.

> . . . *in place of the monies owed to me by your esteemed self, due the first day of this month and already late, I request that you make available to my friend the use of your horse.*

Arnaldo bit his knuckle anxiously as he quickly tried to come to a decision. It could be easily done, but did Palaggio even have two horses? He had to make up his mind. It was now or never. He decided to risk it. He took up the pen and carefully added two letters, skilfully imitating Verrocchio's hand. When he was done, he read it back through. '. . . *to my friends the use of your horses.*' That should do it. You would never know that the words had been altered. He thrust the paper into his tunic and hurried after his friends.

∞

Palaggio scratched the back of his head as he read the note. 'Hmph!' he grunted. 'Verrocchio drives a hard bargain. Two horses. When can I expect to see them again?'

'Do we need two?' Leonardo seemed surprised.

'We do,' Arnaldo said quickly as Palaggio looked up suspiciously. 'Verrocchio reminds you, signor, that the money you owe is already late.' His desperation was making him brave and a moment later Palaggio nodded moodily and called to his stable hand to fetch two horses.

'Treat 'em well, mind,' said the surly Palaggio. 'These are two of my finest. I don't want no knackered old nags back in return.'

Leonardo slung his bag across a horse's back and then hoisted himself into the saddle. He leant down and held out a hand to Arnaldo.

'I wish you well, my friend. I never got to see your painting. I am sure the fair Alessandra is better than my humble efforts.'

'Not at all!' Arnaldo clasped his hand. 'Yours is perfect. At least it will be until we put Orsini's head on it.'

'Then we shall call it even!' cried Leonardo. With that he let go of Arnaldo and reined in the horse. The hooves clattered on the cobbles and echoed around the courtyard as the animal turned. 'Goodbye, my friend. We will meet again soon.'

'Farewell, Leonardo,' cried Arnaldo as the sight of his friend retreated. 'Though I doubt we will ever meet again,' he added sadly when he was gone.

He could not be downhearted for long though. He had the horse. Now all he had to do was get word to Alessandra of when and where to meet. His spirits soared as he made his way to a nearby inn to leave the horse until it was needed.

∞

Verrocchio surveyed the painting that Leonardo had left him to complete. 'There is none like Leonardo,' he said, repeating his earlier sentiments.

'Why has he painted the wrong face?' One of his assistants stood at his shoulder and studied it with him.

'Who knows?' shrugged Verrocchio. 'He probably wanted to try some new technique. It is a shame we have to paint over it. It is a good deal fairer than the one I have to do.' He sighed as he gave his paints a final stir. 'I am ready when you are, signor,' he said loudly.

'Hmph! What? What?' Orsini jerked awake and blinked away the sleep. He ran the back of his hand over his chin to clear the trail of drool that dripped from the side of his mouth. 'What did you say?'

'I said you are a revolting old swine and it is a crime to give you the beautiful Alessandra,' Verrocchio said grimly.

'Oh yes, I see. Very good.' He sat up a little straighter and tried to look noble. Verrocchio dipped his brush but even as he made the first stroke Orsini's eyes were drooping again.

'This is hopeless,' groaned the artist. 'How am I to work like this?' Impatiently he strode over to where

Orsini sat and taking the old man's stick he propped it under his chin. 'There, now sleep all you like, signor. I will flatter you with my brush. I will make you look ten years younger.' He took up his paints again. 'Which will make you about seventy-four by my calculation.'

∞

Marietta walked briskly along the Via Roma. She could move remarkably fast for one of her size and she wanted to get back to the Palazzo Medici before she was missed. She smiled to herself with quiet satisfaction. She had wondered about the artist but he had proven himself. He had the horse and now she had his letter. It was all arranged. She had even been able to give him a purse of money which the steward had reluctantly parted with. The letter was sealed but he had given her the details. It was to be tonight. He would wait for her at the market from sunset onwards. Then they would make their way north, hot on the heels of Leonardo on his way to Milan. And then on into France. There was always work for artists, painting frescoes and altarpieces in churches. Medici would never be able to trace them.

Quietly she slid through the doors to the palazzo and hurried across the courtyard to find her mistress. Medici's eyes narrowed as he watched her from an upstairs window. Where had she been? He had seen her depart half an hour earlier. She seemed to think she could come and go as she pleased. Well, he would soon put that idea out of her head. He was about to call for her when something made him pause. She and Alessandra were thick like thieves. There might be more to this little journey than met the eye. Perhaps he would go and find Marietta, rather than have her brought to him.

∞

'What news?' cried Alessandra as soon as Marietta was through the door. She could barely contain her excitement and had been pacing the room since her old nurse had left.

'It is all arranged,' the servant said, her eyes gleaming. 'I have it here.' She pulled the letter out from inside her dress and waved it temptingly in front of the girl. Alessandra snatched at it but when she had it in her hands she did not tear it open immediately. Her name was written on the outside just above the blob of red wax that sealed it shut. She traced her finger slowly over the letters which were written in a strong and graceful hand.

'Well, read it then.' Marietta was seething with impatience.

'Hush, Marietta.' Nevertheless, the girl slid her finger under the wax and prised it apart. Then she unfolded and began to read. A faint flush of colour came to her cheeks and a smile played around her lips.

'What does he say? Tell me.'

'He says tonight at the old market.'

'*Madre del Dio!* That much I know. What else does he write? There is a whole page of it, I can see.'

She leaned forward but Alessandra clutched the letter to her breast. 'The rest, I think, is for my eyes only.'

'Not fair,' wailed the old nurse. 'Come, I would tell you if the letter were to me. What does he say?'

'Too much,' said Alessandra more seriously. 'Everything is here. He should have spoken the message to you to tell me. If ever my father should find this then –' She broke off and all the colour drained from her face.

'If ever I should find what?'

Lorenzo de Medici stood in the doorway, his face dark as thunder.

# Thirty

*H*OWEVER bad things had become, life had to go on. Elisabetta eventually came downstairs. Her eyes were puffy as if she had slept little and cried a lot. Nonna fussed over her but she wouldn't eat anything. She took a cup of coffee and sat forlornly at the table. Her fingers were wrapped tightly around the cup as if she drew comfort from its warmth. All the while the old woman watched from her chair in the corner, her eyes darting from one to another. She seemed half angry, half afraid. Maria looked at her often, determined to ask her more about the stories she knew when she got the chance. Father Romano bade them farewell and promised to visit John in his cell later that day

'You never know,' he said to Nonna as she saw him out. 'Things might be better than they seem. This strange behaviour, it could be just stress. Men can do funny things when they are under pressure.'

'Oh, Father, I hope you are right.'

'I will do what I can.' He smiled encouragingly but as soon as he turned to leave his face fell again.

In the kitchen, Giorgio was struggling to his feet. 'What do you want?' asked Nonna as she returned to the room. 'One of the children can fetch something. You only have to ask. Beppe, help your father, you ungrateful boy.'

'What did I do?' protested Beppe.

'Nothing. That's the problem.'

'But –'

'Leave the boy alone,' growled Giorgio. 'I don't want anything.'

'Then what are you doing? You need to rest.'

'And I don't want to rest. *Porco Zio!* I have had enough rest. I am going to the basement. I may as well clear up this mess and take a look at this painting.'

'No!' Nonna paled and quickly moved to stand between her son and the doorway.

'What? Get out of my way, woman.'

'No,' said Nonna again, more quietly. 'You are not to go down there. No one must go down there.' Her face was resolute and after glaring at her for a few moments, Giorgio gave up and sat down again grumbling.

'Stupid superstitious rubbish,' he muttered.

Just then the telephone rang. Nonna answered it while keeping her eyes firmly on her son. It was the police and after a brief conversation it was agreed that Nonna would take Elisabetta down to the police station to make her statement. As soon as they were gone, Giorgio hauled himself out of the chair again and hobbled towards the door. 'I'm going down to the basement,' he said, daring anyone to disagree. Maria watched him go, and when the door closed the children were alone with the old woman.

She still looked angry and her lips were pinched firmly together as if nothing would open them. But Maria was angrier. 'I want to know the stories,' she said at once. The old woman said nothing so Maria went and stood right in front of her where she couldn't be ignored. Tommy looked anxiously from one to the other. 'The ones about Saint Arnaldo and the White Lady.'

'What do you want to know?' the woman suddenly snapped. 'You are just like all the others. You blame her for everything.'

'That's because I don't know anything about her.' Her voice was fierce.

'That is right. You know nothing.'

'So why don't you tell me? If you think you know something.' Maria threw out her challenge and waited.

The old woman fixed her with a penetrating stare. Maria stuck out her chin and gazed back defiantly. 'Very well,' the old lady said at last. 'If you really want to know then I will tell you.' She drew herself up and rested her hands on her knee very formally, as if she were a storyteller of old. Maria felt a sudden thrill of excitement. This was it. Not only had she got her own way, she was finally going to learn who the mysterious girl was. She hurriedly pulled up a chair and even Beppe left what he was doing and came to sit on the floor. Tommy stayed standing by the old woman's side. When they were settled, she began.

'Some call her the White Lady, others the Witch, but when she first met Arnaldo she went by the name of

Alessandra.' The woman's voice was low and melodic. Her eyes were closed and she swayed slightly with the rhythm of her words. 'She was beautiful then, a girl on the cusp of womanhood. She loved Arnaldo and he returned her love but the fates had decreed that their love could never be. For their families were the deadliest of foes and –'

She was interrupted by Maria giving a squeal of excitement. 'This is the story the man sang at the festival, except he didn't say it was about Arnaldo, he just –'

The old woman's eyes snapped open and she glared at Maria. 'Who is telling this story?'

Maria put her hand to her mouth guiltily. 'Sorry.'

For a moment it seemed as if the woman was too offended to carry on, but then her eyes closed again and she took up the tale where she had left off. 'Her father had given her to be married to an old man . . .'

Maria closed her eyes too and such was the power of the old woman's words that she found herself transported back over five hundred years as she learnt for the first time the fate of the White Lady.

## Thirty-One

'If ever I should find what?'

Lorenzo strode across the room. Alessandra gave a scream and quickly tried to thrust the letter out of sight but her father was too quick for her. He caught her by the wrist, gripping her so tight that she winced with pain. Then with his other hand he tugged the letter from her fingers. His eyes scanned the page as his face grew darker with anger. He had suspected there might be something between them but never dreamed it had gone this far. When he had finished reading he carefully folded it and pushed it into his tunic. Then he turned on Marietta and without warning struck her hard across the face with the back of his hand. She staggered at the blow but did not cry out. She drew herself up and stared defiantly at her master. There was a red mark next to her eye and already it was swelling.

'I will deal with you later,' he hissed. 'Now go.' She glanced at Alessandra, fearful for her safety but there was nothing she could do. Without even a bow, she turned and left. Alessandra watched her go and as soon as she was alone with her father he turned on her viciously.

'Stupid girl!' he spat, coming nearer as she shrank back against the wall. 'Foolish, disobedient, ungodly child!' He raised a hand and she flinched, bracing herself for the blow. But it never came. Instead Lorenzo clenched his hand tightly into a fist and gritted his teeth until he could control his rage. Then his hand dropped to his side.

'No, I will not strike you,' he said. 'It would not do to be seen at your wedding with bruises on your face.' He leant forward and thrust his face very close to hers. 'Because married you *will* be.' His voice was low and menacing. 'To Signor Paolo Orsini as arranged, and not to some low artist who has turned your head with his sweet words and good looks.'

'I would die first,' she said.

'Don't be stupid. You are just a girl. You will do as your father wishes. Who apart from Marietta knows of this?'

Alessandra set her mouth in a determined scowl. He would see just what she could do, even if she was only a girl. 'Nobody,' she said.

'Good. And nobody else must hear of it, least of all Signor Orsini.'

'Little to fear there, Father. He can barely hear at all.'

'You will not speak of your husband that way.'

'He is not my husband.'

'He will be, which is more than can be said for your painter.' He looked so furious that Alessandra was suddenly afraid for Arnaldo.

'What will you do to Arnaldo?' she asked weakly.

Lorenzo said nothing.

Alessandra had slid her half of the coin into her sleeve for safekeeping and she laid a hand on it now. 'What will you do?' she asked again. 'Tell me.' She stared hard at her father, meaning to get an answer from him. For a moment she saw indecision flit across his features and she pressed her advantage. 'You love him, Father. You know you do. I've seen the way you talk and . . .'

'Silence!' The girl's words were true. He did not need this painful reminder. He quickly continued before he weakened. 'I will keep your appointment with him tonight at the old market. I will explain that you have recognised the impossibility of a match with him and that you have abandoned any foolish plans you had to marry.'

'No! He will never –'

Lorenzo raised his voice above her protests. 'If he sees the sense of *your* decision and accepts it then he may continue to live and work here in Florence. You will be in Rome and there will be no temptation to see you. If he chooses not to accept . . .' His eyes grew hard and resolute. '. . . then he will come to regret the day he ever turned against the House of Medici. That is all I have to say.'

With that he turned and left the room. A moment later there was the sound of a bolt being slid across into its socket. In despair Alessandra realised she was a prisoner in this room with no way to get word to Arnaldo. She had stood up to her father while she thought there was hope but now her strength left her and she sank weakly to her knees. Her shoulders began to shake as sobs of grief and anger seized her body. Never had she felt so alone.

It was late evening when Arnaldo arrived at the old market. The sun had dipped below the horizon and the sky had turned to deep blue, almost black. Lamps were on in the houses and some of their light streamed out through the slats in the shutters. The few people who remained outside walked quickly with their heads down, hurrying to their homes. The city could be a dangerous place at night. Arnaldo tied the horse's reins to a post and patted it on the flank as he spoke quietly in its ear. The animal snorted appreciatively and stamped a hoof on the cobbled ground.

He had one last look in the bag slung across the saddle to check that he had everything they would need. There was food and water, enough for a day or two. They would have to buy more on the way. The money made a comforting clinking sound as the purse rolled around in the bag. He strapped it shut again and pulled his cloak tighter about himself. His hand wandered to the hilt of the sword he was wearing. The roads around Florence were safe enough but beyond that who could tell what troubles they might meet. Alessandra was young and beautiful and sure to attract attention. He gripped his sword harder as he waited. They would have to get past him first.

It was half an hour before anyone approached him and his legs were beginning to get stiff with standing still for so long. It was clearly a rich man. His boots were of soft, supple leather and the hood of the cloak that obscured his face was trimmed with fur. Arnaldo was wondering what he was doing out so late, alone, when unexpectedly the man stopped and spoke.

'Arnaldo.'

Arnaldo's stomach lurched with fear. It was the voice he least wanted to hear in all the world. The man pulled back his hood to reveal the face of Lorenzo de Medici. 'What an unexpected pleasure . . .' His voice made it sound anything but that.

'Signor Medici. What are . . . I mean . . . it is late. I . . . had not expected to . . .' His sentence tailed off, unfinished.

'I could say the same for you, though a little more eloquently I hope. What keeps *you* out so late?' Arnaldo could not answer. 'And you have a horse and provisions I see. Perhaps you are going some-where.' Arnaldo thought desperately for something to say. He had to get rid of Lorenzo. Alessandra might be here at any moment and that would be dis-astrous. He could not help glancing around to see if she were anywhere in sight. 'Ah! You are waiting for someone.' Medici made a show of looking as well before turning back. 'For my Alessandra I think.' His voice was hard and fierce and in a moment Arnaldo knew that all was lost.

His face went deathly pale and the dryness in his

throat made it hard to speak. 'I see we are found out,' he said dully.

'Found out?' Medici looked surprised. 'You make it sound as if somehow I had uncovered your secret. No, it was not like that. Alessandra has asked me to come.'

'What?'

'After she received your note. She showed it to me.' He gave a dismissive laugh. 'It was quite amusing. While your feelings were made plain I found its style somewhat . . .' He searched for the right word. 'Gushing?'

'What are you talking about?' Arnaldo asked weakly. He felt as if his world had been tipped upside down.

'Alessandra wishes me to give you her apologies,' said Lorenzo coldly. 'She realises now that this wild scheme to elope with you was no more than a childish dream. She is sorry to have given you false hopes but she only desires now to do the will of her father and marry the man intended for her.'

'No! That's not true.'

'Are you suggesting that I am lying?' frowned Medici.

'Yes,' cried Arnaldo wildly. 'You're lying to me. Alessandra would never say such a thing.'

Medici stiffened at these words and his hand flew to the hilt of his sword. 'Be careful, signor. You insult me. Men have died for less.'

Arnaldo instinctively gripped his sword as well. 'I speak the truth.'

There was a moment when it looked as if Medici

would draw his sword and charge Arnaldo down but then he seemed to change his mind. 'No, *I* speak the truth,' he said quietly, 'and you defame my honour. But because of your youth and obvious distress I'm willing to overlook this slur. I'm sorry to have brought you bad news but you should have known this could never be.'

He turned to go even as he was still speaking and Arnaldo was filled with a sudden rage. All the old hatred for his father's killer returned in an instant. He drew his sword and Medici stopped at the sound of sliding metal. 'Put it away, boy, or you'll regret it.' His back was still towards Arnaldo.

'Turn and face me if you dare.'

'I do not have time for this.'

'Turn and face me, damn you! Do I have to call you coward as well as liar?'

Medici made a sudden move but again stopped himself. 'You try my patience to its limit, you really do. Go home, boy. This will not seem so bad in the morning. I bid you good night.' His words were final and he began to walk away.

'You wouldn't go if you knew who I am.'

That got Medici's attention. He finally turned to face Arnaldo, wearing a slightly curious expression. 'You are Arnaldo de Rossi, artist and my former friend,' he said, though his voice lacked certainty.

'No! I am Arnaldo de Pazzi. And you killed my father.'

There was a moment of stunned silence and then Medici's face twisted with bitter rage. Then he too drew his sword. 'If that is true,' he said, 'then let me finish what I started seven years ago. Be warned, I will show you no mercy, Arnaldo de Pazzi.'

'I won't need it,' said Arnaldo. Quickly he unclasped his cloak and threw it to the ground. Medici did the same and the two faced each other, swords at the ready.

'This is just like old times,' said Medici. His eyes were cold and hard.

'Not quite,' said Arnaldo. 'Only one of us will walk away from this fight.' They were still circling each other warily when a cry went up and two guards hurried to the scene.

'Hey! What's all this?' Their weapons were drawn and they were ready to break up the conflict and drag both the troublemakers off to the cells. Medici turned on them sharply.

'It is nothing,' he spat. 'You saw nothing, you were never here.'

'Signor Medici! I am sorry. I . . .'

'You are wasting my time. Now go, and see that no one else disturbs us. This will not take long,' he said grimly, turning back to Arnaldo. The guards looked doubtful for a moment then reluctantly turned to leave.

Arnaldo did not wait a second longer. As soon as the guards were gone, he lashed out at Medici who barely had time to defend the blow. The first clash of metal sounded around the deserted square and bright sparks flew into the night. Again and again Arnaldo struck. His fury doubled his strength and Lorenzo was forced back under his advance. There was no grace or skill in what they did. Arnaldo held his sword in two hands and slashed around randomly – left, right, high, low. The blows rained down but each one connected with Medici's sword, not his flesh. Then after one particularly wild swing Medici managed to side step so that Arnaldo missed and was unbalanced by his own momentum. He staggered forward, half running across the cobbles to stay upright. Then he recovered and turned but now Medici was upon him and *he* had to defend.

The man was angry, perhaps as angry as Arnaldo, but he was also older and wiser. He did not let blind rage affect his judgement. He fought with cold and devastating accuracy. Each attack was precise and followed by another and another that left Arnaldo disorientated and confused. Desperately he parried each blow with a half-instinctive jerk of his blade. Each finger-stinging strike seemed to get closer to its mark. The man was relentless. Bitterly Arnaldo realised that Medici had been holding back in their previous fights. Now he showed what he could really do. He lifted his sword again as a vicious stroke stopped inches from his head. His arm felt like a lead weight and despair began to creep into his soul. He drew great ragged breaths and the cold night air burnt his lungs, bringing the taste of blood to the back of his throat. A cruel, satisfied smile spread across Medici's face as he saw his opponent weaken.

'Your passions have been your undoing again, signor.'

Arnaldo did not have breath to answer but something about Medici's remark helped him. It reminded him of their fencing bouts when they would talk and laugh as they fought. And some of what he learned in the courtyard of the Palazzo Medici came back to him. Lorenzo struck again but instead of frantically bringing his sword up to intercept, Arnaldo turned on the ball of his foot and allowed the thrust to pass through the air where his body had been a moment before. Now it was Medici who was exposed. Arnaldo thrust his blade at him and there was a sound of tearing cloth as the edge caught in Medici's tunic. A quick spasm of pain passed over the man's face and even in the low light of evening, Arnaldo could see there was blood on his sword.

They backed off, both of them shocked. Medici carefully touched his side and then examined his hand, rubbing the blood between his fingertips. 'Very good, signor. I once drew blood from you. Now we are even.'

Arnaldo felt a stab of emotion as he remembered that afternoon but he pushed it away. 'You are not thinking of quitting now,' he snarled.

'Quitting? On the contrary. We have only just begun.' He darted forward with a sudden thrust at Arnaldo's shoulder. But he was ready for him. He deflected the blow and put in one of his own. And what followed was a much more even battle. Back and forth they went, their steel blades clashing and ringing. The square was empty but from side streets and behind shutters anxious eyes watched as the two shadowy figures moved like panthers as they circled and fought. Sometimes Arnaldo would gain the upper hand and it would seem as if there could be no escape for Medici. But then with a clever trick the older man would deceive Arnaldo and force him back. Then he would have to defend. For quarter of an hour it continued until both were near exhaustion, fighting for their lives. Sweat streamed down into their eyes plastering their hair to their faces. There were grazed knuckles and bruises but no more blood.

Then in a moment it was all but finished. Arnaldo desperately swung his sword up to deflect yet another blow from Medici and then saw his chance. Their blades were locked at the hilt and Arnaldo gave a sudden twist and then a flick and Medici's weapon was ripped from his grasp and spun away into the night. With a burst of joy Arnaldo knew he had won. This was it. The man who had killed his father, the man who had taken Alessandra from him now stood defenceless before him. There would be no escape. He watched amazed as the sword sailed up into the sky but that look was his downfall. Even before the sword had hit the floor, Medici had pulled a dagger from his belt and thrust it deep into Arnaldo's side.

## Thirty-Two

ARNALDO knelt on the ground. One hand rested on the floor the other clutched his side. Blood seeped through his tunic and congealed around his fingers. Slowly it began to drip on to the floor. He had never known pain like it. Each breath seemed to send fire shooting through every nerve in his body. He was dimly aware of Medici bending to pick up his sword and coming to stand before him. All he could see was his boots and the sword tip hovering inches from his face.

'You never taught me that trick,' he gasped.

'Always keep something back,' said Medici, breathing deeply. He was master of the situation again. His tunic was ripped and bloodied, his face was smeared with dirt and sweat but he was unmistakably Lorenzo the Magnificent. 'Although I suppose that advice comes a bit late to help you. I promised you no mercy.'

'And I expect none.' Each word was a struggle and Arnaldo could feel himself becoming faint. 'You showed none to my father.'

'As he showed none to my brother.'

Arnaldo was silent. He couldn't dispute that. There

was a long pause while the sword tip twitched a few times and blood continued to drop in big splatters on to the cobblestones.

'But that was a long time ago,' Medici said at last. He sounded suddenly weary. 'A lot of blood has already been spilled over that and I regret that it has come to this. I wish things might have been different.'

'It is a little late for regrets now,' gasped Arnaldo.

'But regrets always come too late,' said Medici quietly. 'That is why they are called regrets. But it is not too late for mercy I think.'

'What?' In his surprise Arnaldo looked up and immediately wished he hadn't. A new wave of pain washed over him.

'I offer you your life,' said Medici.

'You would spare me?'

'Yes. Choose quickly before I change my mind.'

'And would you also give me Alessandra?'

'No!' he roared. 'Do not provoke me. She marries Orsini of her own will.'

'Then kill me now,' said Arnaldo dropping his gaze to the floor again.

With a frustrated curse, Medici gripped his sword tighter and angrily swung it up over Arnaldo's head. Arnaldo waited for the blow to come to end his life. But it did not come. Medici's breathing was quick and shallow. His hand jerked as if he were going to bring the blade down but each time he stopped. In the end, he threw the weapon down with a clatter and stormed off. The last Arnaldo saw of him was his back as he stooped to snatch up his cloak. Then he faded into the dusk and Arnaldo slumped to the ground, unconscious.

∞

Alessandra was waiting at the window when her father returned. She hadn't moved since she watched him go less than an hour before. He was hooded for secrecy but as he walked the scabbard of his sword pushed through the folds in his cloak, and the knot of anxiety tightened in her stomach. She was still alone. Marietta was not allowed to see her. Another servant had brought her food but it stayed untouched on the table. In one hand she held her half of the coin, warm and comforting. She had that feeling again – as if it were the one solid thing, holding her to this life. Without it she would simply drift away. In her other hand she clutched the bottle of poisonous hemlock which remained cold and chilling however long it nestled in her palm.

The great doors slammed and her father strode into the courtyard. Alessandra could not help but cry out when she saw him. His clothes were ripped and dishevelled, his cloak slung across his arm. In his hand he carried an unsheathed dagger. Quickly she stood and leaned closer, pressing her forehead against the glass. Then she thrust the half-coin into her sleeve and rushed to the door and rattled on the handle in frustration.

'Let me out!' she screamed. 'Let me out of here!' She

beat on the wooden panels with her fist and then noticed the hammer, still lying among the tools on the floor. She seized it and swung it hard against the door. Twice it rebounded leaving dents in the wood but on the third blow the bolt gave way and the door burst open. Flinging it wide she stumbled down the stairs and fell into the arms of her father. 'What have you done?' she sobbed. 'Tell me what you've done to him.' She began to beat him on his chest and he dropped the dagger and cloak and caught her by the wrist.

'Get off me,' he snapped. She continued to struggle and scratch but his grip was too strong. Finally she became quieter and raised her head to look her father in the face. Tears streamed down her cheeks.

'What have you done?' she asked again.

'What I had to do.'

He could not look her in the eye. She stared at him for a moment longer while his words sunk in. Then her eyes dropped and she saw the blood-stained dagger lying on the stones at their feet.

'No!' She tore herself away from Lorenzo and staggered out into the courtyard.

'Alessandra,' he cried, 'come back.' But she was not listening. She raced across the paved floor and out through the door. Without a thought for her own safety she fled into the dark and quiet streets. With a curse Lorenzo followed her.

Her one thought was to get to the old market and find Arnaldo. She hurried past the great cathedral and along the Via Roma till it opened out into a wide square. 'Arnaldo!' she cried. Her voice echoed and came back to her, but there was no answering call. 'Arnaldo!' she screamed again. She ran up and down, her eyes darting this way and that, but there was no sign of him. Finally she stumbled upon a cloak lying discarded on the floor. She picked it up. A bit further away lay a sword. There was blood on the blade and the edge was notched and scratched. Then she saw him. Limp and lifeless, he lay on the cold hard ground. Unable even to cry, she sank to her knees beside him. She cradled his head in her lap and brushed the hair out of his eyes. They were closed and his face was deathly white. She shuddered at the coldness of his skin.

'Alessandra!' Lorenzo rushed into the marketplace. She glanced around and saw her father hurrying towards her, angry and fearful. 'Alessandra come home. This is no place for you.' In despair she looked at Arnaldo. Was she not to be left in peace with him just for a moment? He was so beautiful, even in death. She smoothed his brow tenderly. Her fingers brushed the gentle lips that would never speak her name again. There was nothing she could do for him now. And there was nothing left for her in this world.

'Goodbye, my love,' she whispered. She bent and kissed him, first on his forehead and then on his mouth. Then gently laying his head on the floor she got up and turned and fled.

'Alessandra!'

She ducked into a side street and hid in the shadows

of a doorway. Moments later her father rushed by, still calling her name. Gradually his voice faded into the distance. When he was gone, she stepped out and made her way back to the Via Calimala and headed south towards the Arno. Where before she had run headlong, not caring who saw her, now she went stealthily – hurrying but keeping well into the shadows. In her hand she still clutched the bottle of poison.

Within minutes she had reached the river where it was spanned by the Ponte Vecchio in three great stone arches. All along the old bridge there were houses and workshops built on the bridge itself and hanging precariously over the water supported by wooden struts. Quickly she made her way down between the rows of shops until halfway across where there was a gap in the buildings. Here she paused to gather her courage and then climbed up on to the low stone wall. She steadied herself against the side of a leather workshop and looked down. Below her the river flowed slowly by, its waters black and oily. She gripped the cork of the bottle between her teeth and wrenched it out. Then she took a deep breath and composed herself for the end.

Lorenzo de Medici ran headlong through the streets of Florence, cursing his bad luck. It appeared that the boy had died anyway and it was going to take all his considerable influence to get himself out of this one. But before then he had to find his daughter. It was late but there were still enough people around to have witnessed her behaviour. If ever word got back to Paolo Orsini then the marriage would certainly be off.

'Alessandra. Where are you?' He spoke through gritted teeth. Finally he came out on the waterfront and stopped, breathing hard. He winced with pain and felt the wound in his side. It wasn't deep but it needed attention. He kicked the wall that ran along by the river and swore to himself. He would never find her like this. She could be anywhere.

No, she wasn't just anywhere. He saw her now and his mouth fell open in despair. There she was standing on the bridge. 'Alessandra! Be careful!' he shouted to her, no longer caring if people heard or not. She looked up at the sound of her name and for a moment stared straight into his eyes. Then she put something to her lips and tipped her head back. He began to run along the river towards the old bridge. She threw aside whatever she had just drunk and put her hand to her heart. She swayed as she stood precariously on the edge and her hand fell away from the wall that supported her. 'Alessandra!' Her name died on his lips and he staggered to a halt. He leant on the wall, his eyes wide with horror. He held out a clawing hand but it was no use. Alessandra had fallen gracefully into the water. He had a brief glimpse of her as she rolled in the current. Then she slipped beneath the surface and he saw her no more.

# Thirty-Three

'*A*ND that is' the *true* story of Arnaldo and Alessandra,' said the old lady.

'Then it was all her father's fault.' Maria had tears in her eyes as she finished listening to the old woman's tale.

'It was nobody's fault.'

'Yes, it was,' Maria insisted. 'He should never have made her marry the old man.'

'But times were different then. He did what any father would have done.'

'No! You're only saying that because you can't remember what it's like to be young.'

The old lady's eyes immediately became hard. She leant forward and spoke in a low hiss. 'But I do remember,' she said. Then she sat back and folded her arms.

Maria bit her lip. That had been a bit rude. 'Sorry,' she said. The woman did not answer other than to make a small noise in her throat. But her glare softened a little. Maria was impatient to know more. 'Is there any more to the story? What about the curse? What happened to the portrait? Have I . . .' She hesitated and glanced at Beppe. 'Have I really been seeing the girl from the painting?'

'I don't know what you have been seeing, but there is no curse. Not what you think is the curse.'

Maria got the feeling that the old woman was not telling them everything. 'But that can't be the end of the story. There's more, isn't there? You must tell me.' The old woman was silent. Then she leant back in her chair and closed her eyes.

'I am so tired,' she murmured.

'Are you going to sleep? You can't! Not now.'

'I told you I never sleep.' She opened one eye and glared at Maria. 'I am tired of talking.' Her eye closed again and her breathing became relaxed and slow. If she didn't sleep she appeared to do a pretty good impression of it. But then she began to talk again, quietly, almost to herself.

'Some say that was *not* the end of the story. Some say Arnaldo and Alessandra were seen again but never together . . .'

Arnaldo slowly drifted towards consciousness. A smile played about his lips as he relived the dream from which he awoke. 'Alessandra,' he murmured. Then the smile faded. Goodbye? He opened his eyes with a start. She was gone. For one bleak, blank moment he wondered where he was and then the pain returned. With a groan, he rolled over on to his side and pushed himself up on to one elbow. The square was deserted.

He didn't know how much time had passed, but the moon had risen and the town was full of soft blue light and sharp black shadows. Gingerly he began to lift his shirt to see how bad the wound looked. He knew how bad it felt. But the blood had dried and the fabric was stuck to the skin. He gasped as he tried to pull it away and then gave up. Something glinting on the cobblestones caught his eye. He picked it up and his heart gave a jolt as he recognised the half-coin that Alessandra had given him. He gripped it tight in his fist and felt some of his strength return.

Slowly he got to his feet and stood unsteadily until the dizziness passed. He was still very weak. The horse was tethered at its post and for a while he leant against its side while his mind went over what had happened. He could see nothing in his future. He was alive but he might as well be dead. Alessandra was to marry Orsini. Painfully he dragged himself on to the horse. The effort exhausted him and he slumped forward against the horse's neck, nearly unconscious. 'Take me away from here,' he mumbled. The horse snorted and, finding someone in its saddle, it began to walk. The hooves clattered on the cobblestones as Arnaldo left Florence for ever.

The darkness overcame Alessandra. The last thing she knew was the warm drowsiness of the drug and the cool touch of water on her skin. Even as she slid into unconsciousness her hand fumbled for the half-coin still safe in her sleeve. She would die but she would be true to her word. She clasped it tight in her fingers and the words of her vow to Arnaldo drifted through her mind. I will not rest, I will not know peace, I will not be whole until these two halves are joined again.

Ugo, the fisherman, slung his bag over his shoulder and set off down the path towards the river. It was early morning. Birds were calling from the marshy reed beds and mist hung over the water. As usual Ugo was first up. There was a good living to be made from the river and the early birds caught the juiciest worms. That was his motto. His boots thumped hollowly as he stepped on to the landing stage and he whistled as he began to untie his boat from the mooring post. Then the whistling stopped. He was not expecting a worm quite that big.

There was a body in the water. A girl by the look of it. She was caught against the posts that were driven deep into the mud. Her long auburn hair drifted like weed in the current and her eyes stared glassily from a few centimetres below the surface. He glanced around anxiously, wondering what to do. This sort of thing could be trouble. He would have to inform the justice and half the day would be wasted before they were through with questioning him. Perhaps he should just push her away and let someone else find her downstream. He half reached for his boathook but then his conscience got the better of him.

Reluctantly he hauled her out of the water, cursing at the weight. Her body flopped face-down as water streamed off her and formed a puddle on the wooden planks. Then he rolled her over to take a better look. He untangled her hair which had become wrapped around her face and when he could see her he clicked his tongue and shook his head sadly. She was pretty, and so young. It was a shame. She can't have been in the water long. Less than a day. His eyes ran up and down the length of her body, taking in the rich cut of her dress. Things were looking up. This was no peasant girl – she must have come from a wealthy family. And that meant there might be a reward. Ugo looked around again, to check if he was still alone. He would go for the justice in a moment but not before he had had a quick search. Nobody would miss a jewel or two.

There was a ribbon around her neck, but when he tugged at it, all that emerged was a tiny key. He swore and moved on. No brooch, no bracelet, no rings. He was about to give up in disgust when he saw that her hand was clamped tightly shut. Perhaps she was holding something – something valuable. He lifted her limp arm and studied the hand more closely. Then he smiled a slow delighted grin. He could just see something gold glinting there. He slid a finger in to prise her hand open but it wouldn't budge. He frowned. The rest of her was still quite limp. He applied a bit more force, trying to bend her fingers back. Then he got the fright of his life.

The girl gave a sudden jerk that made Ugo drop her hand and jump to his feet in terror. Her body twitched and convulsed and finally her back arched as she took a huge breath that was more of a shriek. Then she lay back again, still unconscious but breathing. Colour returned to her cheeks. Slowly her eyes fluttered and opened and the first thing she saw was a man peering down at her. Her face froze. This was not right. She was dead. Or at least she ought to be. She sat up, watching the man warily.

Ugo had got over his initial shock but still felt very uneasy. 'Why aren't you dead?'

'A fine greeting for a lady.' Slowly she climbed to her feet. Ugo backed away. 'Did you pull me from the river?' He nodded. She looked down at herself, disorientated and confused. Just at the moment she couldn't remember why she was here or even who she was. She noticed she was holding something tight. She could feel it small and warm in her hand. Slowly she opened her fingers and studied the half-coin.

For a moment she was blank and then suddenly images started rushing through her mind – a room, a white dress, a painting. Faces – a man with black hair and fierce eyes, a round-faced, middle-aged woman, the gentle smile of a young man. Arnaldo! Then there was a gold coin, and a hammer blow that split it in two. She remembered it all. But why was she here? Something had kept her alive. Or brought her back.

She became aware that the fisherman was staring

~ 275 ~

intently at the coin as well. She clasped her hand shut and drew herself up proudly. 'This does not interest you, signor.'

The man scowled. The gold coin *did* interest him. 'Fine thanks I get for pulling you out of the water.'

'I did not intend to be pulled out when I threw myself in,' she snapped angrily.

The fear came back to the man's eyes and he edged further away until he was standing right on the edge of the jetty. 'Like I said, you ought to be dead. It's not natural.'

Her eyes flashed and she advanced on him. Something about her filled him with dread. 'You would do better to keep your opinions to yourself, and attend to your boat.'

He stared at her mesmerised, and then looked down at his boat. The drainage plug was out and water was bubbling up into it. Slowly it began to sink. With a curse, Ugo leapt into the boat and fumbled to push the plug back in before it disappeared altogether. The girl turned to go.

'Witch!' the man screamed after her. 'You leave this place. Do you hear me? Witch!'

The girl did not turn back. But despair filled her heart. The coin seemed to burn into her palm just as the words burned in her mind. I will not rest, I will not know peace, I will not be whole until these two halves are joined again.

∞

'That is the curse of the White Lady. She walks this earth for ever, knowing no peace and no rest. And she will not until two sundered halves are joined again.'

The old woman stopped speaking and Maria stared numbly at her. 'That's a horrible story. Why did you tell me that?'

'You wanted to know,' the old woman said severely.

'But they were both alive and could have found each other, but they didn't know. It's horrible.'

The woman shrugged. 'It is just a story. You should not upset yourself.'

'No, it's true. I know it is. Alessandra didn't die. Something kept her alive and she's still alive now. I know. I've seen her.'

'Have you?' She stared curiously at Maria.

'Yes.' She squirmed under the old woman's gaze. 'I . . . think so.'

There was a sound from the stairs that made everyone turn. Tommy came into the room. Maria had been so absorbed with the story she hadn't even noticed him go. He came and stood shyly by the old woman again and she gave him a rare smile.

'For you,' he said. He held out a closed fist.

'Another present? Why thank you. The other one was so beautiful.' She held out an open palm and he dropped the object into it. There was a flash of gold and then everybody gasped. There was half a gold florin lying in the woman's hand.

## Thirty-Four

'THAT's the coin!' shrieked Maria. 'Where did you get it, Tommy? Tell me.' Tommy drew back, afraid at her sudden shout. His eyes filled with tears and Maria forced herself to calm down. 'Sorry, Tommy. Didn't mean to frighten you. But please, you must tell me where you found it. It's really, really important.' Her brother shook his head and nothing would make him say where it came from.

The old woman meanwhile was gazing at the coin in her hand as if mesmerised by it. Maria stared as well and without thinking, put out a finger to touch it. Then the old woman closed her hand and snatched it away. 'It's mine,' she said fiercely. The little boy gave it to *me.*'

Maria was taken aback. 'Sorry. I only wanted a look at it.' Cautiously the old woman opened her hand again and everyone leant in curiously. It was an old, heavy gold coin, almost completely worn down as if it had been handled a great deal. The break along the middle was just as smooth.

'It is a gold florin,' said the old woman. 'I have seen others like it, a long time ago.'

'D'you think this is really half of that coin?'

The woman wrinkled her nose. 'It is just an old coin. There must be thousands like it.'

'No, this one's broken in half.'

'So somebody broke it. Now it's worth half a florin.' She spoke dismissively but Maria noticed that her hand was shaking slightly.

'I think we need to give it to the White Lady,' she said seriously. 'Then the two halves will be back together again and the curse will be lifted.'

Beppe immediately gave a great hoot of laughter. 'You want to give this coin to the painting? How are you going to do that?'

'No, not the painting,' said Maria irritably. 'To . . . to the girl I saw.'

'Even better. You want to go to a total stranger and say, "Please, I want to give you this gold coin. Now will you stop the curse on my family."'

Maria reddened at her cousin's teasing. She knew it sounded stupid, but she was convinced she was right. 'Yes!' she said defiantly. There was a moment of absolute silence.

'OK,' shrugged Beppe. 'It might work.'

'Except that the coin is mine.'

Maria turned back to the old woman, frightened. Surely she wasn't going to stop her. 'But I've got to find this girl.'

'No.' The old woman was adamant. 'It will achieve nothing.'

'It might. Please.' She couldn't stop the tears from

coming to her eyes. 'Don't you understand? My dad is in real trouble. This could be his only hope. We have to lift the curse.'

The old lady wavered. She opened her hand and looked at the coin resting in her palm. 'It will not work,' she said decisively. Maria's heart sank. 'And after it has not worked, I want this coin back.' She spoke sternly as she held out the coin to Maria. The girl smiled slowly, before snatching the coin and rushing out of the door.

'You are welcome,' said the old woman as the door slammed.

In the street Maria had to stop. She had the coin but no idea what to do next. So she wanted to give this coin back to the White Lady. But where did you go to find a five-hundred-year-old girl cursed to walk the earth for ever when you needed one? She looked around sheepishly and saw Beppe grinning at the window. She frowned and set off again purposefully, trying to look like she knew exactly what she was doing. Walking around, hoping for a glimpse of a girl in white seemed to be the only plan.

An hour later she was still walking but not hoping. It felt like she had been down just about every street and side alley in San Arnaldo and she was completely fed up. She kicked at an old can in her frustration and got disapproving looks from two old women who were walking behind her.

'Young people,' muttered one as they passed. 'They have no respect.'

'She would not kick that can if she had my feet,' agreed the other.

Maria scowled after them and gave the can another kick. It wasn't supposed to be like this. She didn't know exactly what she was expecting. She had a vague picture in her mind of finding the girl and offering her the coin. Then the girl would hold out the two halves and press them together. There might be a bright light or something and the girl would disappear, or disintegrate like sand blown on the wind. Something like that. But this couldn't be right. Not wandering around, getting hot and tired.

What she really wanted to do was go home. But she had rushed out of the house just an hour before with big talk about lifting curses. She couldn't creep back in now saying she couldn't find the girl. Beppe would never let her forget it. Besides, she really believed that returning the coin was the key. She had to keep trying. For her dad's sake. So where was she? Any other day she would have dreaded seeing the girl and seen her anyway. Today she was desperate to find her and she was nowhere in sight.

She was on the point of giving up when she saw something move in the corner of her eye. Something white? She turned quickly but who or whatever it was had gone. Just into the next street perhaps. She rushed to the corner and looked. There were crowds of people, shopping, walking, sitting outside cafés and drinking coffee. Old men sat on seats enjoying the morning sun, stylishly dressed women chatted with their friends as they moved from shop to shop, young mothers fussed over fat contented babies in pushchairs. But there was no girl in white. Maria stared, her eyes darting this way and that, searching for the girl. There was nobody remotely like her. She was about to turn away defeated when she thought she caught another glimpse of her. Very briefly at the far end of the street, but it was enough. She set off running again.

People watched her curiously as she dodged through the crowd. At the end of the road she stopped at a crossroads and gazed down each street hopefully. Left, right, straight ahead, left again. What was that? She spun around. Something had moved. Maria smiled. It was as if the girl was playing a game with her, leading her on. She raced after her, not stopping to wonder what the girl might be leading her to. All the time the coin burned in her hand.

At the end of each street it was the same. Maria waited, caught a glimpse of something or heard a sound and hurried off in that direction. She raced through the streets of the town, not even sure where she was. Then finally she emerged on to a busy road at a crossing. Cars and lorries rumbled past and there were fewer people on the pavements. Maria waited as usual, looking all around, waiting for a sign. But this time it didn't come. She gave a puzzled frown as the minutes ticked by and nothing happened. Perhaps she had imagined it all.

A few people gathered at the crossing, the lights turned red and they all streamed across the road. The lights turned green and the traffic roared into life again. Bit by bit another group began to congregate. Two or three times this happened and still Maria waited. Then it dawned on her where she was. She was standing on the same corner where she had seen the girl twice before. Once in the doorway opposite and once staring from the window. This place must be important. The girl had led her here. But what should she do now? Why didn't she appear? In the end Maria concluded there was only one thing she could do. She was going to have to knock on the door and see who or what answered.

The lights changed and brought the traffic to a halt. She crossed the road with her eyes fixed firmly on the door. Everyone else moved on, leaving Maria standing on the pavement. There were two steps up to the door which was painted blue. It looked like a perfectly ordinary house. Did these people know they were haunted? She looked at the half-coin resting in the palm of her hand. It seemed so small and innocent. She clenched it tight in her hand and reached up to ring on the doorbell.

The chimes died away and then she heard footsteps on the other side of the door. The handle rattled and the door swung open. Maria felt a sudden knot in the pit of her stomach. It was all she could do to stop herself from screaming. The girl was standing in the doorway. It was her exactly – the pale skin, the deep brown eyes, the auburn hair tumbling around her neck. She was stunningly beautiful. It was as if she had walked right out of the painting. Maria stared, open-mouthed. She tried to say something but the words wouldn't come. Then the girl spoke.

'Hi.'

Maria was brought back to earth with a jolt. That was not the greeting she was expecting. She closed her mouth and her heart sank as she began to notice some more details that didn't quite add up. There were the girl's clothes for a start. Her top was white but the jeans and trainers were definitely twenty-first century. So were the wires dangling from her ears. The girl pulled one of the speakers out and touched a switch on the shiny box at her waist.

'Can I help you?'

'Who is it, Caterina?' A voice drifted out from another room.

'I don't know, Mamma,' the girl replied, turning briefly.

'Then find out. What are you going to do? Stand there and look at each other all day?'

'OK. Mamma.' She turned back to Maria. 'Well? Who are you? What do you want?'

Maria didn't know what to say. This was all wrong. This must be the girl she had seen but she wasn't acting at all like she should be. It didn't make sense. She realised that the girl was looking at her, confused, waiting for a response.

'I . . . I found this coin,' she said. Part of her was still hopeful as she held out her hand. The girl looked at it curiously but there was no flash of recognition. 'I wondered if it was yours.'

'Why would you think that?' Maria was silent. Why would she think that? 'Did you find it outside?' Maria nodded dumbly. It seemed the only thing to do. The girl picked it up. 'I never saw it before. Mamma?'

'What is it?'

'There is a girl here. She says she found an old coin outside. I never saw it before?'

A middle-aged woman appeared drying her hands on a towel. '*Buongiorno*,' she smiled. 'What have you found?' Her daughter handed her the coin and she looked at it with interest. 'This is very old. It is gold too. Where did you find it?' Again Maria was speechless. She looked at the floor in embarrassment. 'Just here? On the step?' Maria nodded, wishing she was miles away. This was all going wrong. It was just an ordinary girl. No! It couldn't be. She had seen her twice on opposite sides of town. Either this girl could fly or there were two of them.

'Perhaps Papa knows,' said the girl.

The woman nodded. 'Mario!' she called. There was no answer and the woman clicked her tongue in irritation. 'Where is he? Francesca, where is your papa?'

'I don't know, Mamma,' came a new voice. Another girl came to join them at the door. 'I think he went out.' She stood by her sister and the truth finally sank in.

'You're twins,' Maria said blankly.

~ 285 ~

'Yes,' smiled the mother.

'There's two of you.'

'Yes. That is the way with twins. Although how I am going to pay for both their educations I just don't know. And always they must have the same. Caterina has a new coat. Francesca must have a new coat. And will Mario get a job? *Mamma Mia!* Sometimes I ask myself, how am I going to cope?' Maria stared from one girl's face to the other while their mother talked. They were completely identical. How could she have been so stupid?

'Are you all right?' The woman became concerned as she noticed Maria's face.

'I suppose so,' she mumbled. 'If you don't know anything about the coin, I guess I'll just take it to the police.' She held out her hand and accepted the half-coin. 'Thanks for your help anyway,' she said flatly. She turned and walked away.

'That girl is crazy,' said Caterina as they watched Maria go. 'I have seen her before. Always she is staring at me.'

'Hush. She is English,' said her mother, as if that explained everything.

## Thirty-Five

MARIA came into the kitchen and stood miserably by the table. Her hopes had been raised for a short while but her disappointment left her feeling worse than before. Elisabetta and Nonna were back but thankfully Beppe had gone somewhere else.

'Well?' the old woman asked. Tommy was still at her side. In answer, Maria held out the half a florin to the old woman. Her eyes gleamed as she eagerly took it from her. 'So it did not work.'

'She was just an ordinary girl,' said Maria in a small voice. 'Two ordinary girls actually.'

'I thought as much. I am sorry.'

'What are you sorry for? You told me it would never work.'

The old woman gazed steadily at Maria until she became uncomfortable and had to look down. 'I am sorry because your father is in trouble and you hoped to put an end to it.'

Tears started in Maria's eyes and she could not speak. 'It is not always that easy,' said the woman. 'I will do what I can to help.'

'W-what could you do?' She did not add, 'you are

just an old woman', but it was in her face.

The woman gave her an enigmatic smile. 'I am old. I know some people.'

'But –'

'And now I am tired. I think I will take some sleep.'

'You said you never sleep.'

'So I changed my mind. Today I think I will manage a little.' She leant back in her chair. 'Just a little . . .' Her voice was becoming softer. Maria stared at her thoughtfully. There was something about this woman that she didn't quite understand. Something familiar yet strange. She found a cushion for her and placed it behind her head. The old woman smiled appreciatively and rolled her head until she was comfortable. Soon her breathing became deep and slow. Maria turned to go away but the woman's eyes blinked wide open suddenly. 'Stay with me, little boy,' she said, staring. There was fear in her voice. 'Stay with me . . .' Her voice tailed off and her eyes drooped again. Maria nodded to Tommy and moved quietly away.

John sat at a table in a bare room. Inspector Morelli sat opposite him and leafed through the file of papers shaking his head gravely. 'This does not look good, Signor Clayton. Not very good at all.'

John said nothing.

The policeman took out a packet of cigarettes and put one between his lips. Then he fumbled in his pocket for his lighter. 'You want one?'

John stared blankly.

The inspector shrugged. 'You are probably right. My wife, she tells me I smoke too much.' He puffed a cloud of blue smoke into the room as he picked up the top sheet of paper. 'It looks like you will be charged with dangerous driving. The old lady lives, which is good, and I hear she stays in your house, which is also good. But this other incident . . .' He shook his head again. 'This is much worse. If Zappini dies, the charge will be murder. There are no witnesses but the circumstantial evidence, it is very strong. Signor Clayton, have you nothing to say in your defence?'

John had nothing to say.

The old woman was dimly aware of the world around her. She had the coin comfortably in her hand and she felt heavy and peaceful. It was as if years of lost sleep were creeping up on her all at once. Years. How many years had it actually been? She had forgotten long ago what it was like to sleep, even to rest. Always she was wide, wide awake. No peace, no rest. Slowly she slipped lower and lower into unconsciousness. And as she did, she began to dream . . .

. . . lightly she tripped through the streets of Florence. Just as she had when she was a girl. How free she felt. Stiff joints and tired limbs were all but forgotten. She had her cloak about her. It was blue and its dark folds blended with the shadows. The moon was full and round and bathed the city in a soft quiet light. She threw back her hood and let the cool night air wash over her face. Then she laughed out loud. The few people who were still about turned and watched curiously the girl who laughed and ran. It was night but she knew no fear. What could harm her now?

The doors to the great cathedral were open and the light of numberless candles spilled out on the steps. The sound of singing filled the square, sober and solemn. What were the priests doing? Singing a dirge on a night like this. She crossed the square with a different song in her heart. Then she slowed down as she came to the old market. Would he be there? Of course he would. She only wanted to savour the last few moments as he came into sight. There he was, waiting with his horse, alone.

Slowly she made her way around the square. He faced the other way and did not see her until she stood right behind him and murmured his name close to his ear. Then he turned, his eyes sparkling. 'You came,' he said, picking her up and spinning her off the ground. Their laughter drifted across the rooftops until they came to a stop, breathing hard as they clung to each other.

'Of course I came,' she said breathlessly. 'Didn't I say I would?'

'You did. But it seems as if I have been waiting for ever.'

'Then let's not wait a moment longer.' She held out

her hand and he lifted her on to the horse. 'Have you everything you need?' she asked.

'I have you,' he replied simply, climbing up after her. She slipped her arms around his waist as she sat behind him and rested her face against his shoulder.

'Then take me away,' she said. 'And nothing will part us ever again.'

He grinned as he reined in the horse. It turned, hooves clattering on the stone cobbles and then they were away. Together they galloped into the night.

The old woman stirred in her sleep. What a lovely story. That was a much better ending. She must tell it to the young girl. What was her name? Maria. Yes, she would like to hear it. But later. Not now. Now she was so tired. She must sleep. Just a little more rest . . .

A hush descended on the kitchen that afternoon. As the sun passed over to the west, its light streamed in through the window and despite everything the house was at peace. Elisabetta dried her eyes and helped her mother and Aunt Adriana to prepare the evening meal. Tommy pulled up a stool and sat by the old woman as she lay quietly in her chair. Uncle Giorgio eventually emerged from the basement saying he had cleared up the mess and he didn't know what all the fuss about the picture was. It was nice but nothing special. Nonna simply nodded and didn't even scold him for going down there. His leg seemed a bit better too. Even Beppe seemed content to sit and play cards with Maria. Only John was absent but he was in each of their thoughts. Somehow the despair was lifted.

Eventually the sun disappeared and the lights were turned on. Nonna called for the table to be cleared and laid. Maria sorted out cutlery while Beppe got the glasses. Then Nonna lifted the huge pan on to the table and the meal was ready.

'How is the old lady?' Nonna asked. 'Does she want to eat?'

'She's still sleeping,' said Maria. 'Should I wake her?'

'I don't know,' said Elisabetta. 'It is good that she sleeps.'

'It is good to eat too,' argued Nonna, 'though she eats like a bird and it hardly seems worth it. *Santa Pan-zanella!* What an appetite she has.'

'I don't think she is going to wake up,' said Tommy quietly.

Everyone turned and stared at him as he stood by the old woman, holding her hand. Then Elisabetta dropped the spoon she was holding and it clattered on the tiled floor. She crossed the kitchen in two strides and seized the woman's wrist between her fingers. She held it for a moment and then let go with a gasp. She put an arm around Tommy. Her other hand was clutched to her mouth as she looked distraught at the body of the old lady lying in the chair.

'Come away, darling,' she said quietly. 'Leave the old lady to sleep.'

'She's never going to wake up, is she?' His voice wavered but his eyes were dry.

There was a lump in Elisabetta's throat. 'No, darling, she won't wake up now.'

'I liked her.'

'And she liked you. You were good friends and you made her happy. You should be pleased.'

They stood and watched over her for a while and then Elisabetta bent to lift the woman's arm. It hung limp over the arm of the chair and she wanted to arrange it more naturally in her lap. 'What is this?' she said, surprised. 'She's holding something golden.'

'That would be the half a coin that Tommy gave her,' said Maria in a subdued voice.

'Tommy gave her? Where did he get a gold coin?'

'Dunno. He wouldn't say.'

'How strange.' The woman's hand flopped open and Elisabetta frowned. 'Did you say half a coin?'

'That's right.'

'Well, there are two here now.' She gently picked them out of her hand and held them up together. They were a perfect match. 'No, not two . . .' She stopped confused. Maybe it was the light but for a moment it seemed as if they were not two halves but one whole. She shook her head and blinked. The illusion passed. 'Yes,' she said. 'They are definitely two halves of the same coin.'

Maria stared at her mum and then at the old woman. 'Then I was right.' Her voice was hushed and reverent. 'I *have* seen the White Lady.'

## Thirty-Six

' . . . Signor Clayton. Signor, we have some better news.'

John blinked and slowly became aware of his surroundings. He appeared to be in a police interrogation room but he couldn't quite remember why. He stretched and massaged the back of his neck. Then he scratched his chin. When did he last have a shave? Or eat for that matter? The inside of his mouth felt furry and tasted like something he had once discovered at the back of his fridge when he was a student. He looked up at the man speaking. He was middle-aged and harassed-looking. There was a priest standing next to him. Father Romano, wasn't it?

'I'm sorry, were you speaking to me?'

Inspector Morelli looked surprised. 'You are talking now? This is progress. I have brought Father Romano. He wanted to see you.' The priest nodded and smiled. John smiled back vaguely. Now that he was a bit more alert he was becoming anxious. He was in a police cell and he didn't know why. He tried to recollect the events of the past few days and found them a worrying blank.

'So, as I said,' the policeman continued, 'it is good news. Zappini has regained consciousness. Our doctors have studied his injury and believe it was sustained by him falling against the bench. There is no evidence that you hit him with the spanner. We hope to interrogate him when he is well enough.'

Zappini, bench, spanner. John looked blankly at the inspector. 'I'm sorry, signor, I haven't got a clue what you're talking about.'

Morelli frowned. 'This is still a serious matter, signor. You would do well to cooperate.'

'Yes, of course. But really . . . I can't remember.'

The man leant forward on the desk and brought his face close to John's. His teeth were stained yellow with tobacco. 'Then let me remind you of some things,' he said seriously. 'Dangerous driving, assault, resisting arrest. Do you want me to go on? These are –' He stopped as Father Romano laid a hand on his shoulder. He turned to him impatiently.

'What?'

'Perhaps we should talk,' the priest said gently.

'Perhaps we should talk? Perhaps we should all hold hands and dance a fandango. Why don't you . . .' He tailed off under the kind but penetrating gaze of the old man. It was true that he was a senior police officer, but then Father Romano was the priest. Father Romano had once caught him as a boy putting a lizard into his motorbike helmet. As well as giving him a few choice words he had dragged him by the ear all the way to his mother and she had given him such a beating that he had walked funny for a week after-wards. It is hard to forget incidents like that. They leave their mark.

'Please excuse us, Signor Clayton,' he said wearily. 'I won't be long.'

The priest drew the inspector to one side and left John alone. There was a plastic cup of water on the table and a dog-eared newspaper. John drained the glass grate-fully and rubbed his eyes. A headline in the paper caught his attention. ORSINI PORTRAIT RESTORATION SHOCK. He picked it up and began to read.

'Be quick then, Father,' said the inspector in a low voice. 'These are important police matters. You shouldn't even be here.'

'Yes, yes,' said the priest. 'Tell me, how bad are the charges against him?'

'Not as bad as they were, but still bad. It's not mur-der any more. Zappini broke into the house, he tripped and hit his head. Clayton had the spanner though. What would he have done if Zappini hadn't tripped, eh?'

'So it's your job to charge people for things they might have done is it?'

'No,' he retorted angrily. 'Are you telling me my job? You're driving me crazy. There is still the danger-ous driving. We have witnesses who say he was doing thirty kilometres an hour over the limit. And resisting arrest. One of my men has a black eye now.'

'This is true,' the priest nodded. 'He should not have resisted. But you have to remember you were arresting him for something he hadn't done.'

'What are you saying, Father? Is it all right to punch a policeman?'

'Which policeman?'

'*Which policeman!* What does it matter, which policeman?'

'You are right. It doesn't matter. But do not judge a man until you have walked a mile in his shoes.'

Inspector Morelli shot a glance at John's shoes. Comfortable brown leather. Needed a bit of a polish. 'With respect, Father, what are you talking about? What have his shoes got to do with all this?'

Father Romano sighed. 'What I am saying is this. Put yourself in his situation.'

'What is his situation?'

'He has the painting of the White Lady.'

The policemen paled. 'What?'

'That's right,' said the priest.

The inspector had a sudden image of the painting in the basement of the Rossini house. How she held you with your eyes and made you forget everything around you. His eyes glazed over even as he remembered. Then he shook his head, resisting. 'But . . . those are just stories. Anyway it was destroyed years ago.'

'So we all thought.'

'You are certain of this?'

Father Romano nodded and the policeman scratched the stubble on his chin thoughtfully. This could explain a lot. He turned and looked at John again, quietly reading the paper. He seemed harmless now. Could he really have been under that girl's spell?

'Let's say he has got the White Lady,' he said turning back to Father Romano. He looked troubled. 'What do you expect *me* to do about it?'

'You could forget any of this ever happened.'

'What? But these are serious charges, Father. You're suggesting I simply lose the file?'

The old priest nodded slowly.

'But . . .' He looked at Father Romano, struggling inside. 'I can't . . .'

'Can't you? Why not?'

Why? There were a million reasons why he couldn't. But somehow with the priest staring at him, none of them seemed good enough. He gave in with a sigh. 'All right, Father. You win.'

Father Romano smiled broadly. 'I knew you would understand. It is for the best.' He laid a reassuring hand on the policeman's shoulder before turning to John. 'You are free to go now, Signor Clayton.'

John looked up, surprised. 'Am I?'

'Yes. It was all a big misunderstanding. Shall we go?'

'OK.' John pushed back his chair and stood up. He held out his hand to the policeman. 'Sorry to have troubled you, signor.'

Morelli took his hand. 'Really, you have been no trouble,' he said weakly.

John turned back to the priest. 'Do you know. I've just been reading in the paper about the Orsini portrait from the Uffizi. It's been restored and during the process something incredible happened. The whole of his face simply peeled away. It was in a terrible condition. It would have been a disaster but – you'll never believe this bit – there was another face entirely underneath . . .'

His voice faded as they walked down the corridor. The policeman was left standing, holding a file of papers. He shook his head, not quite believing what he had just done. Then he dropped the whole file into the waste bin and pulled out his packet of cigarettes. How did his wife expect him to give up when things like this happened?

∞

' . . . *in nomine Patris et Filii et Spiritus Sancti. Amen.*'

Father Romano closed his book and stood with his head bowed. No family attended the funeral of Alessandra, last of the Medici. Just a few friends. It was on a warm and languid, sunny afternoon. The sky was blue and there was a light breeze. Maria gave Tommy's hand a squeeze as they stood together by the graveside.

'Don't be sad, Tommy. She may have died but I think she was ready to go.'

Tommy nodded in reply. Maria looked at him curiously. It was hard to tell how much he understood but she got the impression that he had known all along. After a moment's reflection they turned to go and others moved forward to pay their last respects. Hundreds and hundreds of people crowded into the small, walled cemetery and more waited outside. No one had said anything but somehow the whole town knew. They had all turned out to say goodbye to the White Lady. From the oldest, snowy-haired ninety-year-old right down to the newborn lying in its mother's arms – they were all there. Two girls with dark brown eyes and auburn hair stood with their mother.

'Did you find the owner of your coin?' she asked.

Maria smiled. 'Yes, thank you. She was very pleased to have it returned. It had been missing for a long time.'

'Good. I am pleased.' The lady smiled as they passed.

John and Elisabetta walked side by side behind their children. Occasionally she let her hand brush against his but he did not respond. She glanced at him anxiously. He was still not himself.

'I feel so bad,' he muttered.

'Hush, darling,' she said. She slipped her arm around his waist and would not let him resist. 'It wasn't your fault.'

'That's what you say. But I don't remember. They tell me there was a car crash but . . .'

'Never mind. Everything is just fine now.'

He turned to face her. 'Are you sure?' His face was troubled.

'I am certain.'

'But –'

'Hush.'

She put her finger to his lips and they stood there together as the crowd of mourners moved slowly past them. Gradually his face became calm.

'Do you know?' he said at last. 'I think you might be the most beautiful woman I've ever seen.'

'Is that right?' Elisabetta looked intrigued. 'You have never seen *anyone* more beautiful than me?'

'No.'

'Not even, say, a picture of someone?' He shook his head and a smile lit up her face. 'Perhaps you would like to take me out to dinner then.'

'Are you asking me for a date?'

'No, you are asking me.'

'Am I? OK. Are you free tonight?'

She looked thoughtful for a moment then nodded. 'I could probably make tonight.'

'It's a date then.'

They began to move again, arm in arm. Nonna watched them go.

'*Santa Maria!*' she said. 'I am glad that is all over.'

## Thirty-Seven

Next morning a newspaper lay open on the table while Maria ate her breakfast. Nonna was busy at the sink and John and Elisabetta had yet to appear. Maria had heard them come in late the night before, or was it early this morning? Bumping into things and giggling like teenagers. Her dad singing snatches of opera. She smiled briefly at the thought but her attention was on the picture in the paper. It was in full colour and took up half a page. She had never seen the young man before but she knew who he was. His features were kind and sensitive and he held a garland of flowers in his outstretched hand. The report beneath it told the story of the discovery and went on to speculate on how the young man came to be painted over. One theory was that the picture was commissioned to mark the marriage of the man to the young woman known only as the White Lady. The old photograph from the textbook was also reproduced with a brief history of how it was destroyed. If for whatever reason, the marriage didn't take place, or the fee for the portrait was never paid, then it was quite possible that Verrocchio would have reused the portrait by painting a new face on it. Maria nodded as she read. The idea made sense and sounded quite likely. But she knew it was also completely wrong.

She stood up impulsively when she had finished reading and headed for the basement. Moments later she returned and lay the White Lady on the table next to the paper. Nonna winced when she saw the portrait but didn't object. The original masterpiece looked stunning next to the grainy newspaper reproduction. This was the nearest the two had come for over five hundred years and Maria's heart quickened as she saw them together. Just then her parents finally emerged. They were holding hands and Elisabetta was laughing but the sound died on her lips when she saw the portrait. She glanced nervously at John and gripped his hand tighter. But he let go of her and came to stand in front of the table. The kitchen fell silent, all eyes fixed on him.

'Incredible,' he murmured. He picked the portrait up gently and took it to the window were he could see it better. 'It's like it was painted yesterday. I did a good job on it, didn't I?' He looked up, grinning. The atmosphere relaxed. His face was calm and there wasn't a trace of the madness in his eyes.

'What are we going to do with her, Dad?' Maria came and stood by him.

'That's the question,' he replied. 'She'd look great in our hall wouldn't she?'

Maria's heart sank. 'Yeah. I suppose so. But isn't it too important to be kept at our place?'

'It certainly is,' said Elisabetta. She wasn't ready to share a house with this woman. Not after all they'd been through. 'Anyway, how could we afford to insure it? The premium, it would be hundreds of thousands of pounds.'

'I don't know,' replied John. 'You can't actually replace something that's unique, so insurance is a bit pointless. Besides, nobody knows we've got it so burglars won't be attracted to it.'

'But what about fire?' Maria had a fleeting vision of a grand Tuscan country house ablaze, with a servant staggering out through the smoke clutching a painting. 'Or what if Tommy broke it? You know what he's like.'

'Yes, and who says nobody knows? What about our friends, eh? Most of them just happen to be art experts. Are they going to come to our house and walk right by and say nice painting and then forget all about it? I don't think so. Or perhaps you don't intend to invite anybody around. Perhaps you don't need anybody now you have this precious painting.' Elisabetta's face coloured as she spoke.

'Well, what do you suggest?' said John shortly.

'It should go to the Uffizi,' Maria put in quickly. 'She should be with Arnaldo.'

'Who?' Both her parents turned and stared at her.

'Um . . . Arnaldo. It's just a name. I think the young man in the picture looks like he might be . . . called Arnaldo. I think they belong together,' she finished up quickly. She could feel the red creeping up her neck as she realised how lame this sounded. John continued to look at her doubtfully but Elisabetta quickly agreed.

'Maria is right. The portrait belongs in a gallery. Where everybody can see it. The Uffizi would be best, of course, providing they can afford it. How much do you think we should ask?'

John shrugged. 'It would have to go to auction, but I'm not sure I want to sell it. It *is* mine remember.'

'Oh, so it is yours, is it? And the fact your wife stands by you while you get taken away for attempted murder means nothing to you. Is that right?'

'Of course it doesn't mean nothing. What's that got to do with the painting? Stop trying to manipulate me.' John's voice was raised and Maria stared at her parents as they glared at each other. It was all going wrong again. There was a tense silence that was broken by a knock at the door. Nonna disappeared into the hall and a moment later she returned with Father Romano. Something about the smiling little priest made John and Elisabetta feel suddenly ashamed.

'*Buongiorno!* Am I interrupting something?'

'Nothing at all,' said John sheepishly. 'We were just thinking about what to do with the portrait.'

Father Romano nodded. 'Yes, it is important. She needs a home. Have you decided?'

'Not quite,' said John.

'No where near,' muttered Maria and got a sharp look from her mum.

'While you are thinking perhaps you would like to see something.' They turned to him expectantly. 'You

~ 305 ~

will need to come to the church, but I think it will interest you.'

Twenty minutes later Nonna had changed into her best dress, Beppe and Tommy had been rounded up and the whole family were on their way. Halfway there they had to wait at a crossing and while the traffic rumbled by a girl with long hair and soft brown eyes came out of the house opposite. She slammed the blue door behind her and waved when she saw them waiting. Then she set off towards the piazza.

'That's Caterina, isn't it?' Elisabetta turned to Maria. 'Do you know her?'

'Yeah. We've met. It might be Francesca.' Maria stared at the ground.

'She looks a lot like the girl in the portrait, don't you think so?'

'A bit, I suppose. Hadn't really noticed.' Beppe sniggered and Maria jabbed him in the ribs.

'Ow!'

'Beppe. Leave your cousin alone.' Nonna turned on him angrily.

'What did I do? She hit me.'

'Don't be cheeky or *I* will hit you, so help me.'

'Why is everything always my fault?' Beppe demanded.

'I ask myself the same question every day. Why is everything your fault? You will be the death of me Beppe Rossini, I swear it.' The lights turned red and Beppe muttered bitterly to himself as they crossed the road.

Things were still tense between John and Elisabetta

and they did not speak to each other all the way. Inside the church the sun shone through the eastern window, flooding them with warmth and light. Maybe it was this that caused the deep sense of peace here this morning. Maybe it was something else.

'The wall paintings,' Maria cried in amazement. She rushed forward and stood before the fresco of St Arnaldo and the Witch, or rather where it had been.

'It's not possible,' said John as he stood behind her. The painting of Arnaldo and the Witch was gone. In its place was another picture, seemingly just as old as all the others. In this scene the saint was a youth and he was holding hands with a girl. She was dressed in white and auburn hair fell to her waist. John reached out and brushed his fingertips over the surface. It was no illusion. It was real.

'Did you uncover it like our painting?' Maria asked the priest.

'What did I tell you?' said John. Frescoes are part of the wall. You can't peel them off.'

The priest shrugged. 'I don't know how it happened. I was here yesterday evening, praying at the altar. I heard a noise but when I turned there was nobody there. Then I noticed the painting. I think it might be time to change our play,' he added.

'It's not possible,' John said again.

'That's not all. Come with me.'

John tore his eyes away and followed Father Romano with the rest of them. The priest pulled out his bunch of keys and Maria felt a lurch in her stomach. She knew where they were going next. She gulped as each of them took a candle and the priest unlocked the door to the crypt. It was just as it had been before although the walk did not seem so long this time. At the end of the tunnel the coffin lay on its slab. Nonna curtseyed and made the sign of the cross. Father Romano stood to one side with his candle held high. Cautiously Maria approached the saint.

Shadow filled the space where he lay. She could just make out the shape of the saint's head where the light gleamed on it. He looked whiter than ever. She lifted her candle a little higher and let the thin light fall on his face. Then her eyes widened and she drew in her breath sharply, swallowing her scream. A skeleton lay in the place of the saint.

'*Madre del Dio!*' Nonna stood behind Maria, the colour drained from her cheeks. 'How has this happened?'

'I was hoping Maria might know,' said the priest.

For a while she said nothing her eyes fixed on the saint. 'His waiting is over too,' she said finally.

'His waiting?'

She nodded. 'It's time to lay him to rest.' She turned and faced Father Romano. The old man studied her for a moment, then placing his candle on a ledge, he retrieved the coffin lid from where it leant against the wall. Together they carefully covered up the remains of Arnaldo de Pazzi.

'Sleep well,' she whispered.

'I think you know a lot more than you have told us

already,' the priest said gently. Maria nodded. 'We would like to know too. I will have some explaining to do next time the bishop comes.'

'Not here,' said Maria.

Back at home she sat on the chair in the corner where the old woman had sat. She closed her eyes and waited for the words to come. 'Some call her the White Lady, others the Witch, but when she first met Arnaldo she went by the name of Alessandra.' Slowly the tale unfolded while the family listened, unmoving, held captive by the words. Only once did somebody stir. Halfway through the story Elisabetta felt a hand creep into hers. She turned and smiled gently at John. They didn't speak but both knew what they had to do.

# Epilogue

On the wall of room fifteen of the Uffizi Art Gallery there hangs a pair of portraits. On the right is a young man in a red tunic facing towards the left. The other is of a beautiful girl with a twisted braid of auburn hair. She is wearing a white dress and a circle of gold around her brow. They look into each other's eyes and both hold the end of a garland of flowers which seems to span the space between the pictures and make them one. Many visitors stop to look at the pair and wonder who they were. They read the plaques beneath the paintings but these offer little. *Girl in white, unknown subject. School of Verrocchio. Young man, unknown subject. Andrea del Verrocchio, and Leonardo da Vinci*. Those who are more interested can read their guide and discover that the young man was hidden for many years under the face of Paolo Orsini, and how the young lady had been missing, presumed destroyed for over a century. How they eventually came together is a story in itself. But most just gaze at the paintings and enjoy the delicate beauty of the girl and the quiet strength of the young man. Eventually they move on.

Only a few know who they were. They walked the streets of Florence many centuries ago and are long gone from the earth. Their names may be forgotten but in the Uffizi, Alessandra de Medici and Arnaldo de Pazzi will be together always.

# Historical Notes

THE earlier half of this story takes place in 1485 and many of the events and characters are real. Lorenzo Medici the Magnificent was undisputed leader of Florence until his death in 1492. He was head of the Medici bank which brought the family their fortune but he was also a man of culture. He was a poet, patron of local artists and an accomplished swordsman. He was married to Clarice Orsini. They had at least seven children but none called Alessandra. Neither did Clarice have a cousin called Paolo. The events in chapter nine, when the Pazzi rose up against the Medici and were violently put down, are almost completely true. It happened in 1478 and is known to historians as the Pazzi Conspiracy. The only time I have departed from the historical version is when Lorenzo personally went to the Pazzi palace to seek out Francesco de Pazzi. In reality he sought refuge at his own home while others went to retrieve Francesco. He was hanged along with Archbishop Salviati and others involved in the plot. There is no evidence that Francesco had a son called Arnaldo. Lorenzo's rage against the conspirators was so strong that it wasn't until ten years later in 1488, when the last plotter was killed, that he was satisfied.

Andrea del Verrocchio was a master artist who, among other things, made a bust of Lorenzo, the most recognisable image that we now have of him. He died in 1488. His most famous apprentice was Leonardo da Vinci, painter of the *Mona Lisa*. He moved to Milan in 1482 but there was plague there in 1485. The historical record is quiet on what Leonardo was doing at this period and while there is no evidence that he returned to Florence, there is nothing to suggest he didn't. He was perhaps the greatest genius who has ever lived. Despite having no formal education he became a renowned artist and sculptor and also a great engineer, scientist and inventor. His notebooks record plans for parachutes, hang-gliders, deep-sea diving suits, tanks and many other machines. None were built but modern experimenters have made many of them to his specifications, including the parachute in this story, and found them to work. Unfortunately his notebooks were not much help to the rest of the world. Not only were they written in mirror writing, they were neglected after his death and many of them were lost for hundreds of years. Because of his restless genius, he found it very hard to retain interest in one project for any length of time. This made him quite unreliable and probably contributed to Lorenzo Medici's prejudice against him.

Girolamo Savonarola was a fanatical Franciscan monk who preached publicly throughout the 1480s and 1490s. After Lorenzo's death in 1492 he managed effectively to take control of Florence and crushed many of the artistic developments that were flourishing in the city at the time. His popularity did not last and he was excommunicated from the church in 1497. He was tortured, hung and burnt to death the following year.

All the descriptions of the city and its wonderful buildings are accurate and you can visit these places today, along with thousands of tourists from all over the world. Sadly, you will not find portraits of Arnaldo and Alessandra hanging in room fifteen of the Uffizi.